LOVE LIKE THEIRS
DOESN'T HEAL, IT KILLS.

Blood
Stained
Kisses

L. RENÉE
RICHARD

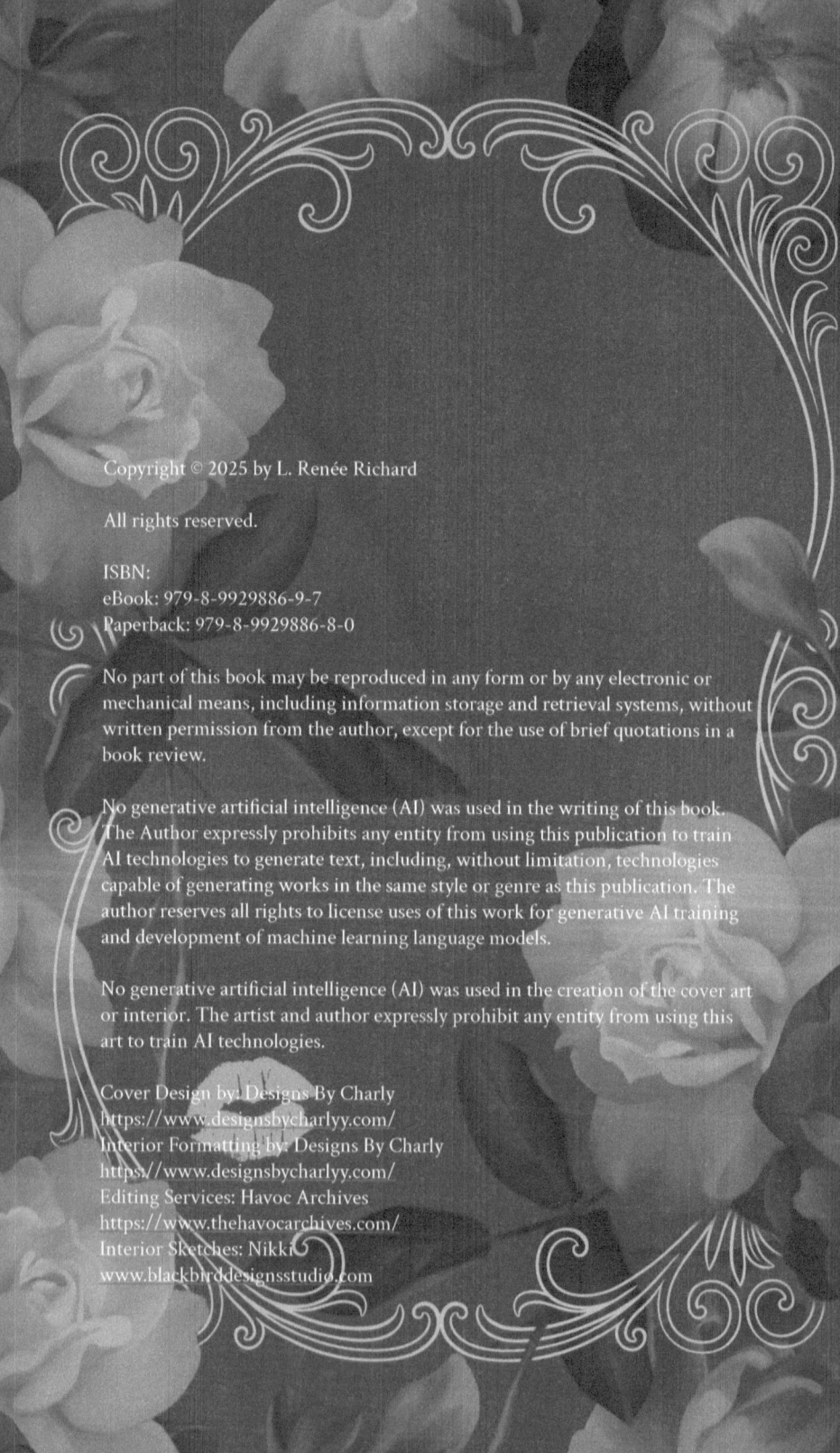

Cover Design by: Designs By Charly
https://www.designsbycharlyy.com/
Interior Formatting by: Designs By Charly
https://www.designsbycharlyy.com/
Editing Services: Havoc Archives
https://www.thehavocarchives.com/
Interior Sketches: Nikki
www.blackbirddesignsstudio.com

Dear Reader,

    Thank you so much for choosing to read this book. This story is a work of fiction and follows morally grey characters whose choices and actions don't always reflect real-world values or behaviors. It also explores dark and sensitive subject matter that may be triggering for some readers. If you'd like a detailed list of specific content warnings, please visit my website at L. Renee Richard. Please take care while reading. If you choose to continue, I hope you enjoy Vic and Dani's story.

    L. Renée Richard

Blood-Stained Kisses

BY: L. RENÉE RICHARD

By day, Victor Flores is the perfect student—quiet, focused, and determined to escape the violence at home. At night, he faces the monster made from bruises and a life he can't control. Until Daniella Andrade moves in next door. She becomes his light, his anchor, and worst of all, his obsession.

Together, they dream of medical school, of freedom, of a future untouched by Vic's toxic past and a secret they swore to bury. But when Dani disappears, she leaves behind only broken promises and shattered dreams.

Years later, Vic has become a brilliant surgeon, saving lives by day and hiding behind the scalpel by night. Beneath his calm façade lies a darker urge for control and vengeance. When Dani finally returns with secrets of her own, she realizes the boy she loved has become a man split in two. But what if the monster is exactly what she needs?

Love like theirs doesn't heal. It kills.

Part One:

"THE SCARIEST MONSTERS
ARE THE ONES THAT LURK WITHIN
OUR SOULS..."
EDGAR ALLAN POE

LA MUERTE

THE PAST

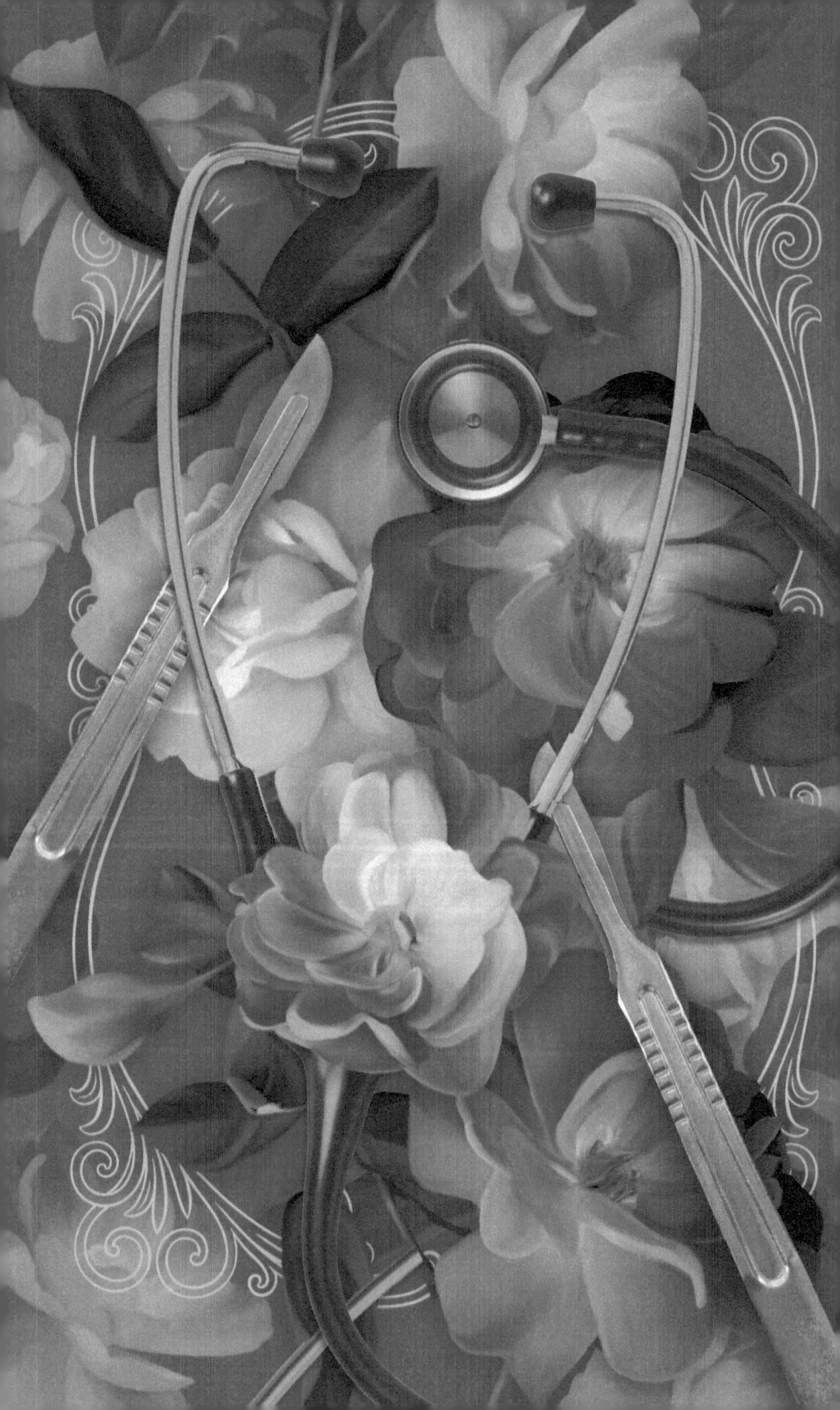

CHAPTER ONE

VIC
16 YEARS OLD

"Do you want to go over it one more time?"

I look up expectantly at Dani, studying her as her eyes dart over the diagram of the class handout, ping-ponging between it and her notes for our exam tomorrow. She bites her bottom lip and pulls it into her mouth like she always does when she's thinking hard about something, as I wait for her to answer me. Her head tilts side to side with indecision. This shit comes easy to me, but I know she struggles sometimes, and if I can do anything to make her life easier, I will. She makes my messed-up life better. More than she can ever know.

"Just give me a sec," she murmurs as she continues to peruse the paper. I nod, but I'm already leaning forward. I'm drawn to her like a sunflower is to the sun, turning toward her, always inching closer.

We've been out here for an hour, and I have done everything in my power to keep my hands off her because I know that she needs to make a good grade on this exam, but damn it's hard. A breeze stirs the air, bringing with it the scent of coconut from her bath gel and the undertones of her freshly laundered clothing. Her dark brown loose curls lift, brushing gently across her cheeks like the breeze's phantom fingers caressing her face. I inhale deeply, memorizing the smells that are inherently hers, wishing I could stay like this, but I know that it will be short-lived. He'll be home soon, destroying everything good in my life and crushing my hopes and dreams, making me want to rearrange his half of my DNA.

From the moment she moved in next door, my miserable existence was transformed into a glimmer of hope. I watched from my window as she helped her mom carry boxes inside. Her presence was larger than life, and when she looked up, she noticed someone in the window staring at her. She raised her hand to shield her eyes from the sun's rays, and that's when she saw me. Our eyes met. Then she smiled, and it stirred something in me for the first time.

It was warm. It was inviting. It was an electric shock that ran through me, causing my heart to skip a beat, much like it did when I was anxious over something, but it wasn't just a smile she gifted me with that day. It was the beginning of a beautiful type of bubbling madness within, and only she was my antidote.

Ever the gentleman, or at least I told myself that was the intention, I was eager enough to help out in the hopes of talking to her. From the first look, the first smile, I knew she would be my first love, too. I craved any excuse to know her better.

Even now, sitting beside her, I'm drawn to everything about Daniella Andrade. She mesmerizes me. Her presence is always at the forefront of my mind, clinging to the edges of my daytime thoughts and fading into the dimly-lit corners of my subconscious at night. Her soft, plump, pink lips, which form the perfect shape, have a way of undoing me. Whether they're pursed in concentration or wrapped around a straw, they remind me of all the unspeakable crimes they commit in my dreams that wake me up in the middle of the night, cuffed to my bed by a mess of sweaty sheets and longing. So many times I lie awake, gazing out the window to where her room is just across the lawn from mine, and it leaves me aching for something that is just barely out of reach.

Just as she is about to speak, the sharp slam of a car door next door breaks the spell, which causes my fantasies to crumble instantly. Dani's eyes widen, snapping her head back to me in fear. I close my eyes, wishing he would just disappear from our lives, but that isn't my reality.

"Shit!" I curse under my breath, not needing this right now. I snap my book closed and quickly shove my work into my backpack, trying to control the tremble that overtakes my hands.

"Maria!" My father's loud, harsh voice cuts through the air like the thick tension brewing between us. I know she's afraid for me, so I try to downplay my worry. The memory of my mom shrinking beneath his insults striking just as profoundly as his fists. Dani reaches for me, and I flinch instinctively, already feeling his invisible reach for me.

Dani stands beside me, nervously rubbing her hands together. Is it with worry for my mom or me? My father is much bigger than I am. It leaves me feeling broken and powerless against him. But when his threats spew forth, most vicious especially when he's drunk, his fury is all-consuming, leaving no trace of recognition in his eyes. In those moments, it's as if he no longer sees you at all, or anyone—only his relentless pursuit to destroy everything in his path.

I fling my backpack over my shoulder, giving her a quick kiss on the lips. Before I can pull away, she cups my face between her hands, holding me there for more seconds than I can spare, but I grant her this moment of calm before the storm that awaits me next door. Placing her forehead against mine, she exhales, eyes closed. I watch as her eyelids slowly flutter open as she whispers up at me, "Be careful, Victor."

I guide her hands away, holding them briefly, giving them a quick, reassuring squeeze and half smile before I release them. I won't promise her that. Not when it comes to my mother. If I can take the blows instead of her, then it's a small price to pay, so that she can stop hurting. Without looking back, I scurry away like a mouse, nimbly slipping through an opening in the fence between our houses, and disappear into the shadows that await.

CHAPTER TWO

VIC
16 YEARS OLD

We were buried in our Anatomy and Physiology notes, studying for our exam, when my asshole of a father got home from work, shattering our peace. He's good at that—causing chaos. I didn't want to leave her. When she told me to be careful, it gutted me. So many times she'd play nurse, and not in the way I fantasized about. She helped patch me up. Tending to my battered and bruised body when I stepped in the path of my father's fists. If it wasn't me, then it would have been my mother. I'm not stronger than my father, but I am bigger than she is. I've learned to stand up for myself. To absorb the blows he deals out. I'm just not a big enough match for him yet, but one day I will be.

I slip along the side of the house, past the flaking paint and dying flowers my mom planted years ago. Left to wither among the weeds where nothing thrives. Boosting myself through the window, which I left partially open, I slide in quietly into my bedroom. I lift my bookbag over to the side, hitting the floor with a loud thud. Just then, I hear my father's sharp, accusing voice cut through my mother's desperate pleas echoing from the kitchen.

The sound freezes me in place.

The escalating argument jars me into action, reminding me to close the window. I look behind me and shut it, praying that no one calls the cops this time, but it doesn't matter. Setting the latch in place, I see Dani across the way, her eyes stricken with worry. This isn't the first time she's witnessed this behavior from my father, which makes her concern for me all the more valid. She mouths a "Please," and blows me a kiss, her hand lingering on the window pane like she can hold me there and keep me safe. Her earlier plea to be careful, left unsaid. I hold her stare and nod once without looking back. Then I walk toward the sound that will forever haunt my dreams—a blood-curdling scream.

I run toward the kitchen, with my heart beating rapidly, threatening to come out of my chest. As I round the corner, the first thing I see is blood. It's a stark contrast to the black and white retro tiles lining the floor. My father stands frozen over my mother's body, his expression is a mixture of shock and rage. His hands lay by his side, fists flexing and unflexing uncontrollably.

I run over to my mother, without thought for my safety, and see that she is still breathing. "Thank God. Thank God," I murmur as I take in her shallow breaths, but she's still alive. My father stands motionless, making no move to help. I shoulder past him, ignoring him, and call for help. The dispatcher's calm, methodical voice comes over the line, asking questions about my situation. I manage to tell them that she's still breathing, but barely. But she needs help now. I know because I see it. The light fades from her eyes as her blood spreads beneath her, its warmth slipping away with her last breath. Dispatch says an ambulance is on the way, but it doesn't matter. Because a quiet truth brews inside me, bubbling silent and merciless, but I push it down. I realize that it will be too late, and I can't save her. My hope dies, and some part of me knows that this moment will forever change me.

I reluctantly release my mom, remembering all the times she kept me out of harm's way. Standing, I turn toward the cause of all our pain and suffering. "What happened?" I scream at my father as he stands there in a daze, still unmoving. He doesn't acknowledge me. Then the wailing sound of approaching sirens and someone banging on the front door prompts a reaction from him now. He shifts, blinking as if waking from a dream, but this is no dream. It's a nightmare I can't escape, and I'm trapped in the final act of my own Shakespearean tragedy.

I don't hesitate as I rush over to the door, throwing it open. The paramedics pile in, gear slung over their shoulders, assessing the scene as they move in. I motion for them to follow and hurry toward her. They drop to their knees beside my mother. Their training takes over as they check her vital signs and start an IV, moving with practiced urgency. All I can do is stare. Then they slide her onto a stretcher, rushing toward the waiting ambulance. I catch snippets of their words like "Quick, we have to go!" and "We are losing her!" as they disappear out the door.

As they load her into the back of the ambulance to take her to the nearest hospital, I know that she won't be coming back. That she is gone despite their effort to resuscitate her. I stare out the window, watching as my father leaves with them, escorted by police, no doubt gathering further evidence of what they witnessed.

What lies will he spin? Will he tell them the whole truth, partial truth, or all lies? I know better than to expect honesty. He'll save himself, no matter the cost. At that moment, I make a silent vow to learn the skills necessary to assist those who cannot help themselves. I never want to feel this helpless ever again, standing and watching instead of acting.

Something shifts inside me. It's as if my very molecular composition is rearranged, reprogrammed into someone else— no, something else—that is colder and harder. I feel detached from my body. A cold numbness replaces everything I once felt. Through the window, I watch the ambulance disappear into the dark. Its red lights become engulfed by the awaiting claws of the hot, humid night.

I turn away. Back in the kitchen, I crouch, staring at the crimson splatter on the otherwise pristine porcelain flooring that my mom had mercilessly cleaned time and time again. She was always on her hands and knees, keeping the house clean for him. I drag my finger through it, feeling the blood, sticky between my fingers, and watching it smear like paint along the floor. The blood that was once flowing through my mother's veins is still warm, now left poikilothermic on this cold, hard surface as a stark reminder of what happens to those who can't fight back.

I rise from the spot steadfast and reborn anew. That's when I see her watching me.

CHAPTER THREE

DANI
18 YEARS OLD

Victor Flores has been my everything since I met him as a scrawny fourteen-year-old boy. Not yet a man, but growing into a body he was trying to navigate. He was all long limbs and a squeaky voice. His hair had a ruffled appearance, like he couldn't be bothered to comb his tousled locks. He was my first friend when we moved to this rural town in Texas. He became so much more as we evolved.

Our friendship is twisting into something deeper between us that can no longer be contained by innocence. An inevitable bond that possesses my mind, body, and soul, until love and obsession become indistinguishable. Maybe that's why I cling to him so completely. I'd spent too long learning what it felt like to be left behind.

After my parents' divorce, I never heard from my dad again. He had a new life, a new wife, and a brand-new family. I didn't fit into that. I pretended that it didn't sting. Being dismissed so easily by someone who used to care for me was a bitter pill to swallow. Now here I am, in a different town with a new life, watching this amazing boy grow into a man. Except now he isn't just a man—he's a killer. I watched it happen before my very eyes. I watched what was always bound to happen.

Right now, I know what's going through his mind. He's reliving that moment two years ago when he witnessed his father kill his mother and walk away free, protected by a successful legal defense and the convenient explanation of his mother's history with depression. In his withdrawn state, he drags his finger through his father's blood as he paints circles along the flooring like a finger painting. I flinch at his clinical detachment, but I've known Vic and watched those same fingers that wiped away tears from my eyes, or touched my face so tenderly after he made love to me in the witching hours of the night.

"Vic," I call out his name, and that seems to snap him out of his trance. He blinks slowly, looking around and then up at me. A question on his face as if to say, "*What happened?*" as I stare at his blood-covered hands. That's when he becomes aware of exactly what happened as the events start flooding in. He scoots away from his father's dead body with urgency and sits with his back against the wall, his hands shaking in front of him as he takes in the scene before him. He's vanished inside himself completely in a self-preservation mode.

I approach him cautiously, much like a wounded animal in need of urgent medical attention. If you move too fast, they will get spooked. So with the utmost restraint, I glide quietly across the kitchen floor, careful to avoid the blood around his dickhead of a parent's corpse. I can't say I'm sorry that he's dead, and I need to convince Vic that it's all going to be alright.

I kneel in front of him and take hold of his wrists. His bloodied hands drip, and as I raise them toward me, a small drop of blood lands on my white blouse. I watch it hit the fabric and spread out across the threads, soaking in, taking root, blooming into a larger circle of destruction. Vic watches it all with transfixed horror, like he doesn't want to taint me. However, the truth is that like attracts like. I am tainted inside in more ways than he can imagine. He doesn't scare me. In fact, I'm more drawn to him than ever before.

I bring his hands up to my face, mere inches from my cheeks.

They hover there, and he stares at me, his expression on the verge of panic. I turn my head to one hand and kiss it, then I repeat the same action on the other hand. I smile at him as the blood stains my mouth, soaking into my lips. It's coppery, and the metallic smell almost repulses me—not because of the blood, but because of the man it belonged to. The suffering *my* man has gone through at the hands of his father is unfathomable. My father just left, and that hurt, but this unholy abomination physically hurt Vic and killed his mom. I wanted him dead for so long. Vic could have been the next victim if he hadn't been strong enough. This time, his mistake would cost him everything.

"I love you," I say as I close the space between us. My words reach for him, drawing him back from some desolate place within himself. I try to coax the half of him that still remembers how to feel. He stirs from the sound, yet what returns is the other half of him that was lost when his mother died. That was the night he was remade into a boy stripped of innocence and consumed by the grief of seeing her die in such a way, and being forced to carry a burden too heavy for his years. And now, standing before me, I see both men I love—the scarred man, and the boy who will never fully escape the memory of that moment.

Yet, despite that, he moves, meeting me the rest of the way. His lips touch mine in a frenzied kiss. It conveys all the emotions I have for this strong, resilient man, whom I will love, regardless of the atrocities he may commit. We pull away, our blood-stained kisses lingering, splashed on like battle paint.

"Listen," I tell him. "I need you to trust me, okay?" He nods, searching my eyes for answers. "I have to call the police. I want you to follow my lead. Do you understand?" He nods again, and I smile at him, placing my hand on his face as he leans into my touch. I pick up the landline and call the police.

Minutes later, I see the lights before I hear the sirens coming down the road. The echoing sound of multiple doors slamming outside the window makes my heart race. I look at him and extend my hand to help Vic up from the floor. I guide him over to a chair while I go to get the door. I turn back to see Vic sitting there with his head in his hands. I know he thinks he's being taken into police custody, but I'll do everything I can to prevent it. I wipe my mouth, smearing the blood, and start crying, letting the tears flow, not for the crime he committed, but for the suffering he endured when no one bothered to help him.

Then I let the police into the house. EMS was called, too. Little do they know that no help is needed. They just need to take his father's dead body to the morgue. If the bastard wasn't dead, I would have seen to it before they got here, just to be sure he isn't around to hurt him ever again. I told the police what happened, how Vic saved my life.

His father got away with murder that day his mom died, but I suspect they all thought he was guilty despite his award-winning performance at the hospital. I shake, I cry, and none of it is an act. I was scared shitless when I walked into this scene, and it all comes pouring out in the play's final act. The police have the body removed. They call Vic a hero, and he shakes his head, not understanding how they are not arresting him. How could they? I was his witness. His alibi. No one will miss his father, especially not me.

I help clean up the mess, and Vic and I shower, removing the blood that has now dried and caked onto our flesh. We scrub each other clean, and I peer up to find Vic looking down at me through hooded lashes. Water droplets lay along his long eyelashes like unshed tears. When I don't think that he is going to say anything, he speaks.

"Why?" is all he says. I understand. He wants to know why I lied for him, became his accomplice in murder, forever tethering me to him through this necessary act of violence.

I sigh, looking up at him, needing him to understand the depths I would go for him. "I will always be your alibi. Your accomplice in life. Your partner in crime," I pause, afraid he might pull away, but I continue, "should you need me." He smiles down at me. He kisses me softly.

"Thank you." He pulls me close. "I love you" are words whispered against the hollow of my neck in the darkness of his room when we don't bother to dry off after the shower. I shiver as he leads me through his bedroom, but it's not from the cold.

And when he takes me to bed, it's not tender. It's impulsive, fueled by primal desires. It's a desperate plea falling from his lips as he enters me in one quick thrust, taking my breath away, echoing throughout a house that has now gone quiet except for the sounds of our slapping skin. I arch beneath him, my fingernails scratching his back, leaving my marks on him like the jagged runes of a spell cast under the full moon's light. We hold each other, and for once, he sleeps peacefully. No monsters that keep him awake at night, because that is what we have now become, whether he realizes it or not. He's a temptation too dangerous to resist.

It's in that pensive silence, then, that I know that I would do anything to take away his pain. Not just for him, but for others if I can. I make a promise not to tell him the truth I suspect today. I won't hold him back. I vow to ensure that he doesn't have to put someone first anymore and pursue his dreams, even if it means letting him go and becoming a ghost he won't mourn.

CHAPTER FOUR

DANI

I gnaw at my fingernails, fidgeting with restless energy as I try to keep my hands busy and my mind occupied, preventing me from unraveling in front of my mother. The waiting room smells of antiseptic, covering up the cloying reek of despair that hovers around us. I look around at the sunken faces with ashen grey complexions, letting you know that they are being destroyed from the inside out by an invisible killer, some more merciless than others.

Now seated beside my mother, her frail hand in mine, I understand that there is nothing to do but hope. Hope for a cure, news that our loved one is going to pull through, and that the words we will hear soon won't break us. My mother underwent an endoscopic ultrasound to biopsy a suspicious mass that they saw on a scan. As the needle slipped adjacent to the probe and through the layers of tissue into the looming mass on the screen, cells were gathered onto a slide and sent to the pathology department. Now the hard part begins. We wait. I pray to a God I barely believe in, still close my eyes, hoping whoever is listening will give us good news. Yet the truth grips tightly around me like a crushing weight.

"Mrs. Andrade?" My head whips up, taking in the nurse standing before us with a clipboard in her hand. She holds open the office door, allowing us entry, a gesture that will determine my mother's path forward. I nod and rise from the chair. Extending a hand to assist my mom up from her seat, her fingers feel so light in mine. It reminds me of all the times she held my hand to help me up when I was a child. Now, the roles are reversed, and I am the one helping her. After my parents' divorce, she used to walk with such strength. Her head held high, knowing she had bettered her life, despite having to start over. But illness has a way of stripping pride away so easily, reminding us that life is fragile and that life is inevitably terminal. She has become so weak over the last few months. She insisted that she was fine, and told me this over and over until one day she wasn't. Together we walk slowly to the door, one heavy foot in front of the other.

"Take your time," the nurse says kindly as she patiently waits for us, propping the door open. Her eyes flick briefly over to the wheelchair, folded neatly against the wall. I catch the movement and shake my head no. She nods, saying nothing, but I can see that she understands. My mom already feels like her independence is being stolen from her, so she continues this slow, relentless walk. Making her way across the short distance means more to her than the action because it's a declaration that she's still alive and still fighting.

The nurse places us in a small, sterile room, impersonal and devoid of color. The white walls and muted grey trim provide little comfort, and I wish that I could change the vibe. If I was delivering test results to patients, I'd want the room to be comfortable, with a warm tone and soft light. The temperature in here is too cold for patients who lack muscle mass and are in various states of fragility. I place my mom's cardigan around her shoulders as she smiles up at me with gratitude in her eyes. I return her smile, but inside, I just want to scream at the cruelty of it all, how illness strips your dignity and hope is the only thing that's left.

The doctor walks in with a chart in his hand, and his expression tells me everything I don't want to know. He is accustomed to giving this type of news, and I can tell it weighs heavily on him. His kind but tired eyes gauge our emotions as he provides a well-practiced speech. We leave the office without a word said between us. Even on the way home, no music or conversation ensues. Our silence persists, and when we get home, my mom quietly announces that she is tired and is going to bed. We don't talk about what we heard. But the doctor's words keep echoing in my mind—she is terminal. He couldn't give me a timeline of how long we have, just a vague estimate of the borrowed time left and options to prolong the inevitable. Some treatments that could extend her life are available, but they are costly. The only thing left to do is help my mom. I'll be there for her, just as she has always been there for me.

I walk down the steps, glancing across the yard over to Vic's house. It's still quiet, and that's not surprising, since I left his bed around three a.m., careful not to wake him. I had to be up early this morning to take my mother to her doctor's appointment. The air is humid, and I can feel my shirt sticking to me as I make my way to the mailbox. I grab the small stack of mail and head back to the house. Inside, I begin sorting through the envelopes, placing the bills in the woven basket my mom has set aside for them.

And that's when I see it. My breath catches in my throat when I see one stamped with the Dartmouth College crest. Vic and I both applied there, hoping to get into school together. We knew it was a slim chance we would both get in, but since both of our grades met the requirement, Vic encouraged me to apply.

I look at the letter before me, tracing the emblem with my fingertip. For a brief moment, I forget everything else. I open it with a large rip along the fold and remove the contents. My mouth curves into a stunned smile. I did it. As I read the acceptance letter, I feel the joy I haven't felt in months since having to care for my mom and dismissing her illness as just a virus. But then it hits me, like a shot through the heart. I can't go. My dream school with my amazing boyfriend is just that—a dream, because I can't leave my mom. She needs me, so it's no longer an option. Now the paper that I'm holding in my hands means nothing anymore. It's just a paper.

I grab the lighter and the ceramic tray, turning the lighter over in my hand. Without another thought, I hold onto the corner of my acceptance letter and hold it to the flame. It catches quickly, and I set it onto the tray, watching it burn along with my future. The paper blackens and curls inward as the flame consumes it. My dreams go up in smoke with a quiet finality. I light the envelope next, and the flames take hold, slowly devouring the paper. Half of it is gone, and the flame is almost out. I grab the other end, just about to relight it, when there is a knock on my door, so I let it burn out. The room smells of smoke and the end of my life as I know it. I walk to the door with a heavy heart, knowing what I have to do.

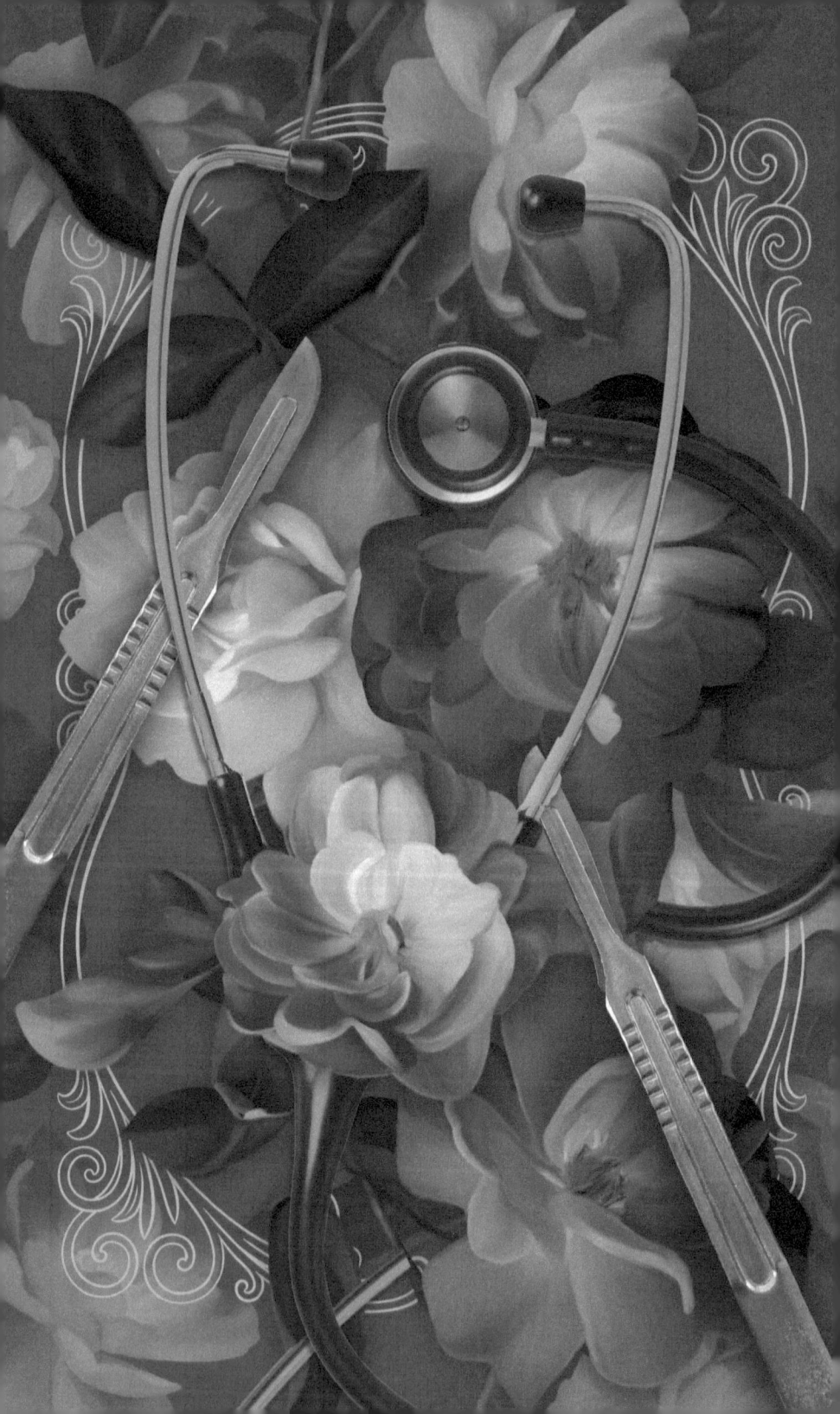

CHAPTER FIVE

VIC

I hold the letter with trembling fingers, quickly noticing it is from the college I applied to not long ago, but now it seems more like a lifetime ago. The green insignia etched along the stark white envelope of the esteemed medical school lies heavy in my palm, or perhaps it's just that it holds the weight of my future, with the potential to crush it all. I notice it's thicker than I would expect, giving me a moment's pause to feel hopeful. My breathing quickens in anticipation as I mentally prepare to read their decision. It would be thinner if it was a rejection letter, because brevity can be cruel and concise, needing only a few words to strike you down.

I tear at the folded edge, and the paper rips as the envelope flutters to the floor. I inhale deeply, bracing myself, before scanning the words on the page, but my heart stops when I read the first word.

"Congratulations," I say aloud and then stop reading. My world stills, and my knees threaten to buckle. The room tilts slightly, but I force myself to refocus. I blink, as if the acceptance letter might disappear or their typed words rearrange to announce my rejection from the school instead, because I just cannot believe the words written in bold lettering before me. I throw my hands on top of my head with the letter still clutched firmly between my fingers. Leaning over, I let out my breath in a long, ragged sigh. Still clutching the letter like a lifeline, my grin spreads wider and wider as I force myself to read the acceptance letter in its entirety. All I can think of is that I can't wait to tell Dani.

With that realization, I bolt out the door, letting it slam shut behind me. I race across the short distance to her house next door. I'm banging on the door before I stop moving, bouncing on the balls of my feet in feverish anticipation. I'm laughing manically because, despite all I have endured, I did it. I really fuckin' did it. I am finally going to make my dreams come true.

I hear footsteps approaching, and I lean forward, ready to take her in my arms. I can already picture how this will go. She gets accepted, she throws her arms around me, and we celebrate. The door creaks open, and when she steps through the doorway, I thrust my acceptance letter toward her with a huge grin. Then I notice her face. Her eyes are red and puffy. Her skin is blotchy, like she's been crying. My letter drops to the floor forgotten as I bring her into my arms.

"Baby, what's wrong?" Her sobs are the only thing I hear shattering the silence as she clings to my hoodie. She fists the fabric and pulls me closer to her as if she is trying to climb onto me. Without thinking, I scoop her up, and she wraps her legs around my waist, latching onto me like she can't get close enough, as she buries her face into the curve of my neck. I feel the warmth of her wet tears and the hotness of her breath against my throat.

My breath quickens as the monster within threatens to annihilate whatever dared to hurt her. I swallow the lump forming in my throat, thick with emotions flooding to the surface. Only she has that power to thaw the ice encasing my heart in its cold, protective exterior after years of seeing the worst in humans, exposing the beast within that would tear apart the world for her, yet stills at the sound of her sobs.

I cradle her tightly, one arm under her thighs, and the other strokes her hair with soft, gentle movements. I carry her through the house I know as well as my own, heading toward the worn couch that rests in the middle of the room. I sink onto it, still holding her like a child, whispering soothing words.

"I'm here, baby. I've got you." She doesn't answer and starts crying harder. I press my lips to her temple, gently coaxing her to tell me what's wrong. "Talk to me. Please, tell me what happened, Dani."

I wait patiently for her to speak. As her breathing becomes regular and the sobs abate into quiet shudders, I notice a tray smeared with ash. A half-charred Dartmouth envelope sits next to the ash alongside a lighter. It's as if it didn't finish burning, but the letter inside did.

I shut my eyes as the realization washes over me. And just like that, the joy I felt about my own acceptance slips away. Now, all I feel is a sense of sadness, and something far worse—loss. I'm filled with the weirdest feeling, a premonition that this is the instance where everything changes, so I need to stay and be there for her, just as she was for me, because if I don't, my future is uncertain when it comes to her.

I pull her closer to me, not wanting to ever let her go. I would stop time if I could, so that we could live in the moment forever with her in my arms and not me moving to the East Coast, so far away. Unfortunately, we need to have a conversation about our future. I want her to understand that I will stay with her here. I will choose her.

I tilt her chin upward, imploring her to look me in the eyes, conveying all my thoughts. Instead, she drops her gaze downward, severing our connection. Something cold settles in the pit of my stomach. An unease I've never felt before from Dani makes me want to throw up my breakfast because I don't want to hear her say those words.

"I'm not going without you," I say resolutely, holding her by the shoulders as she averts her eyes. She shakes her head in protest, her body stiffening as I hold onto her before she returns my stare.

"Vic," she whispers, lifting her hand to my face and brushing my cheek with a tenderness that feels more like a farewell. Her fingers tremble as if she's trying to memorize me, knowing it might be the last time. I lean into her touch, letting her warmth seep into the coldness that is overtaking my body like a biting frost against my humanity.

She is the balm that soothes my soul, and without her, I'm afraid of what I am. She has been my anchor after my mom died, and the only constant in my life, since the incident with my father. That's what we refer to it as "the incident," so that we never speak of what happened again or bring up his name.

She opens her eyes, and with fierce determination, her words cut me like a knife. "You're going to Dartmouth," she says, as if it's the only choice. We both know that's bullshit. I shake my head, fast and desperate, pleading with her. But she grabs my head, stilling it as I squeeze my eyes closed, refusing even to entertain the thought of leaving her behind. She's my everything. Doesn't she even realize? There is no me without her.

CHAPTER SIX

DANI

Now, I have to admit that I'm terrified of what the future holds. We both decided to skip our graduation because my mom was too sick to go, and Vic didn't have anyone to see him off. I wonder if he is starting to suspect something is up with her. If he does, he doesn't comment on it. The weight of this secret is almost too much to bear. I feel myself crumbling, wanting to confide in him, but that would be selfish of me.

With that thought, I add a few more items to the box. When it's full, I place the flaps down and run a strip of tape along the crease, sealing it shut. "There," I murmur as I grab the black Sharpie, labeling it.

I continue to help Vic sort through everything, deciding what to donate, keep, or sell. We've been at it all day, and the repetition is oddly comforting. I want to keep my mind occupied, and this task gives me something to focus on besides my imploding life. I grab another box and place it near the growing donation pile of items, loading it piece by piece, just as I did before. The task is mundane, but it keeps my hands busy while my thoughts threaten to spiral underneath the calm façade.

"I'm going to take a gap year!" I yell, as I lift the box and stack it with the others. The lie slips from my lips with practiced precision. I had rehearsed what I was going to say to Vic ever since we got the call to come in and discuss my mother's biopsy results. I already knew what they were going to say. Something in the nurse's voice implied that the news would not be good.

I think back to that day when I received my college acceptance letter. It was a kick straight to my heart. There was no rush of joy or breathless moment of excitement after realization set in. My broken heart wanted to hope, but to continue would be delusional.

Honestly, I didn't expect to get into Dartmouth. I knew Victor would, and that's what makes this harder to accept. It's like the universe lined this up perfectly to be a little bitch. I hang my head a bit lower, trying to calm my breathing at life's cruel joke and bitter fuck you because it wasn't just a school acceptance letter. It was the future Vic and I used to whisper about in the quiet hours of the night, wrapped around each other as the moonlight filtered through the windows, spilling onto the floor. We'd lie there staring up at the stars, making wishes like they'd come true if we just believed enough. Just a short time ago, when everything felt possible. I blink hard to fight the tears that threaten to fall. Now, nothing is possible with my mom's diagnosis and Vic leaving me.

I stand and repeat the motion of sealing the box and placing it alongside the others. I walk over to a stack of pictures and pick up the ones of us that we set in frames months ago, holding them close to get a better look. This one is my favorite. I touch the frame like a lover's caress. In the picture, I'm holding the phone out at arm's length, grinning like a fool, while Vic is looking at me instead of the camera. I didn't notice it back then, but now, staring at the image, I see it. The way he looks at me, as if I'm the only one that exists, as if he wants to devour me whole. I touch the frame, trying to hold onto that memory so that when he is gone, I will remember that exact moment, when he only had eyes for me.

I close mine briefly, savoring the moment before folding the picture in bubble wrap and placing it in my tote bag. "I'm keeping this one," I mutter under my breath to myself as I continue to glance around at the others, recalling the times when the pictures were taken, and the memories come flooding back.

I sigh. He knows everything about me, and I know everything about him. We were each other's only friends. I rarely had any female companionship, and Vic never had any friends because he was fearful that they would learn of his homelife and later, his mom's death. There were already whispers at school regarding the events of that night, but we chose to ignore them all.

After "the incident," we broke off any contact with our peers. We existed in our own closed, self-absorbed universe, with Dani and Vic at the center, and everything else orbiting around us in irrelevance. Vic never so much as looked at other girls, even when they tried to flirt with him shamelessly. They could never have what we have, so I never worried. I wrap the last of the pictures in tissue this time, my fingers lingering over them before setting them in another box, labeling it *pictures of us*. I set this box apart from all the others. He's going away to college, so maybe I should hold onto these until we meet again.

After some internal debate, I set the pictures aside and decide to keep them, so that I'll have a memento of us and be able to look at them when the memory starts to fade. Then I can remind myself that what we had was real, even though I know that no one will ever look at me like that with the raw passion he did ever again.

I stand looking around at all the boxes. Most of the items are destined for shelters or the town's swap shop to be repurposed. I'm lifting yet another box, setting it down carefully. Rinse. Wash. Repeat. When I turn around, he is there watching me. I didn't even hear him come back to the room. How long has he been standing there?

I push a strand of hair from my face and prop a hand on my hip, refusing to look away from those cold, calculating eyes. "A gap year?" he questions. His arms are folded across his chest in a protective stance. His sculpted muscles are on display as I try not to think about how his arms feel when he holds me close.

I forgot he had asked me what my plans were. I close my eyes, exhaling slowly before returning his stare. "Are you planning to apply anywhere near me, Dani?" He watches my reaction. "You know, there are tons of schools near there, too, right?" I nod steadily. "And you should start looking soon." He assumes I didn't get into Dartmouth, but why would he? He doesn't say anything else. He just waits.

"I'm going to focus on working as much as possible now to save up." I pretend to pick at an invisible thread on my knitted halter top, trying to sound as casual as possible. Without warning, he closes the distance, like a predator stalking its prey, until his chest nearly presses against me. His hand comes to rest under my chin, gently tilting it upward to look at him—his eyes, black as obsidian, narrow, locking on mine. The faint slant at the edges makes his gaze twist into something sharper, pinning you in place with its intensity. He exudes power and demands attention, but to me, he's just my Vic.

My mouth twitches, fighting the urge to laugh. He tilts his head. "Tell me you're going to move near me," he demands, but it comes out more like a plea. I sigh because we have had this conversation multiple times. Now that the time is drawing closer to his departure, he has become more insistent. Without looking away, I lift my arms and loop them around his neck, pulling him closer, so that there is barely any space between us.

"I promise you," I say softly, "I'll move near you." He must feel the truth in my words because his body sags, releasing the worry with it, and when he pulls me back to look at me, his eyes soften, reminding me of the boy I fell in love with. "I love you, Vic," I pull away from his stare, nuzzling closer, my cheek against his, "until I cease to exist." He lets out a short laugh in relief, as if I'd say anything else.

"Now you're speaking my love language, baby." He brings his lips to mine, kissing me deeply, one hand around my waist as the other travels upward to grasp my breast, when a knock sounds at the door, breaking us apart from our lust-filled trance.

CHAPTER
SEVEN

VIC

I know there is something she's not telling me. I've read every emotion on her face for years. It's there in the way her breath catches. I pull back to look her in the eye. Again, in the way she won't meet mine. An intimate silence thickens around us, so I table the conversation for another time as I kiss her instead. And just as I am about to take this further, a knock sounds that couldn't have come at a worse time. It's sound slicing through our perfect little bubble. I grit my teeth, and a pulse tics at my jaw as I hold back the thought of strangling whoever is at the door that dared to interrupt this moment between us.

"To be continued," I state coolly, even as the heat prickles under my skin at the anger I keep at bay. She looks at me quizzically, almost innocently, as if she isn't the one hiding something from me.

I pause, running a hand through my hair as I try to shake off this feeling. I feel her loss immediately, and I feel colder now, without her near, as I walk toward the door to answer it, just remembering about the appointment today.

"Realtor." I toss the word to Dani without looking back. The door creaks as I pull it open, reminding me of the sound of my father's voice that always followed shouting my mother's name. Although the man is no longer alive to threaten me daily, he still haunts my past.

A young man, not much older than us, stands at the entranceway, glancing around the house's exterior, and abruptly turns around as the door swings open, as if he hadn't expected me to answer it so quickly.

His eyes flicker into the dimly-lit interior of the house before returning to mine. "Hi," he says, extending his hand. "Brandon Marx." I look at his hand, unmoving for a second too long, before I finally shake it. His handshake is firm and confident, and something about his smile seems too polished. But I see it.

"Victor." I take his hand, giving it a firm squeeze that comes with a warning, but if he notices, he doesn't let on.

And right on cue, her voice causes my grip to tighten. Brandon doesn't flinch. He nods, showing way too many white, polished teeth. "Come in," I hear Dani say as Brandon notices her, releasing my hand, and walks in front of me. His hand is already outstretched to her, and I bet he has that fake smile already plastered to his face, too.

I close the door behind us slowly, trying to regain my composure. "Hi, Mrs. Flores?" he states it as a question, but it just grates on my last nerve because I know exactly why he asks. A low growl escapes before I can stop it, surprising even me as he holds onto her hand.

She laughs softly and shakes her head. "No, I'm Dani. Just Dani." That's all it takes. Two strides and I'm beside her, sliding an arm around her waist, and pulling her into my side. Her hand reaches around to mine across her waist.

Brandon hesitates, and a frown forms before he is forced to release her hand. Good. I was just wondering what it would be like to break every finger that touched her before severing it from his body.

Dani squeezes my hand, bumping me with her shoulder playfully. Her warm fingers slip through mine, grounding me away from my dark thoughts. I look down at her, expecting annoyance, but her eyes are alight with that familiar mischievous twinkle I've come to love so much. The one that ruins me every time, calling to the darkest part of me.

"Dani is my girlfriend," I state, turning to face him fully, letting a wicked smile form across my lips. The word hit their intended mark as Brandon falters. He stumbles back half a step before regaining his footing, realizing his mistake.

"Well." He clears his throat and clasps his hands in front of him, announcing in his all-business voice, "When do you want to list the house?"

I don't see, but I feel Dani shrink against me. I sigh, pinching the bridge of my nose as frustration begins to build. Without another word, I step away from her. "Come on, Brandon," I say, starting to walk away and beckoning him with my hand. "Follow me and I'll show you around the house so you can tell me what you think."

Brandon nods without looking at Dani again, then begins to walk behind me for a tour of the property. We walk out of the living room toward the kitchen, which leads to the back exit of the house. I push open the kitchen door, as it slowly creaks on its rusted hinges.

We step outside as the warm sunlight shines brightly against the dark cloud that surrounds me. As I look around, a sense of pride hits me because the yard looks better than it has in years. I've tried to keep up the lawn, and with Dani's help, removed the dead plants and planted some flowers, giving the landscaping a much-needed lift. It's incredible how something so simple can make the place feel less haunted. The house has good bones, and I hope the new owners can erase the darkness that lingers here.

I knew this day was fast approaching, and we knew that I would have to sell this house, but seeing the way she shrank against me made it so much more real. The fact that I will soon be leaving her kills me. The feeling in my chest is like a dagger to the heart. It hurts more than my father's shouts and his meaty fists that struck me down more times than I'd like to remember.

Brandon stands with one hand tucked into the pocket of his khakis, casually surveying the exterior upgrades to the house. He pivots in place, glancing over the flower beds, the back porch, and the yard before returning to look at me.

"So…what do you think?" I ask, keeping my tone neutral, because I want to know if I can get a reasonable price for my home. I was able to cash in on some of my father's retirement savings, although it was a small amount. I am also counting on the sale of my house to help pay for college. I am already approved for a work-study program, so that will help a bit, but most of it hinges on this. And despite logic, sadness envelops me because as I look over every square inch of this house, all I can think of is that this was ours—mine and Dani's hard work. The good memories of us and our shared dreams, along with the things we don't talk about, are all to be left behind with a price tag.

Brandon unwraps a piece of gum, pops it into his mouth, and proceeds to chew it loudly. The sound of his chewing grates on my nerves, with each pop and wet snap. I force myself to ignore it. He bobs his head back and forth, continuing to smack the gum between his teeth. Finally, he nods. "I think it will fetch a good price." My shoulders drop slightly at his words, and the breath I was holding escapes slowly through pursed lips.

"That's good news," I say, wiping the sweat that has started to bead across my forehead. The Texas sun continues beating down on us like it has a personal vendetta.

Brandon flashes me a smile. "So…are you ready to list it?"

I nod. "Yeah, let's do it." We head back to the house, where Dani is still in the living room, packing up the boxes of clothes and knick-knacks to donate. She doesn't look up.

I walk Brandon out to the front door. He pauses with one hand on the doorframe before stepping out. "I will get some comps for you," he says, throwing me that fake smile. "It should give you a better idea of what price your house would fetch on the market." He pauses. "I think you will make out well on this sale. And hey, you might even be surprised." I nod once, my hold on the doorknob grip becoming tighter as I hold it open for him. But he doesn't move. He turns toward Dani, who is still crouched over a box. "It was a pleasure to meet you, Dani." He lifts his hand in a small wave.

Before she can reply, I nearly shove him out the door. Shutting the door harder than I should, I stare at it, like I'm waiting for Brandon to come back and ask about my girl. But he doesn't.

I watch him walk over to the car, sparing one last glance at the house, before pulling out and driving down the street.

When I turn around, Dani is staring at me with one eyebrow arched. It freaks me out when she does that. "What?" I play dumb, even though I know exactly what she is thinking.

"Vic," she says with her arms crossed across her chest. "I cannot believe you were so rude to that realtor," she says angrily, but her actions belie her words.

I shrug. "He was trying to hit on you right in front of me." She shakes her head, more exasperated than anything else. "You know it's true," I press, watching her reaction closely.

She chuckles, placing a hand across her forehead. "What were you thinking?" Her voice is weary, and concern laces her following words. "You know there aren't any realtors in this area, at least not one who isn't already overwhelmed with clients."

I stroll toward her slowly with intent. I pull her into my arms, burying my head in the crook of her neck. "I was thinking," I murmur as my lips brush against her warm skin, "what it would be like to sever his hand from his body after he touched you."

Her sudden intake of air makes me smile. I press my mouth against her soft skin there, sucking until I know it will leave a mark. "Would you like that, baby?" I laugh lowly, but there is no humor to it. My tongue follows up, soothing the area where I'm sure a bruise is already forming. She moans. "You'd like that, wouldn't you?" She doesn't answer, but I feel it as her fingers grip my shoulders tightly in response. She's just as turned on by my violent and cruel side as she is by my everyday rational thoughts. I lift her easily, bringing her legs up to wrap around my waist and keep her there, right where she belongs.

CHAPTER EIGHT

DANI

He knows there is something I'm not telling him. He has since that day, when we both received our acceptance letters to Dartmouth College. Vic is perceptive and has become an expert at reading people, especially their hidden intentions. But I may be better.

Now the day I have dreaded has finally come. The realtor was true to his word, and Brandon sold Vic's house for more than he expected, even after he took his commission. As I look around at the empty house, I can't explain the undeniable sadness that overwhelms me. It's as if our book was written without a conclusion. What will happen to us now? Will Vic ever forgive me for what I am about to do?

I just pray with everything I have left in me that last night wasn't our last. We slept on the inflatable mattress in Vic's room that we once thought of as our sanctuary, the walls stripped bare and closed up boxes placed in a corner with the only remaining items Vic keeps. I stared up at the ceiling, but only saw memories, so many that I lost count. I couldn't help but remember all the times we lay there together, making plans for the future. We were so sure of everything, and now nothing is for certain. We stayed that way as long as we could, both of us not wanting to surrender to this moment where he leaves me behind.

Vic's car is packed to the brim, and every last item is loaded up. The car waits, idling until he makes the drive across the country to New Hampshire. He plans to drive most of the way, straight through whenever possible, until sleep becomes necessary, and only then will he stop. There won't be anyone to take the wheel when the highway begins to blur and his eyes grow heavy with sleep, because he will be alone without me to assist with the driving. He also promises to call. And I promise to answer. It shouldn't feel like a question, but I think he can sense it. The distance is already pulling at us, unraveling at something we don't have the words to acknowledge.

He stares at me with a hip pressed up against the metal of his car, like its magnetic hold will anchor him in place, stopping him from coming at me and dragging me along with him. The vehicle is loaded with his sole remaining possessions, except for one box of photos I kept for myself, so I can look back at all our memories, tying me to Vic after he leaves.

I stand there, looking up at him, small beneath the heavy weight of our goodbyes, with my thumbs in each front pocket of my cut-off jean shorts, as if I, too, need something to hold onto—to keep me grounded. We are caught in a silent standoff, each of us unwilling to speak first, afraid to rupture the fragile moment with words. His dark, black eyes are burning into me, holding me steady under the weight of his stare. I can't bear the weight of them, like he can see inside my mind and my heart. But it isn't the man I love that's looking at me now, it's his obsession bordering on madness. His passion has always been dangerous, but now, under his intense scrutiny, it's ravenous.

So I look away, coward that I am, because if I meet his gaze for a second longer, I'll cave. The words clawing at my throat will release with fury. *Please stay, don't go, and I need you now more than ever.* But the problem is that I know what he'll do. He'll abandon the future he fought for, thinking nothing of dismissing the rare opportunity he was given that waits across the country. He may never forgive me if he stays, but I know for sure that I will never forgive myself for denying him this chance.

Vic is the most brilliant man I have ever known, with a sharp tongue, endless curiosity, and a mind that never rests. If anyone deserves a chance to begin a new chapter, it's him. I love it for him, but it doesn't make this any easier.

I swallow back the cry that threatens to rip free of my throat. Instead, I close the few inches remaining between us as my body begins to shake uncontrollably, and throw my arms around him. He catches me without hesitation, folding himself around me tightly and resting his chin on the crown of my head. That's all it takes for the dam to break, as I fall apart in his arms. I expel it all from my body, purging all thoughts. For the uncertainty about our future. For the absence of his touch that I already mourn. For the sickness devouring my mother from the inside out. And worst of all, for the way everything I love is rapidly slipping away through my fingers, just like the tears from my eyes. So I do the only thing I can do—I ugly cry into his chest with all the anguish I've tried to deny feeling.

And he just holds me in his steady, silent embrace—letting me grieve not just him, but what I know is my life collapsing. He rubs my back in a soothing rhythm that speaks more than words ever could. When I stop to pull back and look up at him, his eyes are red, too. Tears are tracking along his cheeks that remind me of the way a hard rain looked against the windowsill as he took me like a man possessed in the backseat of his car while we waited for it to stop. "I love you, Dani." His voice is steady as he looks me in the eye with certainty.

"I love you," I repeat, much like the vows we made together in the dark, "forever and a lifetime more." I reach up, sliding my fingers behind his neck, pulling him down to me. Our mouths meet in a desperate kiss. He kisses me like it's his last breath, and I kiss him like it's my last time I'll ever feel this alive. Because the truth is, it very well could be.

When he discovers what I've done, will he forgive me for lying even if I had the best intentions? Will he see the love in my lie?

He pulls away reluctantly with his hands lingering along my waist as if he is trying to memorize my face in this moment. Then he lets go, turning to grab his bag off the cement driveway, and hurling it into the passenger seat spot that was supposed to be mine. He turns back, his eyes sweeping over me one last time. Then he gently places his fingers beneath my chin, almost reverently, his fingers caressing my cheek, catching a stray tear. Too many fallen to count. He lets his hand fall from my face, bringing his fingers to his lips.

"Until next time, baby." His voice is husky and low, but it rings loudly in my ears along with the rapid beating of my heart. He walks over to the driver's side of the car and opens the door. He places one leg into the driver's seat, and one hand rests on the top of the door. For a brief moment, he watches me and smiles, albeit a sad but hopeful one. Resigned, he hits the top of the car twice and disappears inside. The car door closes with a loud thud, much like the finality of our future. We stay there for what feels like an eternity, in the exact moment in time frozen, not wanting to accept our separation, and just when I'm about to cave and give up, telling him not to go and how I am unable to do this alone, he puts the car in reverse. When he turns around to wave, I lose my nerve. I don't stop him, and lift my hand to do the same.

It takes everything I have not to crumple into a little ball right there on the cracked cement driveway. I force myself to walk toward the end of the driveway and onto the street to continue waving until he turns the corner and I can no longer see his taillights. I drop my hand in defeat, and stand there on the road feeling hollowed out, regretting what I had to do. I hang my head in shame and want so badly to undo everything I have set into place.

I knew that I would feel this way, so I didn't allow myself a moment to wallow in my pity party of one. Instead, I am going to crush that job interview this afternoon, which will allow me to attend school at the community college and have great benefits, so that my mom can stop working and focus on getting better. So I will carry this burden for us and do what she has always done. Take care of us. And maybe, if there is a higher being, they will have mercy on us and allow me to have my future with the man who drove away with my heart, and hope he finds his way back to me.

As I walk past his home, it stands there dark and looming. A reminder of all I lost. As of tomorrow, someone else will be the new owner, and it's something I can't imagine having to witness every day. I walk into my house feeling more alone than I ever have felt since moving here. I think back to that day, when a boy first waved at me from his bedroom window, and I smiled back.

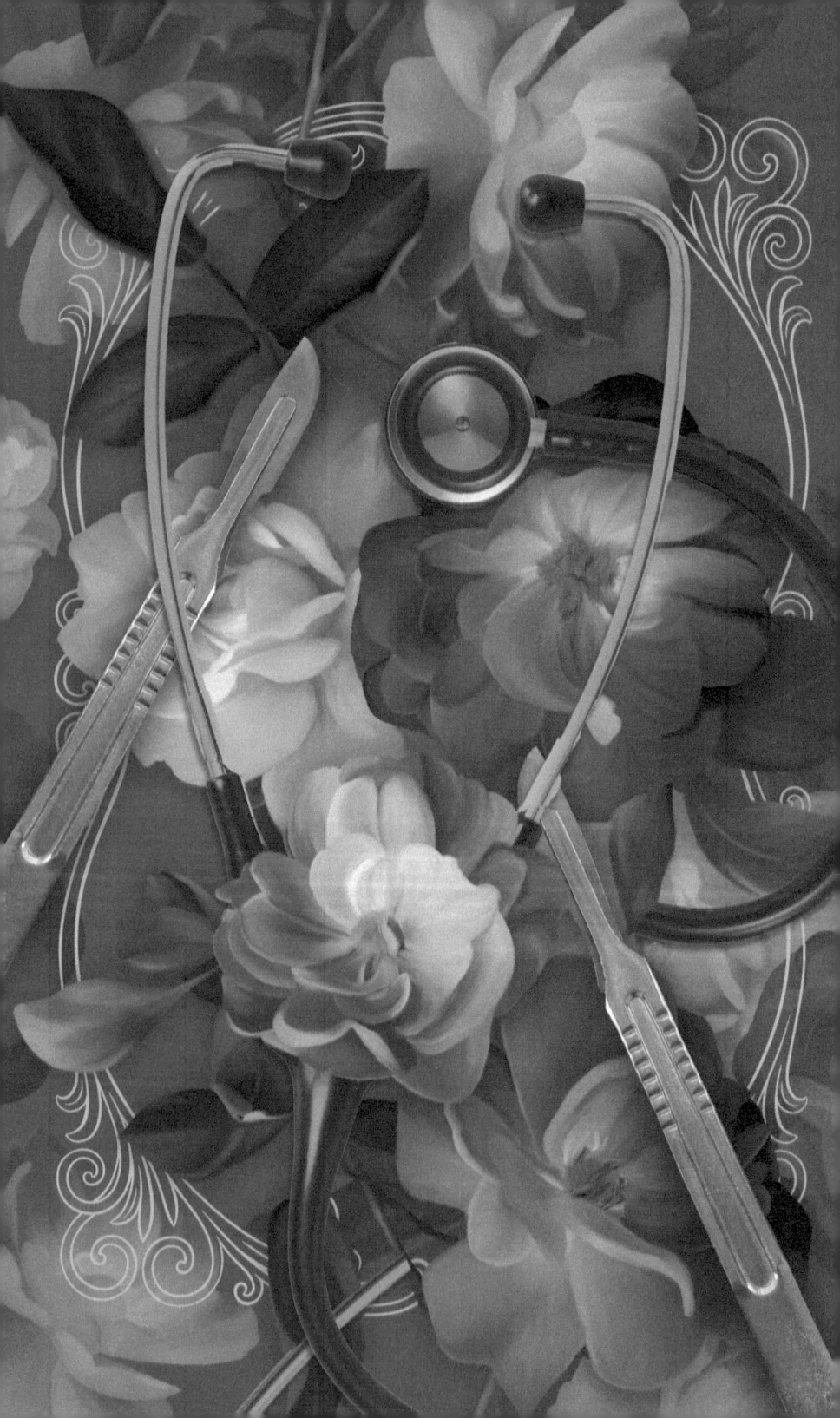

CHAPTER NINE

VIC

It took three long, solitary days to drive to New Hampshire. Three days of endless nights thinking about Dani and a growing anticipation of a dream I had wished to come true for so long. On the final night, as I neared my destination, I booked a hotel, knowing I desperately needed rest. I craved a long shower to wash away the incessant worries that have been running endless circles through my mind.

Stepping outside afterward, I finally took in the scenery around me. I hadn't realized how rural this area was, or how beautiful the mountains looked, cloaked in mist, so unlike the flat, sun-soaked plains of Texas. It is truly something special to behold, and for a moment, it made my thoughts a little less heavy.

I found myself grateful for the foresight to rest because the roads are narrow and winding. If you're not cautious, in one careless moment, you could find your car crumpled against a granite boulder or a moose. When I arrived on campus, I looked around and noticed how the ivy clung to the school's exposed brick. Everything here seems remarkably old, and the school's history dates back to the 1700s.

After I collect my housing assignment and schedule, I make my way to the weathered dorm along the creaking stairs to the second floor that houses my room. When I open the door and step in, I notice another person already occupying half. With nothing left to decide, I place my belongings on the only other remaining bed, where I will live for the remainder of the year and the spring semester. I heard another student in line at the bookstore complaining about the overcrowded quads, so this is a special treat. I pull up my schedule, excited to see how full it is. I can only hope it keeps my mind off the other half of my heart still with her, miles away.

A couple of months have passed in a blur of constant assignments and school activities, and I've settled in nicely, on the surface. I've spoken to Dani, but not as often as I'd have hoped. She seems to be constantly working or otherwise occupied. I am starting to become concerned that she is pushing herself too hard. Her messages are brief and clipped. Without the opportunity to have a decent conversation, I don't know how to approach the pending sense of doom I feel. I plan on surprising her before Halloween. It's our favorite holiday, and I miss her so much that being away from her this season feels almost cruel.

Here, the leaves have turned a majestic shade of crimson, amber, and aubergine, transforming New England into something otherworldly. The cobblestone streets evoke nostalgic memories of a time long ago, with carriages and headless horsemen from the novels I frequently read. I almost expect to see such a scenario because the fall weather elicits these tales of witches and warlocks.

The brisk air brings out all kinds of people walking down the pavement in trench coats, hats, and even the occasional gloves, depending on the drop in temperature. I find myself colder than most, but that's no surprise, having come from a warmer climate, but the air here is so clean and crisp that I can't help but enjoy the scenery. The streets smell of wood smoke, crisp apples, and something earthy. Last weekend, I joined a few classmates for apple picking at a local orchard. We feasted on warm cider donuts and dark, spiced cider with a higher alcohol content than I expected.

Still, through it all, I couldn't shake thoughts of Dani and what she's doing at this moment, especially when I returned to my dorm alone with just my memories to hold onto. I miss her more than I can say, and I long for the day she'll come and visit. Any alone time with her would be worth it, no matter how brief. Maybe I can show her the sights here and remind her of what she's missing. She is always working, and I hope I can convince her to take a much-needed break from it all. I'd like to spend the time showing her around, not to mention I missed my girl and plan on spending a large portion of that time between her legs, too, reminding her of how her body bends to mine and how we fit together so perfectly.

The last session of classes ends for the day right at noon. One thing about New England is that, during the fall and winter months, we lose daylight sooner, and it isn't uncommon for it to be dark by five p.m. I rush back to my room to pick up one more item. I open the dresser and remove the little velvet box, placing it in the side pocket and securing it there. Some of my friends are going into Boston to celebrate the Halloween festivities, so I arranged to catch a ride with them. Without needing anything further, I meet up with them, heading into Boston early before rush hour hits. This gives me plenty of time to catch my flight and for them to enjoy some Halloween festivities in the city.

I've already purchased a ticket, so they'll drop me off at Logan. I tried calling Dani again today, but as usual, she didn't answer. And yet I can't shake this feeling. Something deep inside me senses the secrets she's hiding, leaving me alone in the dark, guessing at what they could be. I hope that I'm wrong, but every time we talk, a quiet tension lingers. I bridge the space between us with stories about my classmates, only to wonder if I'm making it worse by reminding her of what she's missing. It's the crushing realization that she didn't get in. I wish more than anything that she were here, sharing this new adventure with me and creating new memories together.

I almost need her to say something else, anything to fill the silence, so I don't feel like I'm the one making her sad by being here without her. Doesn't she understand that without her, the days are something I endure rather than live? I want her here with me, at my school, close enough to grasp something real instead of clinging to the tormenting memory of her last caress. So I hold onto it, keep it close, and do everything I can to let her know she's constantly on my mind.

I try to stay close to her however I can, but my attempts to stay connected are far from thought out. Like when we tried to have phone sex. Yeah, that didn't go so well. My roommate's girlfriend walked into our dorm room with a friend right in the middle of it. It was painfully awkward, and by the time they finally left, after trying to drag me to their party they were going to, Dani was silent on the other end of the line—cold and almost entirely detached. There was nothing I could do to fix that phone call, so we hung up, and I felt like everything I had was slipping through my fingers.

I wish she could see that no one will ever compare to her. She just has to trust me when I say she is the only one for me, because every thought, every beat of my heart, belongs to her alone.

I can't bear the distance any longer. Words are no longer enough. I have to prove to her, make her see how much she means to me, and the only way to do that is in person. I need to show her how deeply I miss her, and remind her of how well we work together—how we still belong to each other. And I intend to spend the night, and all weekend, proving just how undeniably true that still is.

CHAPTER TEN

DANI

I, in fact, did not crush that job interview. Not getting the job makes the realization of my circumstances undeniable. And now I know with bleak clarity that my situation is more fucked than I'd like to admit. How impossible it is to find work here that offers the benefits that I so desperately need is soul-sucking. Every job opening is part-time and offers little more than minimum wage and a polite slap in the face. None of it comes close to the security I need to keep this household afloat. It's the worst kind of desperation, realizing you can't do anything about it unless a drastic change is made.

Worst of all, I couldn't stand seeing the new family in Victor's old house. Strangers now occupy the house where we shared our first everything. I swear I can still hear our laughter echoing from next door, our whispered promises made in the dark, and our shared sins that continue to haunt my dreams. I see the young couple on the porch sometimes, and their children running across the lawn as night falls. They stay out long past the children's bedtime, stargazing like Vic and I used to.

Now our favorite holiday, Halloween, is fast approaching, and the whole world is dressing up in costumes. I don't need to don a mask because I'm already living a lie. I want to rip down the orange string lights and smash the pumpkins with their taunting, cruel smiles, the same ones I once loved to carve. I want to pull my hair out, just to feel something other than the agony I feel from Vic's absence. It's killing me from the inside out, and as much as I try to put on a fresh face for my mother's sake, she knows the hurt that lies just beneath the surface.

After she confronted me about it, I told her everything—the lies, my fears, and especially how my heart is breaking without the man I love. It all spilled out of me. I cried as she held me because I couldn't be brave anymore, even though I don't think I am. Not compared to her. She is the brave one, the one who gets up every morning, praying it isn't her last, which just makes me feel all the more pathetic. But she continues to hold me and validates my feelings, having the grace to comfort me, as if my heartache is real pain, even though it pales in comparison to hers.

With that, I knew what I had to do. That night, after another endless double shift at the diner in my dead-end job, which smelled of burnt coffee and my broken dreams, I spoke to my mom about the reality of our situation. As we sat at the kitchen table, I spoke of how we would need to move to the city and seek charitable assistance at a well-renowned cancer center to explore better options. I have a job interview at that same hospital, and I have applied to the community college for the spring semester to take my introductory courses. As if the stars were aligning, I was accepted into the college, I got the job, and we were approved for charitable care after providing documentation of our limited financial resources. Now, all that is left is to make one call.

The doorbell rings, and I wipe my hands on my shorts, trying to calm myself. When I pull the door open, there he is, Brandon Marx, the realtor who sold Vic's house, and who Vic also threatened with bodily harm, standing on my doorstep. Except this time, my boyfriend isn't here to interfere. Brandon stands on the front porch as the late sunlight flashes off his designer sunglasses, which he has casually slipped between his teeth as he sizes me up. When he sees me, he flashes that obscenely perfect smile, showing his expensive veneers, because no one's teeth are that perfect.

"Hey there," he says as I open the door fully and invite him in. Closing the door, I turn to find him watching me. But as if just remembering, he quickly scans around, searching as if he is waiting for Vic to assault him from another room.

I shake my head, keeping my voice even. "Vic's away at school. He left months ago," I say. He nods, but doesn't ask anything further, which I am grateful for.

"I have to admit," he tucks his sunglasses in the front pocket of his tailored blazer, "I was surprised that you called me." I walk toward the kitchen.

"Would you like something to drink?" I ask without turning around. He follows me. "I have iced tea, water, and Jarritos." I open the fridge, letting soft light and cool air escape, making me shiver as goosebumps pebble across my bare arms. I reach for a Jarritos, the sweet fizz of the Mexican soda transporting me back to memories of open markets and long afternoons spent on family trips across the border. The glass is slick with condensation as I pop the cap off with a practiced smack against the opener mounted beside the fridge. I don't wait for him to decide, as I take a long pull of the cold liquid. The crisp tang of mandarina fills my mouth, the flavors bursting like liquid sunshine. A small sigh slips out as the cold seeps into my hand from the bottle, and wetness drips onto my wrist.

His smile plays at his lips as he watches me. "I'll take one, too." Without another word, I return to the fridge, retrieving another bottle. I pop the cap and hand it over, tossing the caps in the trash beside the sink. He extends his bottle to mine, and I meet him halfway, clinking the neck with mine. "Here's to getting you the most on this sale." I nod as we have a silent stare-off while drinking our soda.

A moment later, I motion with my hand, repeating words Vic had spoken not long ago. "Follow me, Brandon, and I'll show you the house, then you can tell me what you think."

I take Brandon on a tour of the property, and he notices every detail, offering advice for a quick fix that could increase the value. "A fresh coat of paint here," or "A little swap of this broken faucet knob can do wonders," I hear him say. I consider his advice and weigh my options.

We walk around the outside perimeter of the property, and I take a wilting flower into my hand, twirling it slowly between my thumb and forefinger. He's talking about powerwashing the siding, and I understand what he's saying, but I just shake my head. He turns toward me, patiently waiting for me to speak. "I don't know if I can do that." He stops to look at me, sensing the shift. The question lies unspoken, so I address it. I force it out before I can think about it. "My mom is dying." I cough, trying to force the rising bile down my throat. Brandon's shoulders slump, and I see the way his eyes comprehend my situation. "Vic doesn't know." I look down, kicking at the grass, attempting to give myself something to do instead of standing still, feeling useless.

"Why didn't you tell him?" Brandon asks curiously. His voice is soft, non-accusatory, and it's a valid question. So I give him the truth.

"I didn't want him to put off medical school to stay back and help me," I say, still twisting the limp flower until the petals begin to fray. "He's too smart for that. He got a full ride for his undergrad, so I guess he's allowed at least one good thing in his life." The words hang heavy between us, and I know Brandon is from here, so he must be familiar with the story surrounding the house and Victor's parents' death. It's not something I will ever talk about, no matter who it is. Brandon must sense it, too, because he changes the subject.

"So that's why you need to sell the house?" he asks. "To care for your mom and cover her treatments?"

I nod slowly, pondering my following words. "Yeah," I say barely above a whisper. "It won't save her life, but it could prolong it, and that's all I can hope for, and that she doesn't suffer." Instead of asking further questions, he does something unexpected. He offers me help.

"I can help you fix up a few of those things I pointed out, and I'll do something further." He glances away, rubbing his chin with his hand like he's trying to work something out in his head. "I can cut my commission to the bare minimum, and that will let you keep more of the money to help with your mom." For a moment, I just stare at him, wondering if I heard him right. The flower falls to the grass, forgotten. Tears well up in my eyes at the kind gesture.

"Thank you so much, Brandon. You don't realize how much I appreciate that." He smiles and then turns around, assessing the property further.

"You know," Brandon says, sweeping a final glance at the house, "I think we can get a good price for this place." I huff out a laugh. With that, we walk toward the front of the house to where his car is parked in the driveway. "I'll pull the comps tonight of similar properties in the area," he adds, reaching for the car handle. "I'll let you know, okay?" As he smiles at me, my eyes meet his, shimmering with unshed tears.

"Okay," is all I can manage at this point.

He opens the car door, but pauses midway. "You know," he says, turning fully to face me, "if I were Vic, I wouldn't have been able to leave either. Not if I knew." He doesn't wait for a reply, because what could I possibly say to that? I stand there still as a statue as he slips into the driver's seat and starts the engine. He gives me a small wave before pulling out onto the streets, and then he's gone. The sound of his tires on the asphalt fades, but his words linger, making me second-guess my choices about keeping this from Vic.

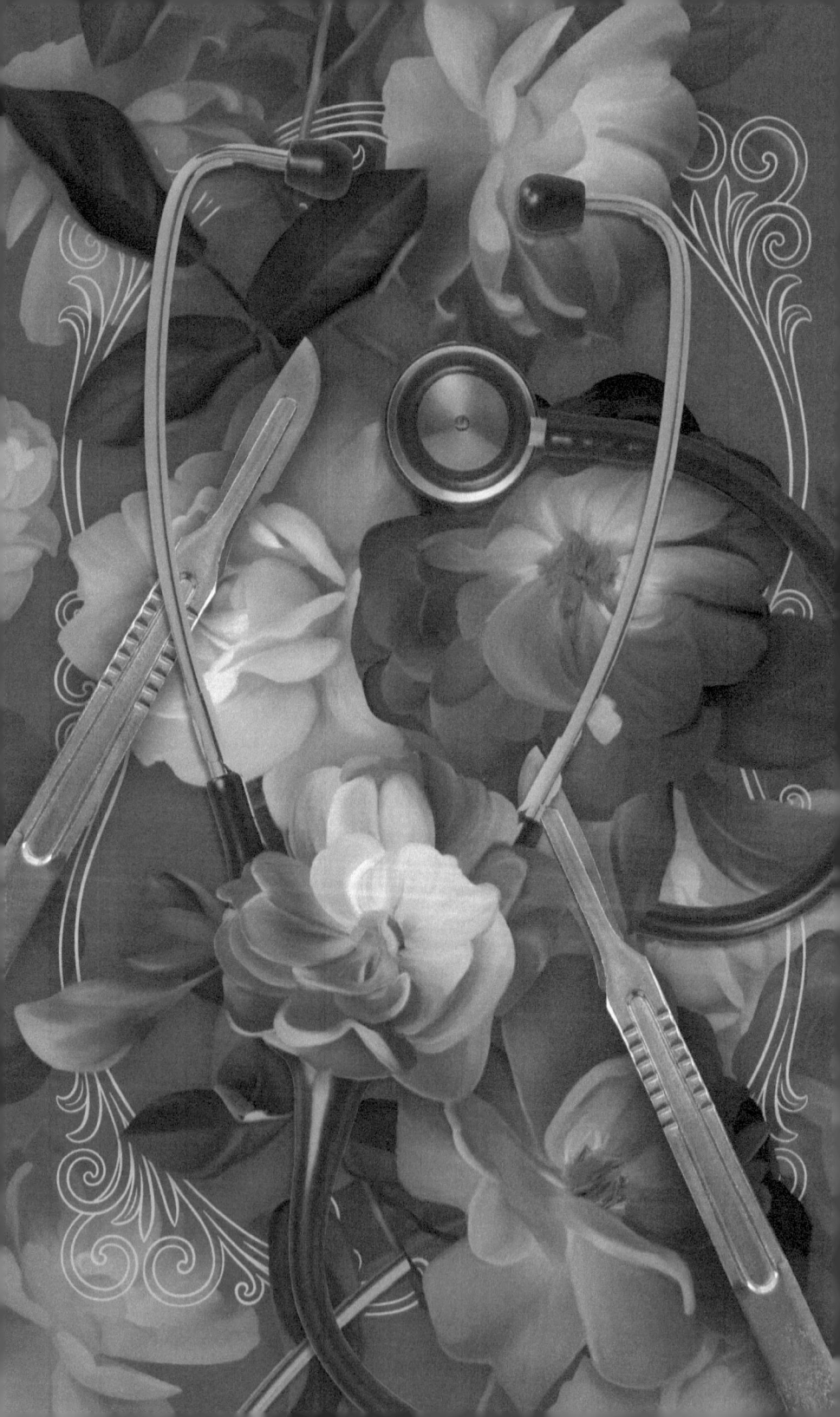

CHAPTER ELEVEN

VIC

I board the plane for a straight connection to Texas, back to my old life, to Dani, and everything that's home. The flight seems to drag on for an eternity, but when the captain's voice crackles through the intercom, announcing that we are making our final descent into the Austin airport, I can't help but feel a tinge of excitement at his words.

I grab my carry-on, and with my pulse thrumming in my veins just below my skin with anticipation, I step into the rental car that is reserved and waiting for me at the curb. The temperature here is so vastly different from up north that it makes me start sweating. I peel off my hoodie, which still smells of pine trees and crisp autumn air, and toss it into the back seat along with my bag before stepping in and driving away to see my girl. The engine hums to life as I start the car, and it zooms onto the highway.

The city lights blur past the windows with each passing mile until I reach farm fields on the outskirts of town, where the landscape of our rural town comes into view. I should be elated, brimming with joy because I'll be near her soon, and if I'm lucky, I'll be enveloped in her warmth for the entire weekend, or longer if I can help it. Instead, unease envelopes me, and a reckless foreboding invades my thoughts.

To settle the whispers in my head, I try calling her again, but it goes to voicemail. Her silence is more deafening, so I don't leave a voicemail. I should let her know that I'm on my way, but for some reason, I choose not to. Now, I'm wondering if I misunderstood. Maybe she is working again tonight, trying to save up that much-needed cash to join me. I know that sometimes she also picks up shifts for extra money because that was the plan, right? To meet me as soon as possible? At least, that was my understanding.

But as I turn onto Dani's street, a twinge of unease settles in me, twisting low in my gut. I lift my foot from the gas, and ease forward, letting the familiar street slowly come into view. The unease continues to grow, and dread begins to consume me. I should be overjoyed that in just a few minutes, I'll finally be holding her. Yet, to settle whatever this is, I try calling her once more, but it goes straight to her preprogrammed voicemail. Again, I hang up without leaving a message.

"I bet she's working. That has to be it," I say, snapping my fingers as if doing so will make it happen. All I need are the magical words with a chant of abracadabra to go with them. I hope that isn't the case tonight, because it will seem like forever until I can see her, but so be it. I'll just show up and surprise her at work and wait until she gets out at eleven. Will she be as excited to see me as I am to see her? I slowly pass along the familiar homes close to ours, and that's when I notice someone in her driveway. At first, I don't think much of it until I realize the car is one I've seen before, but for the life of me, I can't place it. A chill prickles at the back of my neck. "Why can't I place it?" I bring my hand to my chest as I feel it tighten there. I try my best not to overreact and calm the beast inside that knows something is wrong with this situation. The name, the face—it's right there, just out of reach. We have a solid relationship. I should trust her. Although I know I shouldn't worry, something tells me to pull over immediately, so I decide to wait there for a couple of minutes, giving me a perfect view while the engine idles.

I want to see who this is, and I'll wait here for as long as possible.

My legs begin to shake nervously, and I'm jittery. But I don't have to wait too long because that's when I see them together. I do a double-take to see if I'm imagining things. I lean forward as if maybe I can hear the conversation. My ears turn hot, and I swear I can feel my heartbeat thumping loudly in my chest. I try not to jump to conclusions, but it is getting harder to resist.

He's holding a bag. Did he stay the fucking night? My knuckles turn bone white from gripping the steering wheel like I envision gripping his throat, squeezing so tightly as I watch the light fade from his eyes when he realizes the grave mistake he's made. I don't dare move as I try to calm the monster that wants to wreak havoc and ask questions later, breathing in and out like I used to when my father spewed his venomous words.

Then she hands him some keys, and he hugs her, kissing the top of her head, and I fucking lose it. He holds her like she means something to him. He looks at her like she's his, and I wonder how long Dani and Brandon, my previous realtor, have been having this relationship behind my back. I can hardly believe what I'm seeing, but it's undeniable. Did it happen as soon as I left? They are obviously together, and the thought makes me want to vomit. My brain screams in silent protest, rioting inside in what my lips refuse to voice aloud. She's mine. She'll always be mine.

I feel something inside me crack. My fists begin to shake, and I imagine him suffering a terrible fate at my hands. Would Dani help me with the body this time? No. Not for him, her new lover. The thoughts turn acrid in my mouth as my mind races, unraveling every small detail of the past couple of months. I remember old phone calls, and how I thought I was imagining Dani's clipped voice growing detached and distant with each passing day. I blamed myself, calling it paranoia or my increased exhaustion from countless sleepless nights either studying or missing her, as well as having the most fucked up past to resurrect every insecurity I thought I had buried along with my parents.

I feel the betrayal first, knocking the breath out of me, leaving a hollow ache. Then comes disbelief, not because she chose someone else, but that she did it so easily despite our instant connection and shared secrets. Lastly, the rage. It's all-consuming, made ten times worse by the knowledge that I meant so little to her as it implodes within me. Everything I have done, I did for us and the future I wanted to share. However, it was just a dream, nothing more.

I was too focused on climbing my way to the top by finishing medical school, becoming a doctor, forging a life as a partner and a husband. I've been so consumed by my goals that I can't shake the fear that what I left behind might be gone when I return. And yet I clung to our love, stubbornly refusing to question that she would wait for me, even as the thought of her slipping away turned every moment into torment. Maybe I'll never get the reason I deserve, and be forced to accept that I've been replaced. Unable to fathom any reason to further torture myself by staying to watch the rest unfold, I leave just as quickly as I came, my heart heavy and praying for bleach to scrub the scene from my eyeballs.

I drive in silence, my cold hands on the steering wheel, with a clear path straight to the airport, unable to escape the heavy thoughts swirling in a maelstrom of emotions roaring through my head. I move on autopilot, dropping the rental off at the kiosk and grabbing my bag from the back as I walk to the departing terminal, quickly calling the hotel to cancel my reservation and informing them that I have an emergency that requires my immediate attention back home.

Just like that, my old life is gone. This is no longer my home. As I board the plane with a newfound purpose, I feel my new identity begin to take hold of me. It is filled with loathing and a relentless need to destroy, born from a shattered heart beyond repair. There is no recovering, no returning to the man Dani once knew. He is gone and buried, replaced by a coldness that envelops me, solidifying into something methodical and calculating in the wake of her absence. I shut myself off from the emotions that threatened to consume me because I won't allow myself to feel what I felt for Dani ever again or with anyone else. She is the only woman I have ever loved and will love. She holds all the power. Now, I fight the monster within that knows only pain and cruelty. He is the one who has resurfaced, staying to protect me from ever feeling that way again. And I welcome him with open arms.

CHAPTER TWELVE

DANI

I took the day off to help Brandon with the last-minute touch-ups. It's the final day I'll ever spend in this house, and that thought alone has me down. You'd think that I grew up here, but in a way, I did. I found something more real here than in all of my existence. But tonight, I will load up the last of our things, severing my only tangible connection to Vic and the way we fit so perfectly together.

Tomorrow morning, I'll drive my mom and me to a new city, a new apartment, and a new life, leaving behind a place that I will always call my home because this is where I gave my heart and soul to a boy who will forever own me.

I hold the cold, metallic keys in my hand. They feel so heavy as I give them over to Brandon. "Here." I extend the keys to him. He watches me, and I know he sees my throat bob as I swallow down the lump quickly forming there. "I guess there is no need for these anymore, right?" I know it is a rhetorical question, but still, some part of me wants to hold on to them, and in doing so, keep the memory of us alive a little longer here in this place where it all began. Because right now that's all I have left.

And I know that I haven't done a great job of showing Vic how much he means to me. That he is still mine. But I have had so much on my plate lately, and he can't understand because I never let him in. And I'm just so damn tired of it all. There's no real reason to hold on because the house is just a shell of wood and old ghosts. There is no use for the keys, since we just have to lock up and go, so I shake them for him to take. But Brandon doesn't take the keys. He just eyes the keys in my outstretched arm warily.

I watch as he places his bag on the ground—the same bag that holds all his tools. I wish he could take those tools and fix my broken heart that continues to shatter every day that I'm away from Vic. It's so funny to think that he was so jealous of Brandon when he first came over to sell Vic's house. Now, here we are doing the same thing, except it's me now.

Brandon stayed true to his word and helped me fix up the place. He spent countless hours here with me, not just helping me fix things that would increase the value of my home, but also listening to me vent about my current situation. I cry, he listens and offers supporting words, but not once did he ever cross the line and use my vulnerability to his advantage. I couldn't be more grateful for his friendship. As he moves forward, I stiffen because maybe I got it wrong, but then he surprises me. He reaches around me and pulls me into a hug. And I didn't realize how much I needed that. I soften and hug him back, clutching on to the key still in my hand like a lifeline.

"I'll make sure everything else is cleaned up," Brandon says with a soft sigh. "And—" He pauses like he wants to say something else, but instead changes his mind. "I wish you the best, Dani." I cling to him harder, fighting the rising pressure burning behind my eyes. But I refuse to let the tears threatening to fall spill. He presses a gentle kiss to the top of my head. It's tender and comforting in a way that makes me feel worse as his words fall softly, almost whispering, "I still think you should tell him the truth."

I break away from his embrace, placing the key into his hand that holds my past as I embark on an unknown future. I look him in the eye, already shaking my head. "No." He tries to speak, but I hold out my hand to stop whatever he was going to say. "I just can't," I say feebly, resigned.

He sighs. And I hate the way that makes me feel like I am letting him down. Brandon has been nothing but kind, patient, and generous, and as much as I am grateful for all of that, I still can't take his advice. Maybe that makes me a coward. As I start to turn away, I see a car pass by, and for a brief moment, I think it is Vic. My breath catches in my throat. But that's impossible. It can't be because he's a couple of thousand miles away, fulfilling his dreams in a place we both promised to go to together. I huff out a laugh that sounds more amused than anything.

Brandon eyes me warily, brow furrowed, and probably wondering if I'm finally going to lose it, and he may be right. "What is it?" His voice is cautious as he probes further.

"Nothing." I shake my head. "I think I'm seeing things now." He looks around, then glances down the street just as the red taillights of a car turn at the stop sign further down the long street before disappearing out of view. When he turns back to me, I exhale slowly, ready to explain.

"Great," I mutter, forcing out a half-hearted smile as I motion to the empty street and at the car that is now long gone from view. "Now I am hallucinating." I rub my eyes hard, hoping the pressure might help clear my vision, but when I blink, it still looks the same. "I thought I saw Vic," I admit, my voice growing quieter, "driving down our street," I continue, until it becomes a whisper, or more of a wish on my lips. I gesture again, although the car is long gone. "So much for moving on, huh?"

Brandon chuckles. "Yeah, but I know that couldn't be him. I mean, you saw how he looked at me last time. And that was just from looking at you."

I laugh, too. "Yep, you're right." I decide, letting the truth settle. "He would have already been out of the car, ripping you away from me." We both laugh, and when it becomes awkward, dissolving into silence, Brandon spares me one last glance before turning away.

He lifts his hand in a small wave. "Take care of yourself, Dani." With that, he doesn't look back. He just gets in his car and drives away. I stand there long after staring over at Vic's old house, feeling more alone than ever.

As I step into the empty house, the silence swallows me whole. I grab my purse and dig out my phone, desperate to hear Vic's voice. I need something to ground me, something familiar, and that is home, even though my heart is thousands of miles away. I see a few missed calls from Vic. My heart lurches. When did he call? I hit his name, and the call connects. It goes straight to voicemail after two rings.

My brows knit. "That's weird," I say to no one. Thinking it must be a mistake, I try again. This time, it skips the ring entirely and goes straight to voicemail as if he turned off his phone. A chill crawls up my spine, and the air feels heavier around me. Why would he decline my call? My knees buckle at the thought, the ground crumbling around me as my vision goes hazy. It feels like something is piercing my heart, and I don't know what heartbreak is, but I bet it feels something like this. It's as if a piece of that very organ is being torn apart. But that can't be right because he'll always be mine. And for the first time today, I feel afraid. Not just of losing him, but of the possibility that I already have.

So I do the only thing I can, I pick myself up and find the will to move forward. To take care of my mom. To finish school. And one day, when the time is right, I'll find Vic again. When I do, I'm never letting go.

The drive into the city was uneventful. Once I get my mom settled in the lower-level apartment, I throw myself headfirst into all the tasks that need to be completed to make her life as comfortable as possible. I started my new job as a patient care technician in the emergency department. The flexible hours allow me to keep up with school, and for the first time in a long time, I find myself looking forward to something.

I'm just finishing up the laundry when I glance over at my mom to see her watching me. There's something unreadable in her expression, causing me to drop everything and go over to her.

"Mom, is everything okay?" I place my hand on her forehead, feeling the coolness of her skin, and my worry dissipates slightly, but I need verification. "Are you feeling okay, Mom?" I ask.

Her face softens. "Daniella, please sit down for a minute, sweetheart." Her frail hand reaches for mine, and I take it, lowering myself on the couch beside her. She looks at me with those tired eyes, worn from years of carrying pain that she never let me see. I squeeze her hand, silently reaffirming a promise—to make a difference in her life by being here for her and allowing her to rest. Tomorrow is her first appointment with the cancer center, and I cling to the hope that this marks the start of something better.

I haven't had much time to think about Vic, or maybe I'm just intentionally avoiding it. And I am hopeful that things can be better. But deep down, I know that something is wrong. He won't return my calls, and my text messages go unanswered. How does someone go from being your everything to nothing overnight? I have the day off tomorrow, and I will try again. Brandon's words keep playing on a constant loop in my head, because I need to tell him the truth. I just hope it's not too late.

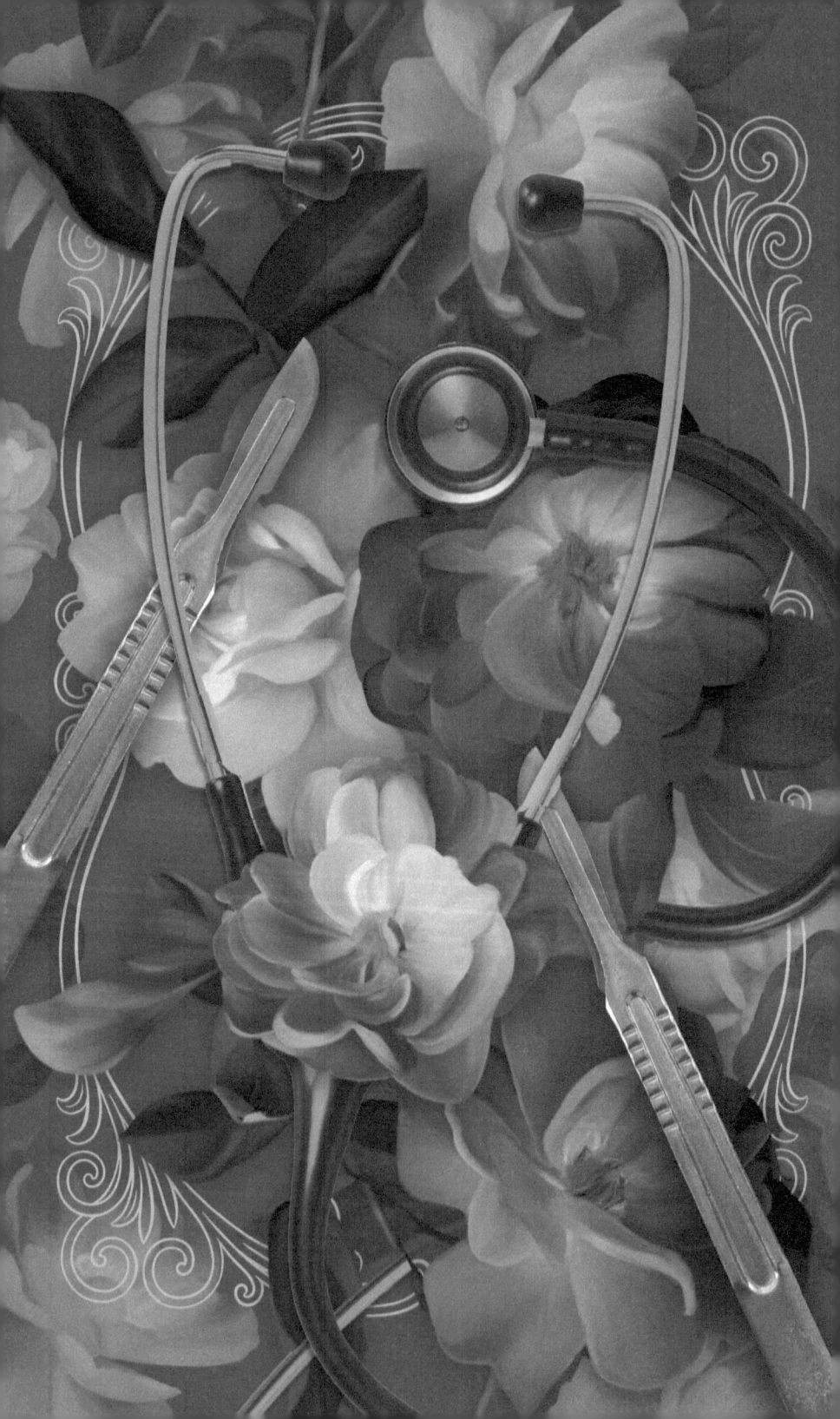

CHAPTER THIRTEEN

VIC

Seeing her with him confirmed every suspicion I had. Every fear. My worst nightmare came true. Dani is—was—my everything, except now she is with someone else. Watching her in his arms was the worst thing I've had to experience, and that says a lot, considering the hell I already lived through.

I know I should talk to her. I should let her explain. I should have a conversation with her. But my anger is too much. I'm afraid that I will say something that I cannot take back. If I take her call, then the hope that I have can't linger on. The call will be final, and I am not ready to admit that.

So I won't. Not until I am strong enough to listen to everything she has to say, even if it isn't something that will tear me apart. I left that night, and ever since, I've been a wreck. My grades are slipping. I'm losing focus. But I can't afford to fall apart and blow this chance I've been given to make something of myself. So I shut it all off. The pain. The memories. The love I have for her. Any side of me that feels, I disengage. Existing on autopilot, I try my best to carry on.

Just waking up, going to school, studying, and then repeating it all over again.

I plop onto the bed, just when my dorm mate Simon strolls in, looking like he's seen better days. He mirrors my position, collapsing onto his bed with a groan. "Damn, that exam was brutal," he moans, rubbing a hand down his face like he's trying to erase the trauma of taking that test.

"Yeah," I grunt. "It kicked my ass."

He snorts. "Sure, it did. That's why you finished first, and walked out while everyone was left in the room sweating bullets."

I glance over at him, smirking. "Really?"

"Bro," he says, sitting up and pointing his finger at me, "you ace every test. Don't act like you don't know that. The least you could do is sit there a little longer so the rest of us mere mortals don't feel so fucking inferior." He pounds his chest dramatically with his fist.

My smile stretches a little wider, almost sinisterly. "Nah," I say, leaning back on my elbows. "I think I'll just do what I do best."

He rolls his eyes, grinning. "Being a pain in my ass?"

"Exactly." I don't hesitate to reply.

Simon plops one hand up against his head. "You know what you need?"

"Is this where I am supposed to ask what that is?" I groan, throwing a pillow over my face.

A moment later, I hear Simon's footsteps approach. He rips the pillow away and tosses it against the wall. "You need to come out with us. There's a party tonight." That's the last thing I want to do, but instead of saying that, I just lie there silent, deciding if maybe I should go. Perhaps a part of me wants the distraction. Maybe I'm just tired of staring at the ceiling, feeling sorry for myself.

Simon must sense the crack in my resistance, because he jumps on it. "You know," he says, trying to play it cool, "Chloe has a thing for you." He hesitates briefly. "I hear she wants you bad."

Chloe is the last thing I want. One night outside the library, I saw her climb out of her boyfriend's car. Her face was pale, and his voice was a vicious snarl as he spat expletives, exiting his car and following her. When she tried to walk away, he lunged after her, grabbing her shoulders and shaking her. The fight spilled into the night, drawing a few onlookers who were curious about the cause of the commotion.

I stepped in, and only then did he back off, cowering under the presence of someone bigger than him, and the piercing, judgmental stares of the surrounding students. He retreated to his car, venomous words thrown over his shoulder, before getting into his vehicle and peeling out. I walked Chloe back to her dorm, though I never wanted to. I also made sure her ex-boyfriend would never carry out his threats. From that moment, I've been on her radar.

Still, Chloe's interest means nothing. My thoughts, my body, my blood coursing through me, will only belong to one person. She is the only one who truly owns me, even in her absence. The only one who can make me hard with just one glance and ignite every nerve in my body is Dani. But I don't say that aloud.

"You're not with your girl anymore, right?" Simon presses.

I shrug, because who the hell knows anymore? We never had the actual breakup conversation, but after what I saw and her behavior, what else can I assume? I should never have confided in Simon about what I saw when I left for Texas to surprise her.

Simon takes my silence as acceptance. "Okay then. Get ready. We're going out." I groan, but push myself to my feet, accepting my fate for the night. He grins, victory at my acquiescence. "Alright," he smiles, rubbing his hands together like he's been waiting for this moment. Then he crouches under his bed and pulls out a bottle, extending it outward for me to take.

I glance at it. "Whiskey?" It's harsh, like it could really kick my ass, and I welcome it. Taking it from his grip, I pull the top off and cock an eyebrow at Simon. Its pungent smoky scent hits me first, curling under my nose, and I pull away instinctively. His smile spreads wider.

"Take a drink and let's get ready." He grabs a towel from the closet and heads toward the door. I take a swig. The liquid burns a warm trail down to the pit of my stomach, where it settles. The heat replaces the cold feeling that I've had since the day I left her behind. I savor the taste, smacking my lips before eyeing the bottle with a little more interest than before. Is this why people drink?

To fill the hollow ache? I replace the knob and set it carefully on the desk.

When I look back up, Simon is watching me with understanding. He knocks his knuckles against the doorframe. "We're going to have a good time tonight," he says, with a pleased look on his face like it's a promise.

I avoided people like him when I was growing up. I had too much baggage. I was afraid they would see where I came from and how bad my home life really was. However, no one here is aware of it. I can be anyone. And right now? Who I want to be is someone numb and detached from any emotion. I pick up the bottle and take another swig. Then I grab my own towel and follow Simon to the showers. Tonight, for the first time since I arrived at the school, I'm going out. And maybe it's long overdue.

We arrive at the party. Music thumps around us as bodies sway to the rhythmic beats streaming from the speakers haphazardly set up along the townhome. It may be fall, but you'd never know from the scantily dressed women in this place and the number of people here acting as a human furnace. Condensation forms along the windows, and I see a few already pushed slightly open, letting the cool autumn night air provide some needed ventilation through the house.

"Vic. Simon." Someone calls out our name, and we see Hudson, another one from our group of friends, beckoning us over with the wave of his hand. We move, single file, through the gyrating bodies in the middle of the living room to the back of the townhouse, where the small kitchen island is set up with a mixture of alcohol bottles and red solo cups. "Hey!" He shouts over the music. "What do you guys want to drink?" I shrug, not really caring what it is. Truth be told, I've already had enough before we even arrived, and I know I shouldn't have any more. But tonight, I throw caution to the wind and set myself on a path of self-destruction.

"I'll take whatever," Simon says, and then looks over at me. "Him, too." He thumbs over at me. Shrugging, I let Hudson know to make one up, and I take a minute to look around. A woman is staring at me, sizing me up. She's pretty with a cute button nose, long blonde hair, and big, full tits. She sees me returning her stare, which causes her to perk up. She leans over to tell her friends something, and they both turn my way, looking at me and smiling. She waves, but I get distracted by a hand extended my way.

"Here you go." Hudson hands me a drink, and I bring it to my lips, taking a long sip. It's strong, and I second-guess my thoughts about coming to this party. Simon hits my arm, and my drink sloshes over my shirt.

"Oh, shit," Simon says as he nudges his head to the side of Hudson. "Bro, those girls are coming over here, and Chloe's with them." I turn to see the women walking this way, confidence exuding in their movements, but as Chloe walks up to me, smiling, it's all wrong. Her lips are thin, unlike Dani's full lips. Her hair is blonde and straight instead of the wavy, dark chocolate curls that ran to Dani's mid-back. The woman moves closer and starts talking to me, but I can't make out a word she's saying. She puts her hand on my arm, and I feel hot all over. Just the thought of Dani left me hard and aching. All the alcohol did was allow me to let my guard down and expose how much I still want her.

Chloe's friend pushes her from behind, and she rocks into me, her hand on my chest and her body flush against mine. She gasps, and I know then that she feels it. My cock, that was hard at the thought of Dani, is pressing into this petite girl's frame, and I see her eyes widen in recognition. Little does she know that it isn't for her. It never will be.

I push her back because she isn't Dani, and because I feel like I might throw up. Suddenly, the music is too loud, the people are too close, and this girl is just all wrong. I refused to think about Dani, pushing her to the back of my mind, where she is tucked neatly into a little box with hearts and bows. Now the thoughts of her flood my mind, and especially those that I never want to think of. Of her hugging Brandon and how he kissed my girl's head. I push through the crowd in search of a bathroom, looking back to see my friends engaged in a heated debate, no doubt about some New England sports team.

I run up the stairs in search of a bathroom. I need to wash my face and maybe get rid of the contents of my stomach at the moment. Hoping this feeling will subside, I see a few people in line for the bathroom in the hallway, but just then someone closes the door from one of the rooms. He must see how bad I look because he hits me on the shoulder. He leans in. "There's a bathroom in there if you need it, bro," he says, then walks off. I don't waste a second in that other line as I enter the darkened bedroom. I tug off my jacket and place my phone on top of it as I head for the dim light in the corner of the room.

CHAPTER FOURTEEN

DANI

Today had already been unbearable, but everything imploded when I came home from work to find my mom face-down on her bedroom carpet. We've just moved in, and some things are still in boxes, awaiting their final resting spot. I'd placed this task on my list for today. But this...This isn't something I thought I'd be doing today. For a moment, I forgot how to breathe. I didn't know how long she had been lying there alone. My hand shook as I rolled her over, bracing myself for the worst, but then relief flooded me when her body still felt warm, her eyelids fluttering open.

"Dani?" Her thin, broken voice cuts straight through me, splintering my heart, hearing her say my name, like a plea on her lips sounding just oh-so-fucking sad. I drop my head in defeat, placing it closer to hers.

"Mom, are you okay?" I ask hesitantly, not really wanting to know anything else that could devastate me so cruelly. Cradling her in my arms, she manages the slightest nod, almost too weak to answer. "What happened?" I whisper. Her tongue swipes over her dry lips, ready to answer, but I place my hand gently against her arm, causing her to pause.

"Don't. Not yet." I pull her up as she stands weakly against me. Her frail body is weightless in my arms as I steady her before guiding her to the recliner. Once she's settled, I rush to the nightstand, refill her water glass, and place it in her shaking hands. Only then do I let myself breathe.

Every morning before work, I make sure she has everything she needs. After I leave, the visiting nurse comes to watch over her and stays until just before I get home. Which means she couldn't have been lying on that carpet for long. I know this, yet the thought still destroys me. Her helplessness, the fear she must have felt with no one there to answer her call, singes my soul, branding me with a shame I'm sure the world can see—the mark of what a terrible daughter I am.

I guide her delicate, paper-thin fingers around the sippy cup, steadying the straw at her lips. She tries to lift it, but even that small act proves to be too much. With my hand over hers, I coax it to her lips for her to sip.

"That's it, Mom," I say encouragingly. Her chest rises with a slow, steady breath, the effort draining what little reserve she had. Her hand slips away, almost too heavy to hold, so I keep the cup steady for her, pressing the straw to her mouth so she doesn't have to lift it again. She drinks slowly, in small sips, pausing in between, as I continue to hold the cup up to her lips. She's too weak, and the sight of it breaks me.

"Now," I whisper, my throat constricting with emotion, "tell me what happened, Mom?"

She looks at me sadly. "I just wanted to pick up my Chapstick." Her gaze flicks to the floor, where the little black tube lies abandoned. I set the water aside and cross the room, placing it gently in her hand, which rests limp upon her lap.

"It fell," she continues, her voice cracking at the last word. A sharp breath escapes, laced with anger, as her feeble finger tips attempt to flex around the offending chapstick as though she might strangle it. "I leaned over just a little to grab it..." She trails off as silence fills the void. She swallows. "But I guess I am too weak to hold myself up. I lost my balance. My arms couldn't catch me. And

I fell."

She turns away, ashamed, and I can't bear the sight of it. I twist the cap from the tube and lift it, applying the balm against her dry, cracked lips. A single, traitorous tear escapes down her cheek, and I know in that moment, this hurts her more than the fall. The humiliation of needing me for something so small hurts her more than broken bones could.

"I'm sorry, " she whispers. The words knock me over as I look at her, stunned.

"Whatever for, Mom?" I ask, shaking my head.

"For being a burden on you." Her voice cracks, and tears form in her eyes. Her words hang between us, threatening to suffocate me as I try to take a breath in and fail. My chest caves in protest as I force the air in as my vision begins to blur from the tears rising in my eyes. I reach for her hand, gripping it as gently as I possibly can, anchoring her to me if I could to this life and the next.

"You could never be that," I tell her, even though my throat threatens to tighten around the words. I hold her gaze, imploring her to see what I see. A strong warrior. A fighter. Unbroken, still now, despite the fragility of her body left ravaged by this terminal illness. She isn't a burden. She couldn't be. How could love be a burden? And I love her fiercely, through the good, the bad, and the ugly. Every day I have left with her is a gift. I clutch tightly because she has already exceeded the initial time frame the doctors gave us, measured out by cold facts and clinical statistics. They warned us that every case is different, not to get our hopes up, but to make the most of the time left. Yet they still provide us with numbers, ranges, and expectations, but she defied them all.

"All those times you took care of me when I was little," I murmur, "you left a loveless marriage and started over, building us a new life." I swallow hard, watching the tears stream down her hollowed cheeks. "You are the strongest person I know. And if I can be half the person, be half the mother you are to me..." I struggle to get the final words out. "I'd have done something right." I wrap my arms around her, holding her the way she once cuddled me as a child. For a moment, I wonder what a person could have done in their life to deserve so much suffering. The thought strikes right through me, but it also sparks something inside. It sparks a fight. A fight to advocate for people like my mom. To ease their pain. To end their suffering.

After tucking Mom into bed, I wander aimlessly through our small apartment, picking up what I can. I wash the few dishes in our sink, robotically fold the towels, and lose myself in thought. I sink into the worn chair at the kitchenette, the tiny space doubling as the living and dining area. I pull out my schoolbooks, trying to focus, but my mind drifts back to her and the events of the day. And then it drifts to him, the man I should've confided in, and the weight of the secret presses heavier with every passing second I sit there.

I step away from the cluttered table full of books and almost-dreams to enter my bedroom and reach for the box tucked into the far corner of the closet. Cradling it carefully to my chest, I carry what could have been my future, placing it onto the dining table. I gently set it down, clearing the books I most definitely won't be touching tonight to make some room. My hands linger on the box, wondering if I am ready to do this. I breathe deeply before ripping off the top, unleashing the memories I've kept contained and tucked in so neatly since he left.

I sit there for hours, sifting through every memory and every photo. I hadn't wanted to do this because the memories are too painful. I miss Vic so much. The ache in my chest burns, and the silence of his absence torments me. What could have made him give up on us? Did he find someone new?

That thought alone makes me spring upward and grab my phone. I bite my lip, imagining him with someone else. No one could ever share a love like ours. The very thought churns my stomach violently. And the idea of him fucking someone else—it forces me to remember him, the way we were together, and how good it was.

The darkness he carried wasn't a result of sadness or anger. It was a pulse of primal desire. The way he gripped me, wrapping his fingers around my throat as we collided, bending me over, thrusting into me with an unrelenting pace, leaves me sinking to the floor, clutching the picture of us that we took after his father died. That was the moment he fully embraced his darkness, and I joined him.

He was uncontrollable in bed, and I was insatiable for his violent nature. I craved him as fiercely as he craved me. But even in our most dangerous throws of passion, there was a pull to each other we couldn't resist. It made every look he gave me and every touch he offered feel like molten fire on my skin. We were a collision of need and pain, morphing into the rawest form of love. His inner turmoil spilled over, dragging me down with him. It was suffocating, dangerous, and thrilling all at once. And I'd never felt more alive.

I was addicted to him as much as he was addicted to me. Our shared madness teetered on obsession because loving him meant embracing our darkest parts, and that's what scarred me the most. Acknowledging that I had them, too, was the most brutal truth to accept. I imagined living with him, and sometimes I pretended that our shared memories, even the blood and the pain, were what made our home. It could never be tainted because our love was the road that led us there, not a physical place. But that dream was fleeting. After graduation, we spent that last summer together, desperately clinging to everything except the reality of the time we had left.

It's with that thought that I do what I know I shouldn't, but rational thought is long gone. So I grab my phone and dial his number. It rings and rings, and with each chime, it chisels into my chest just a little bit more. Just when I think it will go to voicemail, someone answers. At first, there's only silence. I pull the phone back, wondering if the call ended. When I see it hasn't, I call out, "Vic?"

But then I hear it. A small, feminine voice answers, "Hello."

I blink, disbelieving, until I ask, "Who's this?"

Her voice grows louder and a little bolder. I hear a huff. "Who's this?" she counters.

My stomach drops. I collapse to the floor, clutching my chest. I hear a toilet flush, and then a door open.

"Baby, are you okay?" Her muffled voice asks who I can only assume is Vic.

"Chloe, do you have my phone?" he asks, confirming my worst fear.

Then the line goes dead. And so does my heart. The road I thought would always lead to Vic is gone, and I'm left standing alone.

CHAPTER FIFTEEN

DANI
FOUR YEARS LATER
AGE 22

Sighing, I rise from my chair in the auditorium that has been my world for the last four years. I glance around one last time, committing the familiar rows and faces in them to memory, before picking up my test and making my way to the front of the class. I pause for a moment, letting the weight of my accomplishment settle in, savoring this fleeting victory.

Although I wasn't able to attend Dartmouth, I did my best under the circumstances. Soon, I will become a registered nurse upon completing my boards, and I am excited about this new career path. Working as a technician in the emergency department has allowed me to learn on the job and has prepared me for the next step in my career. It gives me the chance to give back and advocate for patients like my mom or those who seek care because they don't have a primary care doctor and lack the financial means to access better healthcare.

My lip twitches as I place my paper face down on the desk for the last time at this school. I walk out feeling lighter than I have in weeks. Taking long strides, I push open the door and make my way toward my car in the crowded parking lot. Our class will hold a ceremony for those who passed the nursing program, and then it's on to the boards, where I'll earn my RN license and move beyond my patient care tech pay. I am beyond excited and more than ready to make it happen.

I open the door, place my tote on the passenger seat, and retrieve my phone, which I then power on. As I start the car, a flood of messages and voicemail notifications pop up, forcing me to put the car back in park to see what's going on. When I see it's the nursing aid who stays with my mom, calling repeatedly, my anxiety spikes. I call her back and rush home.

She answers on the second ring. "Angeline?" I don't even wait for her response before my words tumble out. "What happened? Is Mom okay?" My voice rises as I speed through traffic, my heart pounding as I rush to get to my mom. Luckily, it's still early, and the city hasn't reached its late afternoon chaos yet, leaving the streets mercifully open.

"Dani," she whispers into the phone, "your mom has taken a turn for the worse. When I couldn't reach you, I called the hospice line. A nurse from Horizons Hospice is here now, waiting." I gasp, the words slicing through me.

"I was finishing up my exam," I say apologetically, my voice breaking at the poor excuse. "I didn't know….my phone was off for the exam."

"Dani. This isn't your fault," she replies, her tone comforting, yet firm, trying to break through my downward spiral. "It could have happened any time. We knew this was imminent. It is nothing short of a miracle that she has lasted this long."

Of course, I know she's right. But knowing doesn't soften the blow. If this is true, then the moment I've been dreading has finally come.

"She is on the couch," she continues cautiously, "and the nurse placed a Foley catheter to drain her bladder and make her comfortable." My vision blurs at the onslaught of sudden tears. I let out a shaky breath as the inevitable reality I've tried to postpone finally arrives.

"Okay," I manage to force out the following words. "How long do I have?" I veer off the freeway, taking the next intersection too sharply, as I make a beeline for the apartment complex that has been our makeshift home since leaving our real one behind. "Almost there," I mutter into the phone, though the words feel more like a plea than a statement, as I wait for her response.

"She received some medication to make her comfortable, but I think it may be soon, so please hurry." With that, I end the call.

Ten minutes later, I slam the car into park and sprint toward the apartment. The door flies open, my bag slipping from my shoulder and hitting the floor as I rush to the couch. And then I see her. My mom lies there so still, and the gravity of the situation crashes down on me. This is it. I was given more time with her than I thought possible, but now the moment has come, and I don't know if I am strong enough to let her go. My knees hit the floor, and I clutch her hand in both of mine, making promises into the void to anyone that would answer, letting her stay just another day with me.

"Mom," I murmur her name, afraid that it might be the last time I'll ever call her that and hear her answer. My chest tightens with the ensuing silence, as I pray for her to answer. Then I feel her squeeze my hand as she slowly opens her eyes.

"Baby girl," she says softly. I move in closer, straining to hear her near-silent voice as she speaks. "I waited as long as I could, Dani, and I'm so very tired." Tears fall freely down my face as I stare at the person who gave me life, watching her lose the battle to keep her own.

"Mom, I'm here. You don't have to wait any longer. I know you're tired...and you've been so brave and strong. I love you so much." I lean down to kiss her, and for the briefest moment, her lips curve into a slight smile. I rest my head against her, listening to the beating of her heart and feeling the rising of her chest until both cease to function.

"No. No. No." I rise from the spot, staring down at my mom's still body, all life gone, now leaving only a shell. The same body that I watched be ravaged by a cruel, unimaginable fate from the very beginning. I collapse to the floor, crying for the only person who had ever truly loved me. But that's not entirely true. I have Vic, and maybe, just maybe, he still loves me. Even if he isn't a part of my life right now, I know without a doubt we will be together again. My heart feels like it's splitting in two, and I let myself feel every shred of it before forcing myself upright. I wipe the tears from my cheeks, one at a time, standing there numb.

We had a plan in place for this moment. I called the funeral home to collect my mother's body, and she will be cremated per her wishes. We have no one to attend the service, as sad as that is, so I'll honor her request and spread her ashes on the beach. She loved the water and had an extensive collection of sand dollars, taking pride in the ones she found intact along the shoreline, unbroken despite the unrelenting waves. Those, she said, were the strongest survivors and deserved to be preserved and cherished like a trophy, on display for all to see.

The funeral company called to tell me her ashes were ready. I went without hesitation, carrying them with me toward the coast, toward Galveston. The seawall rises before me, the Gulf waters and sky blur into one by the heavy, humid haze along the horizon. I leave the car and step onto the sand. The wind tugs at my hair, salt in the air mingling with the salt of my own tears. *It's fitting*, I think, as the sting of grief pushes me forward, one step at a time, and leads me to her final resting place.

The sound of waves lapping against the jetties guides my steps until I reach the rocks that hug the water's edge. There, with trembling hands, I draw out the small container that holds my mother. From my bag, I remove her collection of sand dollars, carefully placing them one by one on the cool, damp sand and arranging them into a heart shape.

She always cherished these fragile little treasures. To her, they symbolized the delicate balance between life and death. These talismans of endurance stood as reminders that even in her final hours, strength could be found in what survives the storm.

At last, I open the canister. Ash spills into the heart of the shells. Some rise, caught in the wind, while the tide carries away the rest. The sea reclaims the lifeless, sun-bleached skeletons and folds her ashes alongside them into the foamy spray. And when the tide retreats, carrying away the last of her remains, I stand there staring at the place where her sand dollars and ashes were mere moments ago. But now, there is no trace that she had ever been there at all.

Before leaving, I place the empty vessel in a barrel by the seawall, although my hands linger, unwilling to let it go. Back in the car, I sit for a long time, listening to the cry of seagulls overhead and the steady beating of waves against the shore. The day settles heavily over me, as I struggle to grasp the reality of all I have lost. Before shifting into drive, I vow, with all I have left to give, never again to take love for granted, no matter how brief, because its worth lies in all the fragile pieces. And no matter how beaten and battered by the storm, you still make it out whole.

CHAPTER SIXTEEN

VIC

I know there was more to the story, but instead of confronting Brandon and Dani that day, I let the rage devour me completely. I threw myself into my studies and detached myself from everything else—no parties, no friends, and no women.

As a result, I think I lost a little of my humanity. Confrontation would have been a predictable response for any sane person. To find out the truth and seek those answers to the questions that plague you. But I'm no longer either of those, sane nor predictable. My mother died, and I endured. I survived a hostile home, the sting of his volatile temper, and the punishments dealt out with his fists. Until one night I ended him, and his reign of terror ceased until his blood ran freely on the floor. And then, there was Dani, still cloaked in my father's blood.

My breathing hitches, and my cock grows hard, remembering when her lips were coated red from our shared blood-stained kisses.

I carried her upstairs bridal-style. I took her there in the shower, still drenched in the red coloring of my sins, driving into her mercilessly with the same desperation that had driven me to commit murder. Our darkness collided, entwining in a macabre dance of shadows that cloaked my bedroom, binding us in something deeper than this world. It was darker than love, a contract of our forever, bound through violence and need. Our equal obsession.

My breathing increases, forced and angry.

So when I saw her wrapped in the arms of another man, I couldn't breathe. I couldn't think. She was all I had left, and in that moment, it felt like she was being stolen from me, and my soul was being ripped apart from its ethereal tether, piece by fucking piece.

I look down and see the blood swell slightly at the surface from where my nails bit into the skin on my leg. I watch it bead, and one lone drop forms at the surface, and I place my thumb into it and suck it into my mouth.

That next morning, when I returned from Texas, I woke with a hangover sharp enough to split my skull. Now, years later, as the silence stretched, and as I realized my time at this school is over, one truth surfaced. I couldn't outrun the past any longer. So I made the decision to travel back to Texas before my next move to Massachusetts for residency. Back to the ghosts that haunted it, the blood and the lies I buried there. I needed to see Dani and get answers. I can't move on, and maybe I don't want to.

The first thing on Monday, after securing my place and preparing to begin the next part of my career path, I drive to the Boston airport and leave my car in central parking, resolved to worry about the fee when I return. Four hours later, I pull away from the Austin airport in a rental car, finally doing what I should have done before. I curse my stupidity and berate myself the entire ride there. The old Vic would have never let her go without a fight, and yet I left her that day like a coward. Leaving her was my failure, but now I'm finally doing what I should have done long ago.

The city gives way to long stretches of highway, with city buildings made of steel and glass transformed into pastures and country homes. It's as if time stands still in this place, despite the years that have passed. As I drive onto the last stretch of road, my body twists with doubt about my choices. I hadn't thought this through, not really. I have been a shell of myself since I left her, drifting further with every mile that I left things unresolved between us, and now I was barrelling back without having a single word prepared. What would I even say to her? That I love her? That I hated her? That I would forgive her for anything? All of it was true at the present.

But if Brandon is there, I don't think I can trust myself to walk away without bloodshed. I sigh. Bloodshed could mean jail, and I don't know if Dani would protect me from myself this time. Without that being an option for now, I force myself to breathe long, deep inhales as I fight the darkness that claws just beneath the surface, manifesting it to sink into the deepest crevices of my being. The way that I had trained myself to keep the rage contained in its cage, even as it tried making its way to the surface just beneath my ribcage, battering my heart that only beats for one woman.

So with the help of several more deep breaths—manifesting a calm, clinical detachment, I pull up to her house and get out, and can't stop my eyes from drifting over to the one I'd grown up in. A bicycle leans against the porch rail, along with a couple of toys scattered across the lawn. It paints a picture of a normal home life filled with caring parents and children running amok, content with their childhood. It looks like the way I always wanted my childhood to be, but the only hope remained that I could recreate that depicted fantasy with another person, one person in particular.

The vision clears, and I blink. The dream is gone. As I stare at it more closely, I know that I will always see it as my father's house. The place I'd never called home. But Dani's house? That had always been my sanctuary. She was the place where my jagged puzzle pieces met hers, creating a beautiful, scenic picture of our future. This is the place where I still feel like I truly belong. And I was ready to take back my sanctuary and erase Brandon forever.

I have already decided to forgive her. Truth be told, Dani could do anything, and I'd still love her. So as I bounce up the steps with a hammering heart, ready to knock on her door and win her back. I'm practically readying to throw myself at her feet, just as the door swings open before I can knock.

A young woman, who is very much not Dani, stares at me, her

head tilting slightly, assessing. "Hi." She smiles up at me curiously, my hand frozen mid-knock. Unable to speak, I lower my arm and step back. Confusion pulls my mouth into a frown. "Can I help you?" Her voice is polite, but edged as if she's calculating shutting the door in my face. Her gaze looks past me, scanning the driveway, before her attention snaps back to me.

I clear my voice, the words stuck in my throat as I push them out. "Are you a friend of Dani's?" The question escapes before I can stop it. My eyes search her face when hers crinkle at the corners in confusion. I look at the driveway, searching for Dani's car, but I only see an unfamiliar sedan.

At Dani's name, the woman stiffens, her posture rigid. "Are you friends with Brandon?" she asks, and when I look at her, she must hear the murderous thoughts that cross my mind when hearing their names used in the same sentence, as if they could ever be a couple. She takes a step backward as fear shows in her eyes, but my anger is misplaced. It's not toward her, but pain from the knife that is twisting in my heart.

"Did he send you here to collect rent?" Her words hang in the air between us. My eyes widen in surprise at hearing that Brandon owns this house or is possibly connected to it. I shift forward, my foot pressing to take a step, but she instinctively flinches. I halt my movements, my body seizing at the memory. For a moment, it isn't her I'm seeing, it's my mother. The same recoil and fear bring back so many haunting memories of those dark times in my life, and I try to keep them buried. I push them all down, softening my shoulders and clenched jaw. When I speak again, my speech is softer, and my temper is reigned in.

"Explain." It's the only word I can force past my lips. One that I can let out as the storm brews inside me when it comes to Dani. Each memory collides in a cyclone that ruins me. Her face. Her touch. Her betrayal. On the surface, I am silent and calm, but underneath, everything is coming undone.

"I'm only a month behind, but I have the money..." She trails off, looking over her shoulder into the house. She keeps the door cracked, but I see her finger held taunt on the frame, her knuckles white in panic. If she shuts me out now, I may never know what happened. I press my hand against the door, keeping it open, and stopping her from retreating into the house. Her body stiffens, alarm sparks in her eyes. I know I'm scaring her, and that isn't my intention. But it's desperation that fuels my actions today. One made from a lovesick fool, and I need her to understand my dilemma.

"No, that's not it." I shake my head, sighing, breaking eye contact with her and looking down at the crack in the cement on the top porch step. The familiar jagged fissure mimicking the fracture residing in my chest. "I'm looking for my girlfriend," I explain, trying not to sound as pathetic as I feel. "She used to live here. Her name is Dani."

"Ah," she says. Her body relaxes as she steps onto the porch. I feel her approach me like someone trying to coax a skittish animal closer, a palm extended, full of food. Except hers isn't food in her palm, it's information. "There's no Dani here, but I bet Mr. Marx may know something." I look up, hopeful, and she smiles. "She used to own this house. I do know that." Her eyes crinkle at the corners. Her finger comes up to touch the side of her lip. "He wouldn't be here." She shakes her head. "He just owns the place now, but his office is still downtown." She sees my shocked expression and shrugs. "That's all I got."

And that's enough. I nod eagerly, already turning around and running to my truck. "Good luck!" she shouts after me. I raise a hand in acknowledgement without looking back, already shutting the door to my rental car and throwing it in gear, speeding away to where my answers lie.

CHAPTER SEVENTEEN

VIC

As I drive to Brandon Marx's office, a storm of questions churns in my mind. Why the hell would Brandon own my girlfriend's house? And more importantly, what am I missing?

I know exactly where his office is, the familiar drive to the so-called business districts. A few local eateries and mom and pop stores across from the commons, town offices, and a park unfold before me. Easily finding a parking spot, I stride toward the real estate office, determined to get the answers I came here for. I know the office well, as it is the same one where I first met Brandon when I initially inquired about listing my house for sale before leaving for college. His face stares back at me from an advertisement along with a few properties for sale, placed on the window.

The bell chimes as I step inside, announcing my arrival. And then I see him. He doesn't appear to have aged much. Brandon's face flashes with shock before he quickly masks his emotion. The sight of him turns my stomach. The memory of their embrace loops endlessly in my mind. He rises from the chair, and I close the distance in a few strides. Smoothing the front of his familiar blue sport coat, he extends his hand toward me. I just stare at it before looking up at him. His smile falters, morphing into a frown, as he retracts his arm stiffly to his side. He straightens, his posture stiffening as he locks his body into a guarded stance.

My anger swirls in a violent current between us as our eyes bore into one another in a stare-off. With a curt gesture, he motions to a chair. I remain standing. When he sees that I will not move, he exhales. The sound of air that escapes sounds of irritation, but I don't care as he purses his lips, likely about to lecture a repugnant child. I am neither, but I can envision the dark fantasy now. How I will gut him like a fucking fish.

"I'd ask what brings you here, but I think I have an inkling," he says matter-of-factly, snapping me out of my red haze. Anger radiates off me, hot enough to make my ears burn, as I try to keep it at bay, forcing myself towards a semblance of civil conversation. But when it comes to Dani, all bets are off.

"I need to know what happened." He blinks, confusion flickering across his face. "I went to Dani's house. She isn't there. In fact, she's moved. So where is she?" Shock registers on his face. It's subtle, but unmistakable.

"You haven't talked to her?" he asks.

I shake my head. "She won't take my calls. When I arrive at her house to talk to her, I find out she doesn't live there anymore." My voice rises angrily, and I know speech betrays the other emotion threatening to burst forth. Heartbreak.

"Imagine my surprise," I continue through clenched teeth, "when I don't even know where she is now." Brandon leans back in his chair, exhaling a slow, ragged breath.

"Wow. When was the last time you talked to her?"

"Years." That's all I say as his eyebrows raise, concern flickering in his eyes. Why is he worried? The question hangs silently in my mind, but I can't seem to see past the anger. He asks as if that day didn't destroy me. Like he has no idea. So I let him know.

"Oh, let's see..." I trail off through gritted teeth. "Maybe it was the day I came to surprise her and found you wrapped around her, kissing her fucking forehead." My fists clench and unclench by my sides. Brandon notices, and his attention shifts as he attempts to soothe me, although his awareness of my fury is unmistakable.

"Jesus Christ." He rubs a hand over his face, then looks at me, remorse evident. "You've got it all wrong, bro." His hand rises, pacifyingly.

"Do I?"

"Yeah. You do," he insists.

"So enlighten me then," I demand, arms raising outward, daring him to make me understand.

"Dani called me up, explaining that she needed to sell her house. She needed the money." He shrugs, like I should know. But I don't.

"Why?" I ask. My steady voice is taut with anger.

He watches me. "You'll have to ask her." He bites his lip as if he's trying to hold back a secret. "It's not my story to tell." It's all he says, but his body language betrays him. As we lock eyes in a silent stare, I know that I'm not getting another word from him on that. Still needing to hear the rest of the story, I roll my hands in a coaxing motion, silently urging him to continue.

"The house was in a bit of disrepair, so I helped where I could, but she needed to sell rather fast." He shakes his head, reluctant to admit it, and steeples his fingers together. "I know she needed a certain price, and without the repairs the house needed, she wouldn't have gotten it." He clears his throat. "So..." He hesitates briefly before continuing. "I decided to buy it myself, under a company she didn't know." He pauses, rubbing his eyes, as if this is painful to him. I suspect he has no idea how much it hurts me.

"Where is she?" My voice sounds weak.

He shrugs. "No clue. Houston, maybe."

It's then that I notice his ring. His eyes catch mine, and he smiles widely, waggling his finger. He turns the picture facing him around so I can see it. "Vanessa," he says proudly. "The love of my life. We've been married a year, and we just found out we are having a little girl." He smiles, but he isn't seeing me. He's seeing his wife, and in that moment, I realize just how stupid I've been.

"That day I saw you with Dani, I thought the worst." I bury my face in my hands, then slowly remove them. "I was so jealous I wouldn't even take her calls."

His face tightens as though he just remembered something.

"You know," he pauses, snapping his fingers once in the air, "come to think of it, she swore she saw you. Even joked about how she was seeing ghosts."

I groan. "I didn't even let her explain."

"So you really haven't talked to her since?" he asks, shocked by my admission.

"Oh, she tried calling. But then one night, I went out and got drunk with some of the guys. I ended up sick at a frat house party, and..."

"You fucked someone and she found out?" he asks quickly, shocked.

I shake my head quickly. "No, I was sick in the bathroom. Left my jacket and phone on the bed. This girl picked up her call." I saw Dani's name on the recent call log later when I was sober, and I knew. I knew karma was a bitch, and she wasn't going to answer. "I tried, but she never picked up."

"Wow." He lets out a long whistle. "That's fucked up, bro."

I flop into the nearest chair. "Yeah, tell me about it." I run my hand through my already tousled hair. "She seemed so distant every time I called, and then when I saw you two together, I thought she had moved on." I exhale, deflated.

"She loves you," he says, leaning forward. "She had a lot going on, and I really think you need to find her. You need to get the full story."

I nod. "I just hope she still does." It's been years, yet I haven't moved on. I get up from the chair and head for the door, but Brandon stops me.

"Hey," he says, walking over. "I just want you to know, if she ever wants to come back, I can sell her house back to her. She loved it. She told me it was the only place her heart called home."

I nod, swallowing the lump rising in my throat. "Yeah."

Brandon extends his hand. I take it, and as he releases it, he says, "I do really hope you find her and work it out."

"Let's hope." I step out the door, and the walk back to my car stretches out longer than it should. The drive back to the airport feels even longer, each mile weighed down with the fear that I may never see her again.

I pull out my phone and call her. Once again, it goes straight to voicemail. It's as if she doesn't even have it on. I leave countless messages, each begging her to call me back, terrified that my words will go unanswered forever. This time, I won't stop.

CHAPTER EIGHTEEN

DANI
FOUR YEARS LATER
AGE 26

Not a day goes by that I don't regret my decisions. I brought this on myself. I could have told Vic from the very beginning how much I needed him, and maybe we could have made it work. Now, after all this time, how do I call? What do I even say? It's with these conflicting emotions gnawing at me that I step through the ambulance bay doors and into the chaos waiting inside. The chaos that mimics my internal struggles for a man I no longer call my own, but maybe I will again one day.

Eyes cast downward just as Emma taught me to, I don't look up until I reach the employee entrance of one of Houston's busiest emergency rooms. I place my badge up against the keypad. The light turns from red to green, followed by the sharp click of the lock. The doors swing open, granting me entry into my personal hell for the next twelve hours.

I stash my things in the cramped locker and leave the staff lounge, making my way to the main desk for my assignment. Emma, the charge nurse tonight and my fast-coming friend, takes one look at me and worry etches her face. Her bright green eyes scrutinize me, searching for something I refuse to let her find. There's something about Emma that calls to me. I've found a friend in her, but never let her in. She has her secrets, and I have mine.

I meet her stare, unblinking, until she finally sighs in defeat, directing her attention to the stack of charts in front of her. "Here," she says kindly, picking them up and handing them over. "I'm putting you with Liv in urgent care today. Give these to her, and tell her I said you needed a better day." Her words leave little room for protest. I take the charts from her, momentarily blinded by the flash of her diamond ring. The lightsaber, as I call it. She notices me staring and flicks her fingers flauntingly in a *run-along* motion. Before I can muster a response, she turns away, her long, blonde ponytail swaying as she walks off.

I find Liv in the urgent care area. She drops into a chair, watching me as I approach with the charts Emma gave me in hand. With a slight nod, she gestures for me to set them on the desk. Placing them down, I repeat Emma's words. "Emma is putting me here with you today. Said I needed a better day." Liv eyes me suspiciously.

"Hm." The sound is low as she slips off her clog with a heavy thump as it hits the floor. Rubbing her foot, she never looks away. I stand there in silence, offering her nothing. Her gaze sharpens. "And do you, Dani?"

I shrug. "Who doesn't need a better day?" I retort noncommittally.

Liv's eyes narrow. "Cut the crap." She slips her shoe back on and rises to her full height, towering several inches above me. Next to Emma and me, she looks like a goddess—all tall, regal, and effortlessly elegant.

"I could say the same about you, Liv. You feeling okay?" I ask, genuinely concerned.

"That's what having an active toddler does to you," she says with a smile. She's also happily married, like Emma, whose recent wedding was absolutely gorgeous. Her husband, unlike Liv's, is a bit intimidating, as is Emma's whole family. But hey, who am I to judge?

"Anyway," Liv snaps me out of my thoughts. "Some of us are

going to meet out at the sports bar we always hang out at after work today. Wanna come?"

She notices the hesitation on my face, so she goes in for the kill. "Come on, you never hang out with us. I can't get out all the time, but Dax is off today and watching Kaden tonight." She almost pouts, and it makes me laugh.

"Fine," I wave my hand dismissively. "But I don't get out of here until seven, maybe."

She laughs. "Lucky for you, Emma and I are in charge of this hell pit tonight. Trust. You'll be out in time."

The day passes in a blur of patients and discharges, and before I know it, Emma comes over to let me know she is leaving. I check in with Liv's replacement to let him know I'm going as well. He's a kind physician assistant who's taken a liking to me, but he doesn't hold a candle to Vic.

Once I finish giving my report to the next shift, we make our way to the locker room, excitedly making plans for tonight. As we exit the building, a black SUV waits out front, its engine humming. A burly man holds the door open for her. She winks. "See you there, Dani," she says, sliding into the back passenger seat. I nod and wave. But my thoughts are no longer on fun. The night air stirs with memories, and for an instant, I almost see him. Vic, waiting in the dark shadows that linger outside the building. The ghost of his gaze follows me. I know it's only my imagination, yet the ache of his absence coils around me, tight and suffocating. I have to break free of it, because the weight of missing him presses down on me so fiercely that it causes my steps to quicken and drives me toward the car.

As I reach it, Emma, who was waiting for me to get there, rolls down her window, and I catch sight of her husband, Eduardo, next to her. His gaze is cold, unyielding, and he's staring straight at me from across the seat. "Don't make me come get you, girl," she warns. Her tone is playful, but the edge to it makes me hesitate before she winks, then rolls up the window and disappears down the street.

A shiver runs through me. The rush of danger prickles under my skin. It's sharp, intoxicating, and makes me feel fucking alive.

I realize this is what I've missed. I jump into the car, deciding it's time I had some fun. I'm overdue for my dose of chaos.

I rush out the door in a flurry of excitement. For some reason, I am actually looking forward to tonight. I haven't felt this happy or looked forward to something in a long time. Emma and Liv have been there for me since I started working as a tech in the emergency room while I was in school. They were there for me after my mom died. They didn't know what was going on. No one did. However, when I failed to show up for work and risked getting fired, they discovered my address and showed up at my door. They had also endured their own family tragedies. I found out that Liv's best friend died, and Emma's parents both died in a terrible house fire. Our shared grief bonded us, and in the midst of all that pain, we forged a fast and unbreakable friendship.

Since I plan on consuming more than a few beverages tonight, I decide to take an Uber to the sports bar. Dressed in my favorite skinny black jeans, Doc Martens, and a cropped tee, I sling my crossbody bag over my shoulder and step out. The ride is mercifully short, mainly because the garlicky, tangy smell radiating from the driver's pores in the front seat makes the air feel suffocating. I pull out my favorite travel-sized tube of Black Opium perfume and spritz myself lightly. The familiar scent grounds me, a small ritual I perform before stepping into the night.

The tinted windows don't reveal much as I approach the front doors, but the moment I step inside, a roar erupts from several tables, where people are glued to the action on a football game. The place smells of beer, sweat, and fried food, and I almost consider leaving while I can. But as I scan the large area for my friends, I spot Emma standing on her stool, waving me over, as Liv holds her steady.

"What the..." I trail off as a grin forms across my face at her wild antics. I definitely don't need her husband here. Overprotective doesn't even begin to describe his behavior when it comes to his wife. And isn't that her same driver sitting at the bar, shaking his head? He's on his phone, and I strong suspicion about who he's calling. I hurry over as Emma swings her legs off the stool, one arm still draped over it in balance as Liv holds onto her other.

I push my way through the crowd to meet them, and Emma wraps an arm around me. "I love that you're my height."

Liv comes over to embrace me. "Glad you made it, Dani."

A cough comes from across the table. "Oh, yeah. This is my sister, Evie, and her better half, Jameson. Her eyes narrow at Emma as they both wave. Evie is clearly Emma's twin with the same bright green eyes. But her red lipstick screams danger. And when she smiles, it's my favorite part. I grin back, showing off my own red lips and black nails that mirror hers. She smirks, then pivots her attention to her so-called "soulmate," as Emma once dubbed him. I suspect she stalked him, too, as Emma insinuated. Hm. Another thought to tuck away for later.

A flicker of movement in my peripheral vision draws my gaze downward. "Here," Emma says, sliding a dirty martini my way. The stemmed glass is frosted cold, beads of condensation sliding down its side. I take a slow sip, savoring the taste as it rolls off my tongue and slides down my throat. A soft, involuntary moan slips past my lips. Emma nearly chokes on her own drink. "Well," she snorts, "that wasn't pornographic at all." Her grin is wicked, and her laugh is infectious. And for the first time in what feels like forever, I feel myself smiling, too.

"Great timing," I say, taking another quick sip, careful not to drain the glass too quickly. Emma arches a single brow. It's low-key freaky, but I let it slide because it probably looks like mine. My fingers trace slow circles along the rim of the martini glass. "You nailed it with this drink!" I tease, letting a smile tug at my lips. "Almost like you knew when I would get here and need it then. Perfect timing."

"Oh, that." She takes a sip of her drink—an appletini, its neon green liquid glows in the dim lighting. "I just tracked you getting into the Uber and had Gus order it at the bar." She nods at the burly man still sitting at the bar, watching us with curiosity. That's definitely her driver. For some reason, her comment doesn't faze me as much as it should. I don't press for details, and I don't think she's joking either.

Liv notices my hesitation because her eyes widen and a sharp laugh escapes her, cutting through the noise and drawing Emma's attention to me once again. Her emerald gaze studies me, alight with mischief and humor.

Shrugging, Emma casually says, "Nothing says 'I care,' like stalking your besties." Her eyes narrow in challenge. But before I can process it, Evie pulls her into the conversation. It's there in that statement that I realize, I've found my people, my own besties. Fierce, unapologetic, with just a dash of danger, this recipe contains the makings of a beautiful friendship.

CHAPTER NINETEEN

DANI

Two hours later, they manage to convince me to join them at Emma's husband's club, The Viceroy. Everyone in Houston knows the name, as it's spoken with equal parts envy and intrigue because of its exclusivity. By day, its sleek metal exterior mixes in with the other steel structures in the downtown area, blending into the hustle and bustle of a busy city. But by night, it transforms, shining with decadence, glittering in those forbidden nighttime hours. Whispers create more allure about the hidden club, concealed behind an unmarked door, reserved for only the carefully vetted members who thrive on secrecy and sin.

We slip through the restless line of patrons as the queue curls in an endless S around the block. We move through the crowd like we own the place. Well, Emma kind of does. Inside, the perfumed air thickens with the heat of bodies dancing to the high-energy pulse of the dance music. We weave through the crowded throng of partygoers until we reach the sleek staircase that comes into view, rising into the most coveted section leading to the VIP area above. Security guards stand sentinel, tracking our movements with cold eyes. The VIP area opens up to a sea of velvet and dim lighting.

Plush emerald color couches create the illusion of intimacy, but I doubt much goes on that Eduardo doesn't see. The area thrums with a sense of danger that calls to me, making me sink into the chair as I kick one leg over it. My boot presses against the glass balcony. Gus lingers close by, vigilant as ever over his watch, until another man approaches, trading silent words in the form of a nod before changing places as Gus disappears into the shadows through a rustle of drapes.

Emma catches me staring and tips her chin toward him. "That's Philip," she says casually, as if his name should mean something. "He's single." Her smile sharpens.

I laugh, shaking my head, unwilling to play along with her matchmaking games. It's not the first time. A woman glides to our table, dressed in black, with elegant gold accessories. Not overdone, but stately. Her pose is effortless, but her judgment is poor. Her gaze lingers on Jameson, and beside me, I swear I hear Evie hiss under her breath. The sound jolts me, and I choke on my water. Liv pats my back, smirking.

"Geez, hun," she teases, her tone dry. "We're off the clock here." Then she adds, "But don't worry, Philip can give you mouth-to-mouth." But before I can form a comeback, Emma cuts me off.

"Yeah, Liv," Emma coos, her velvety tone edged with a hint of sarcasm. "We're off the clock, so why aren't you having a cocktail?" She studies Liv, giving her a suspicious look, though there's no actual malice there. Whatever the joke is, I'm clearly not in on it.

A different waitress approaches and sets our drinks down with quiet precision, nodding at Emma in some silent exchange before she leaves without another word. Her indifference is intentional, and the change of waitress a statement.

With the drama concluded, I slip further into the velvety, pillowed cushions, draping my arm over the chair, to indulge in my favorite pastime—people watching. Below us, people dance, their bodies lost in the lights and shadows of the strobe lights. In a quick glance, I catch something meant to be concealed by the dim lighting causing the hairs on my arm to rise. My senses become hyperaware of the danger hiding in plain sight. It's this heightened awareness that lets me take in everything unfolding below.

My eyes zero in on a man leaning close to a woman. His looks are pretty, and his smile is smooth. His hand is deceptively casual as he drops something into her glass. It fizzes slightly on impact, but other than that, nothing else is out of order. She doesn't notice. She only laughs, tossing her head back at some charming line no doubt, as she takes a big swig out of her drink. He raises his in mock salute, downing the rest, encouraging her to do the same. She mirrors him, trusting and unaware of his intentions.

My heart plummets as I see him for what he is—stripped of charm and a well-bred façade. He is nothing but a predator. He presses closer, angling his body, so the crowd shields them from view. She sways against him as her movements dissolve into his control. And to anyone else, it looks like nothing more than dancing. Like she maintains her own faculties, but I see the subtle falter, the slowing of her movements, and I know that at this point the drugs are taking effect, winding through her bloodstream, and rendering her helpless. So he'll make his move soon, and no one will be the wiser. Except for me, because I notice all those things shrouded in shadows.

I lean forward, tracking his movements, and the shift in my body catches Emma's eyes. She looks at me as I stand abruptly. But before she can speak, I yell. "I'll be right back!" over the noise. The velvet cushion falls to the floor as I leap from my seat and take the stairs quickly to the lower level. My pulse beats in time with the bass from the dance floor as I scan the area for them. I continue to scan the crowd, frantically searching for that tall mop of blond hair, until I spot him. His arm coils around the woman, holding onto her tightly as she appears to sway in his arms. He guides her to the exit, and I follow.

I stand in the corner, hidden away, embracing the darkness that provides a protective cover and advantage. He's talking to another man. Irritation flickers across his face as this interruption keeps him from his real intent. I take the syringe out of my pocket and uncap it, holding it in my hand, ready to strike at any given moment.

He slips out the back door, causing my pulse to accelerate. I see him exit into the empty alley. It's then that I know what his intentions are. She's there, pressed against the wall, as she leans limply in his grip. Her movements are unsteady, and her once cute little skirt is hiked up, her panties torn on the ground, discarded as he undoes his pants. His eyes meet mine. His predatory focus is clear, knowing he has her cornered and isolated. I step forward, deliberately slow, keeping to the unlit portion of the wall to disguise my face just in case. His pupils widen when he sees me approaching, thinking his deal got a bit sweeter—a two-for-one, as his lips twist in a cruel smirk.

"What the fuck do you want, sweets? I'm kind of busy here with my girl." The woman leans against him, her head still on his shoulder, as she lies unresponsive to our heated exchange. I keep approaching, steadily gaining footage. I notice her eyes open, as her hand twitches just a little in my direction, in a silent plea for help.

And then I charge. The syringe plunges into his neck as the medication sears through his thick skin and rips through the striated tissue fibers beneath. His reactions are slow to acknowledge what I just did, as he drops the woman and stumbles backward, touching his neck where I stabbed him. He runs it along the wound, and a smear of blood comes away from the site, gleaming in the dim light. I used a big ass needle to push the medication faster and harder into the circulatory system. His eyes bulge with rage and he lunges at me expectantly, seeking vengeance. I stumble back, but he pins me to the wall, forcing me further into the recesses of the alleyway.

"What the fuck did you give me, you bitch?" he shouts, spittle flying toward my face. My lips quirk up in a smirk, anticipating what is coming. His hand shoots to my neck, squeezing as I grit my teeth. I had taken a deep breath, expecting his maneuver, as he starts to choke me. But the joke's on him. This loser is nothing but predictable as fucking clockwork. Two minutes stretch like hours, though in reality, it's less than that. I feel his hands begin to shake involuntarily, then loosen against his will. His body drops like a ton of bricks awkwardly onto the ground, convulsing. I instinctively clutch my throat, gasping as I rub at the sting his grip left behind. The sensation still feels fresh against my cooling skin. I let my hand fall away and lean forward, bracing my palms on my thighs. I'm thankful I had the foresight to hold my breath. I look over to his flailing body as the medication takes hold of him. For a moment, I was afraid it would be a subpar dose, but luckily it's working as intended; otherwise, this could have had a very different outcome.

I sway on my feet before sprinting toward the girl lying on the ground. Just then, I see Emma and Eduardo, along with Gus and his replacement, Philip, merge from the back alley running toward me.

"What the fuck happened?" Eduardo asks, his voice unnervingly calm as if this type of crazy chaos is just another night at the club. He's too calm considering a man is sprawled out on the ground in the alley of his club, and an unconscious girl isn't far away, as if this shit happens all the time. I rub at my throat, still trying to recover from the strangulation attempt. As I try to speak, Philip lifts the girl and carries her around to the back entrance. Her head hangs limply in his arms until she disappears from view.

My gaze returns to the man on the alley floor, his lips tinged grayish-blue. The fight has left him. "Deprived of oxygen and a life-saving breathing tube." The words sound hoarse to even my own ears. I gesture in response to Eduardo's question, extending my hand at the man lying on the cement. I tilt my head, almost hearing his heart faltering. Its rhythm is weakening, as his heart is probably stopping as we speak. Flatlining in that perfectly asystolic line that marks life's end. It grips me with such emotion as I remember my own mother taking her last breaths, her body stilling and breath ceasing.

Emma touches me, and I flinch, yanked back to the present. I sigh, pinching the bridge of my nose. "That piece of shit drugged her. I saw it. He was just about to do terrible things to her before I got here." I attempt to act unaffected, although the adrenaline still coursing through betrays me. Emma rubs a gentle, soothing circle along my back.

She coos softly, "There, there, Dani. It's all going to be alright."

Eduardo strides over to the man still sprawled out on the floor and, for good measure, delivers a hard kick to his ribs. I hear the sickening crunch of bones breaking as he mutters a curse. "Piece of shit rapist," he spews, spittle flying.

I glance up. The door swings open as Evie and Jameson appear. Evie lights up a cigarette between her fingers and strolls toward me. Smoke billows from her mouth as she lifts her chin, exhaling the remainder out in one quick stream.

Emma opens her mouth to speak, but Evie holds up a hand, stopping her.

"Before you chastise me for smoking, sister," Evie says, taking a long drag from her cigarette, "I just came to tell you that Liv was dizzy and nearly fainted."

She crouches beside the man sprawled out on the ground, smoke trailing from her lips as she studies him with calm detachment. With a smirk tugging at her lips, she mutters, "Well, he's fucking dead. What happened?"

But before I can respond, Emma rushes past me. "I fucking knew Liv was pregnant again." Her tone is clipped, but there's no animosity there toward her friend as she raises her hand in the air, addressing Jameson.

Jameson takes out his cell phone, glancing at his messages with a knowing smirk. "Dax is on his way to get her. Just like last time, huh, Emma?" Emma hesitates at the door before rolling her eyes and then turns back.

"Don't worry about it, Dani, we'll take care of it. Evie, can you stay with my friend?" She looks between us. Evie nods, and Emma rushes inside, trailed by Gus.

Eduardo runs his hands through his hair, tension etched into every line of his face. He starts giving orders, and I can see that he is the leader. They, despite being family, all have their own roles in the organization they have established. "Jameson, can you scrub any footage?" Then he turns to Evie. "Can you get rid of the body?" Eduardo asks playfully. "You seem to have a knack for doing that, don't you?"

Evie takes one last drag of her cigarette before flicking it on the corpse. Her smile is sickly sweet, almost deranged, as she presses a button on her phone, lifts it to her ear, and is ready to act. "Mateo, can you come to the club? I need help with a body." She pauses briefly, and I hear yelling on the other end. She doesn't flinch. "Just bring the van and park in the usual spot." She says, then ends the call and pockets her phone.

She eyes me and nods. "You should go. I'll take care of this." Jameson is already on his phone trying to address the security footage, as I am learning is his specialty.

Eduardo sighs, rubbing the back of his neck, and looking upward in a plea, "Can't I get a moment's peace?" he mutters, striding down the alley and stopping mid-step. He glances back at me. "Why aren't you following me?" he asks, and I don't hesitate, following in step behind him. He leads me through a nondescript door and into a long, narrow hallway. I can almost feel a pulse in the air from where the elusive club lies beyond. What is it called? The Hidden Pearl? But we don't go near there, and I'm almost disappointed. Sensing my thoughts, he shakes his head and chuckles.

Instead, he guides me up a dimly-lit corridor. At the end, Eduardo's door to his office is slightly ajar, and I see Liv reclining on the couch. Her posture is relaxed, and it quickly sets my mind at ease. Across from her, a tall man with kind blue eyes kneels before her, watching her with an almost worshipful intensity.

As I enter the office, I hear him chastising her. "Really, Liv, I can't believe this happened again. Can't you just take a pregnancy test like everyone else?" he asks, but there is no bite to his tone. Only warmth, care, and devotion radiate from him. It reminds me so much of how Vic used to look at me not long ago.

As everyone disperses, Emma slips her arm through mine, gently guiding me out of the office through the hallway.

"Come on, killer, let's get you home." We emerge into the alley, now eerily empty. No body. No evidence. Only the shadows remain and the faint buzz of the city beyond.

CHAPTER TWENTY

DANI

I awake before the sun rises, and the sins from last night still cling to me. Sleep doesn't come after what I did. It wasn't a choice, it was a compulsion—a need to help her when no one else would. But it drags up memories I try to keep buried of the night I covered up Vic's father's murder. He was a monster, one who got away with murder and cruelty. He deserved what came to him, yet holding Vic afterward, feeling the scales of right and wrong tip in my hands, reminds me how convoluted everything is, how a man like Vic can be inherently good, yet harbor such a dark side. Now, in a similar situation, having played jury and executioner myself, I ache for Vic, for him to hold me, to whisper that everything is going to be okay, even though the darkness that I've fully embraced tells me otherwise.

I don't know if Vic has called. That night, when I heard Chloe pick up his phone, something inside me snapped at the intimate way she called him "baby." I powered my phone off and tossed it into a box, locked away with all our memories. A black ribbon tied it shut, a symbolic ribbon to be cut only in emergencies—my own personal Pandora's box.

The next day, I bought a new phone. I had a new number. And a chance to start a new life without him. But in the end, I couldn't do it. When the sales associate asked if I wanted to trade in the old phone, the one still crammed with our texts and voicemails, I shook my head. I couldn't sever him from my life altogether, even though it felt like I already had. I needed a return path, however slim the chance might be. I kept the phone and the number active, keeping that lifeline connected to a past I refused to let go. It offered a sliver of hope that maybe, just maybe, a miracle was still possible.

That night after delivering my version of justice to that man, I came home desperate for someone who might understand. I lifted the single framed picture of us and placed it reverently on my nightstand. The phone went on the charger, while the rest of the box's contents lay scattered across the floor. The black ribbon is discarded there in tatters. This will force me to see him every day. To remember him every day. But why does it torment me so much?

I have no idea. Perhaps it's punishment, my penance for never telling him the truth, for letting him believe my disinterest was anything but exhaustion from caring for my mother, working, and attending school. And now, what do I have to show for it? I am alone, surrounded by wonderful friends, yet they have their own lives and families, leaving me with my solitude.

That's how I find myself here, clutching the box that holds my past. One foot propped on the bed, I rest it in my lap, hesitant to open it. Once I do, there's no turning back.

"Fuck it." I rip the top off, letting its contents spill freely on my freshly laundered sheets. The first morning rays peek through the blinds, but I'm not ready for them. I rise and shut them tightly, shrouding the room in the illusion of night. My dim lamp's glow casts a warm, intimate presence over the scattered memories as I lift the first photograph, feeling the weight of all my choices.

And my heart shatters. Memories of us come flooding back as I lift every photo from the box, reliving each unforgettable moment frozen in time. I retrieve some tape from my desk drawer and begin the tedious ritual of affixing each picture to my bedroom walls. Once it is done, I finally step back and take in the shrine I created for Vic. Everywhere I turn, I'm surrounded by him, by the man I still love, and will likely love until the end of time. I collapse onto my bed, tears flowing freely down my face. For the first time in what feels like forever, I allow myself to mourn. I mourn for my mother, for the boy I once loved, and the man who continues to reside in every corner and consume the entirety of my heart.

Finally, I pick up the phone and power it on. One by one, the voice messages ping, each a fragment of the past I tried to ignore. Countless messages went unanswered, and yet I see that it's only been a few months since Vic last reached out. I hit the arrow button.

I graduated today from medical school and am now starting my residency program in Boston. Another four years of nights spent buried in books. Mornings running on fumes. I thought the moment would feel like a victory, but the only thing I felt was emptiness because you weren't there to share it with me. I kept looking, hoping that by some twist of fate, I'd look up and see you in the stands. But now I know that you're never coming.

I tried to find you, you know. I went to your house, but you no longer lived there. I even hunted down Brandon, but he wouldn't tell me what happened. I wished for any breadcrumb of information.

Where did your mom go, Dani? Where did you go?

I need you to know that I'm genuinely sorry. I should have stayed. I should have fought harder for us. That Halloween, when I came down to surprise you because I just missed you so damn much, I saw you outside with him. I saw the way he held you, and I thought, "How could I be so easily replaced?" But Brandon told me it was never like that. That he was just helping you out and selling the house. I kept replaying that night, watching you in his arms, and it broke me. I'm not a good man, Dani. And now all I have are the ghosts of us, and the life we could have had.

The call ends abruptly, and I sit there stunned. I look back at all the times he called, each message a testament to his continued persistence. I was never aware of all the calls. I grasp the phone like a lifeline to Vic himself. After I've cried until I thought there was nothing left, wading through self-pity and despair, I decide to take a shower. Tears continue to fall, and my body shudders with tremors I can't stop. This must be what dying of a broken heart feels like.

After all this time, he thought I cheated on him. Why would he believe that? I never gave him the whole truth, and I will forever regret that decision. It has caused so much unnecessary pain. I thought I was doing the right thing. As I replay the voicemail, the realization hits me. Vic would have stayed behind. I loved him, so I let him succeed, knowing he wouldn't have graduated from his residency this year if I hadn't. My sacrifice and silence were done to give him that chance, yet the cost to us has been detrimental.

Dressed in a pair of pajama pants and one of Vic's old sweat shirts, I step out of the bathroom and scream, clutching my hand to my chest. Emerald green eyes track me as she lounges in my chair, legs crossed beneath her.

She whistles. "Dang girl, I would've never thought." Her gaze sweeps over the hundreds of photographs plastered against every inch of sheet rock, and for the first time, I see how stalkerish it looks. "This shit makes Evie look tame," she chuckles, rising from the chair, walking toward me. "How are you, sweets?"

I plant a hand on my hip. "Are you for real right now?" I fling my other hand outward. "What are you doing in here?" But then maybe, she is here to tell me I need to run. Oh, God. Have the cops found out? Are they looking for me?

As if sensing my wayward thoughts, she snaps her fingers in the air. "Hey, girlie. Where'd you go? You're fine. Everything's fine," she says coolly. She flicks her long blonde hair calmly over her shoulder, tucking it neatly behind her ears.

Her actions are a stark contrast to my increasing agitation. So I restate my question, now that the feeling of dread is gone, knowing that I'm safe. "What are you doing here, Em?"

"Well, isn't it obvious?" She chuckles. "I came to see you, silly goose."

I stare in disbelief. "Obviously." My face crinkles in confusion. "But how did you get in here?" I ask suspiciously.

She shrugs, casually picking imaginary lint from her shirt. "The door was open, so I came in."

I know for a fact that I locked it, but I'll give her this, deciding to let it go. Maybe I don't really want to know. It may be harmless or not, but after last night, I think we all have our issues.

"Right," I mutter, neither buying nor arguing about it. Then she beams at me, knowing she's won.

"So what's all this?" she asks. Her hand slowly sweeps around the room.

I cross my arms over my chest and huff. "How long do you have?" I counter, my voice edged with defensiveness.

"Oh. Is it going to take long?" She seems totally unbothered by this admission, and almost, do I dare say, excited? "I should let Gus know he can leave." She plucks out her phone, sends a quick text, then pockets it just as quickly. "Do you have wine?"

I glance at the clock and then back at her, measuring how much patience I have left after a night of no sleep and now this.

"Seriously," I say, extending a hand toward the clock reading eight a.m.

She snaps her fingers, "Right, mimosas it is." She rises from her chair and, with long, purposeful strides, goes to the kitchen. She swings open the fridge, searching its contents. I can't help but smile when she spots it as she turns back, she grins widely. "I knew you'd have it." She grabs a dish towel I keep ready by the sink and pops the top, as if it were champagne meant for a celebration rather than a confession. She pours us each a glass, topped with just a small amount of orange juice for added color.

I lead us to the couch, but she halts mid-stride, reaching back for the orange juice and champagne, and carrying them to the table with us as she sinks into the cushions. A pillow lands across her lap as she makes herself comfortable, wiggling into the sofa before sighing.

She scoops her long hair up, tucking it over one shoulder, and rests her hand on her legs. Sitting up straight and giving me her undivided attention, she clears her throat before saying, "Okay, I'm ready now," she says thoughtfully, and I realize my friends are completely insane. I'm about to begin when she interrupts. "Start from the beginning," she lectures, "and don't leave anything out."

So I do. I skip over the parts about covering up his dad's murder, but from the sharp look she gives me, I suspect she may have guessed the truth. I also know I didn't exactly handle myself well last night, but she doesn't bring that up at all. She pretends like it never happened.

Afterwards, we talk, and Emma insists that I move to Boston so I can find him. With all my heart, I know she's right. And with her help, I begin to put the plan in motion.

PART TWO

"ALL HUMAN BEINGS, AS WE MEET THEM ARE COMMINGLED OUT OF GOOD AND EVIL."

ROBERT LOUIS STEVENSON, DR. JEKYLL AND MR.HYDE

LAS JARAS

THE PRESENT

CHAPTER
TWENTY–ONE

DANI
FOUR YEARS LATER
AGE 30

Sighing, I stand from my chair in the testing center after taking my Certification for Hospice and Palliative Nursing (CHPN). After years in the emergency department, I finally found a specialty where I could make a real difference. It started one day when a family member brought in their mother, who was dying of cancer. She hadn't had a care plan in place, and ended up intubated, despite a poor prognosis and rapidly declining quality of life. The doctor informed them that she would not likely leave the hospital this time. Later, they chose to withdraw support. Maybe if they had received information about hospice options earlier, they might have been better prepared for that moment. Still, even the best-laid plans can sometimes fall apart.

Can you ever really be prepared? Emotionally, no. However, having a plan helps you think clearly, find a middle ground, and simply focus on being present in their final days, hours, or even minutes. I know that I wasn't prepared when my mom passed away, despite knowing it was coming. The hospice nurse, making her comfortable in those final hours, was invaluable. I hope to provide that same guidance to others—to offer support, clarity, and the information they need to make decisions they can accept and feel at peace with when that time finally comes.

As I slip into my car and start the engine, the drive through the city passes by in a blur of pavement and shopping malls. The streets seem quieter than usual, or it's just the thoughts in my head that are subdued. The late morning sun reflects off the glass of the building as I approach the downtown area, and I let my mind wander. I think about the patients I've helped, my mom's passing, and the uncertain future that still lies ahead. Each mile brings a strange mixture of nostalgia and hope. Am I making the right choice?

By the time I pull into the emergency department, my thoughts have shifted to the present. The familiar chaos of ambulances, paramedics, and nurses rushing about is a setting I've been familiar with for years. I find it strangely comforting, despite the stress it carries, because it always keeps my mind busy.

I enter the emergency department to clear out my locker, and Liv greets me. "Hey, you," she chirps, looping her toned arm around my shoulder as I rest my head against hers. This place has been a familiar setting for years, and the friends I have made here are the best part. "How'd it go today?" she asks, and I can't help but smile.

"Passed like a superstar." I laugh, and Liv claps.

"Well, of course you did!" She does a little hop. "I never doubted it for a second."

"Yeah, now I just need to send off my résumé to a certain hospital in Boston," I say sheepishly. "I'm going to miss you guys," I admit.

Her eyes mist. "I'm going to miss you, too." She starts crying and hugs me, squeezing me tightly. I hear a distinctive clatter of clogs approaching before I see her.

"Oh, ease up, besties." Emma snorts as she walks up to us. "You know Liv, she's so emotional when she's pregnant." She laughs, rolling her eyes and hitching her thumb in Liv's direction.

Liv nods, agreeing. "It's true." She dabs at her eyes with her sleeve, and I cringe, thinking about what it has touched in this place, hoping she doesn't lose an eye. "Are you glad you took a little time off to pack and then make that big move?"

I bit my lip, mulling it over. "Yeah, I'll need the time."

Emma's eyes crinkle in amusement. "Need the time to stalk things out?" she says.

"I think she means *stake*," Liv counters, but Emma just hides her smirk before turning to watch a stretcher rolling past. A paramedic squeezes the bag as they rush the patient into the trauma bay with several people following close behind.

"And that's my cue to go," Emma says as she waves before following suit. Liv insists on hugging me one last time as she reluctantly leaves, taking the hallway that veers off to the right and walking back to her urgent care station. Opening the door to the women's locker room, I open the bag I brought and begin the task of removing my years of memories from this place, which hang in the form of photos and well-meaning gifts. I notice an envelope and see the cursive sprawl of Emma's writing on the front. I place this in my purse to read when I get home. I pick up the stethoscope my mother gifted me the day I was accepted into nursing school and hold it tightly. A single tear slips from my eye, and I can't help the sadness of losing her in such a cruel way. The monster that stole her from this world too soon. Fuck cancer. I place it delicately on the top of my belongings and close the locker with finality, knowing that I won't be returning, and the next time I hang my stethoscope in a locker, it will be in a different city and hopefully, if I plan it out correctly, at the same hospital Vic works at.

I grab my bag of belongings, swing them over my shoulder, and exit the building for the last time. Memories of fun times with my friends, and reminders of how exhausting this job can be, flood me. Yeah, I definitely won't miss it all. I take a moment to savor the accomplishment, letting it sink in, before moving on to what I hope will be the final defining chapters of my life.

Back at the apartment, I can't help but wonder how all this will play out.

I place my belongings in a box that will be taken to my new place soon. I stand around looking at the apartment that has been my own personal prison. Too many sad memories reside here, and I can't wait to be rid of this place. The walls are bare, and my bedroom is all packed. I plan to have a quick night sleeping on the couch and stalking Vic online before the movers come to load my items and bring them to the East Coast. Emma wanted to take me to the airport to catch my flight, but she and Eduardo had to go to her family's house in Mexico. Luckily, Liv is off and volunteered to take me. That prompts me to remember Emma's note. I stand up from the couch and grab my bag and laptop, plopping them on my lap as I fall back into the sofa, crossing my legs over one another. Extracting the letter from the envelope, I open the stationery with a capital E in script. It reads:

Dani,

Over the years, you have become one of my most cherished friends. I want you to know that if you ever want to talk, your secrets are safe with me. Even if you don't want to share, that's okay, too, because I know you and I get it. You are so much like me that the first time we met, I knew we would be great friends. Please know that if you need anything at any time of day, I will be available to answer. Should you need help, I will provide it, no questions asked. Don't be a stranger, and come back home whenever you can.

Love,

Emma Taylor-Ruiz

Home. That word stands out the most in that letter because I only have one home, and that is wherever Vic is. But for the last few years, this place with my found family in Houston has been my home.

I heard rumors about Emma and her husband being in the mafia, but I thought it was just that—a rumor. However, after what I saw that night and the way they helped me take care of the situation with the body in the alley, I knew there was more truth to it. There is usually some truth mixed in with the rumors. The fact that no one was freaked out by what I did was also a big clue. And I know that Eduardo, her husband, would do anything his wife asks, including helping me.

Opening the laptop and typing in Vic's name, I see a picture of him on the medical staff website. Dr. Victor Flores, of the general surgery department, is depicted in his portrait. The boy, now a man, looks so similar to the person I said goodbye to that day, until his taillights faded from my view, taking my emotions with them. His eyes are devoid of any happiness, and his lips form a thin line. His white coat, with his name in black script, stands out. I touch his face on the screen and vow to make the light return to his eyes and his lips to once again find mine.

CHAPTER TWENTY-TWO

VIC

It's been years since I last saw Dani, and yet even at thirty, not a single day passes without her ghost of a memory lingering in the recesses of my mind. I left her there, standing in the street, as I drove away. Both of us were eighteen, with hearts and dreams too big, and an all-consuming love. Time and distance have done nothing to subdue it, and the ache only sharpens with each passing year.

On the rare reprieve from the relentless life of a surgeon, I retreat to my favorite corner table at Café Nero, a steaming cortado warming my hands as I attempt to read the pages of my newest thriller. Her absence has never truly left me, it follows me even in quiet moments such as this, seeping into every corner I try to hide in. I tell myself I come here for the quiet, for the illusion of normalcy. Truthfully, it's in these moments that I feel at peace because they are the only times I can convince myself that I've let her go.

Well, almost, until that peace shatters the moment Bethany walks in and spots me. Her face lights up as she rushes over. "What the fuck did I do in this life to deserve this?" I mutter under my breath, keeping my expression perfectly blank.

"Dr. Flores! I didn't expect to see you here." Her voice carries that syrupy forced-happiness, grating on my nerves like nails on a chalkboard, and I resist the urge to roll my eyes. I stare at her in disbelief because the woman has been circling me like a vulture for about a year now. Or maybe that's when I first started noticing her little games. I'm about to tell her I was just leaving when she rushes off to snatch up her to-go order from the row at the counter. Perfect. My chance to slip out before she corners me again.

Unfortunately, luck isn't on my side today. "Dr. Flores, wait!" She shuffles along in those ridiculous heeled boots, her scarf trailing behind her as she scrambles to catch up to me, heading for the door.

"Bethany, good to see you." I greet, because I'm a respectable person. Or at least that's what I tell myself. Anyone who says that is probably far from it. But hey, her problem, not mine. "Sorry, I was just leaving." Not that I'm actually sorry. I tuck my book under my arm, sparing her a flat-out rejection. But she doesn't quit. Of course not. Instead, she quickens her pace. The blast of cold air hits us as we walk outside, contrasting sharply with the café's comfortable heat. Coffee clutched firmly in hand, I lift the collar of my dark grey field jacket, the chill biting at my neck. I frown, cursing the thoughtless mistake of leaving my scarf at home.

Fall is fast approaching, and the cool, crisp air is a welcome reprieve from the city's relentless humidity in summertime. It's finally sweater weather. I pick up my pace, and she tries to keep up, but I'm not about to be late for my lunch obligation.

"Where are you going? Mind if I join you?" I stop mid-stride and turn to look at her. She halts, too, wobbling as her heel nearly catches on a crack in the sidewalk, but I don't lift a finger to help. If she's going to insist on wearing those ridiculous boots, the least she could do is master the art of walking in them. She steadies herself, flashing me a triumphant smile, like she just won the lottery, but the joke's on her.

"Actually, that would be wonderful," I say, slowing my pace for her to keep up. She looks surprised, but quickly masks it.

"Where are we going?" she asks curiously.

I glance at her, eyes narrowing. "It's a surprise," I say, a smirk tugging at my lips. "Wouldn't want to ruin the fun."

Bethany fucking claps. "Oh, how exciting," she gushes animatedly with fake enthusiasm. I arch an eyebrow and give her my best, *Seriously?* Look, but it doesn't faze her in the slightest. This woman is beyond annoying, but soon enough, I'm about to discover her true character. Perhaps I've judged her too harshly.

"Are you going to the gala?" she asks suddenly, the abrupt topic shift so startling that I can't help but chuckle at her persistence.

I nod once. "Of course," I reply. Bethany leans in closer, brushing her arm against mine as if by accident, and her overpowering perfume nearly makes me gag. "It is for a great cause," I continue, side-stepping to reclaim some space, "helping parents of children needing treatment at the hospital stay on campus for a reduced fee, and making it easier for them to be near their loved ones."

Her manicured hand flies to her chest. "Isn't it wonderful?" she coos, but the sincerity is about as genuine as her knock-off Louboutins.

"Not much farther." I throw her a bone, noticing her wince in those four-inch stiletto boots, as we trek down Boylston Street in downtown Boston. We turn the corner and stop in front of the Catholic charity house where I volunteer. I take the steps two at a time and pull the heavy door open, holding it wide for Bethany to go in first. Only, she isn't there. I turn slowly, exaggerating the movement, pretending to search the landing like she's vanished into thin air. Until I spot her clicking heels retreating down the first step. I let the door close behind me and approach her, already knowing I had judged her correctly from the start.

"Are you not coming in?" I ask, putting on the most sincere face I can muster. She looks around, avoiding my eyes.

"Isn't that a soup kitchen?" she asks, and I can't help but wonder how she ever became a nurse.

"That is correct," I say, watching her, waiting for her just to admit it. But I'm not about to make it easy on her. She ruined my last few minutes of peace, and I could have spent them finishing that chapter.

She looks down at her outfit. "I'm not really dressed to hand out food," she replies, and I can tell it's the best excuse she could come up with. Honestly, it's almost shocking.

"I didn't realize serving people who don't have access to warm meals requires a certain attire," I deadpan, more than a little pissed at her lack of empathy. In short, Bethany sucks as a human. She starts to back away, and I can't help the curl of my lip, almost a sneer.

"I just remembered I have to meet my sister to help with her wedding plans." She nearly misses the last step, and I briefly consider whether it's terrible to hope she face-plants on the granite. Well, that would make me late, so I'd settle for her just leaving.

"Right," I say, expression perfectly unimpressed. "Well, see you never, Bethany," I add dryly, swinging the door open with a flourish, stepping inside, and finally ridding myself of that drab gold digger.

My sneakers squeak against the clean floors as I walk toward the kitchen, where food service is scheduled to begin from eleven-thirty to one p.m. I usually arrive an hour early to help prepare everything. I spot Arthur at the hospitality desk, and he waves me over. I grab my volunteer pass, the lanyard proudly displaying the word *volunteer* in yellow letters, and sling it around my neck.

"How's life at the hospital, man?" he asks, smiling widely, showing off his gapped teeth. It's endearing to him, and I can't help wondering if orthodontia would take away some of that charm. He always jokes that he can fit a buck-fifty in there, though I hope he hasn't actually tried. I shudder at the thought.

"Never-ending," I say, and that seems to please him. His mom was an operating room nurse, and from her stories and firsthand experience, he knows how grueling the workload can be. With a wave of my badge, I walk to the kitchen ready to help in any way I can.

"There you are, love," Betsy calls, waving me over. "Can you be a dear and load the trays with the canned veggies, please?" I nod, offering her a quick smile, and get to work, opening cans and arranging the vegetables in the warming trays. Soon, the metal serving trays steam, and I've loaded all the utensils into bins, along with napkins. Taking my place in line, I prepare to help as the first guests arrive. Many are familiar faces, but a woman and her daughter, about five people down in line, catch my attention. They're new here.

As they draw closer, I notice the woman has a black eye. It's healing now, but it's still ringed with streaks of yellow, green, and purple. I force myself not to stare, but it's hard to look away. The little girl beside her clutches a worn rabbit, its big, floppy ears matted from too much love. Her wide eyes sweep over the trays of food with such wonder that it makes my jaw ache from clenching. She looks at it like a child who hasn't had steady access to food in a long while.

"What do you like to eat?" I ask her, forcing my voice to remain calm while anger claws at my insides, urging me to punish whoever let it get this far because they deserve far worse than hunger.

Her eyes widen in surprise. "I can have whatever I want?" she whispers in disbelief, and my heart aches a little at her question.

"Of course," I assure her softly, but before I can say more, her mom steps in.

"Rose Daniella, just get a couple of things that you know you'll eat. We don't want to waste any food." I freeze with my serving spoon suspended mid-air. She looks up at me and points eagerly to a dish of pasta.

"I'll take that one!" Her little hand extends toward it, and that's when I see it—a bruise. The handprint is an angry purple and wraps around her entire wrist. I fight the surge of anger rising inside me. I grip the spooner tighter, fighting to smother it down, to keep my face composed while every instinct screams out to find the bastard responsible.

She looks at me with those kind, trusting eyes that have probably seen more than her fair share of injustice. Instead, I keep my voice calm for her. "Dani, do you want something else with your pasta? We've got meatballs and some sauce, too," I offer as an afterthought. She nods quickly, her little eyes wide, watching intently as I place a generous scoop onto her plate.

She takes the tray, confused by my nickname for her, but I can't help it. It's too close to home. "Thank you, sir," she offers politely, and her mom gives me a small, timid smile before they leave and settle at a tiny table in the corner. I watch them as Dani—I mean, Rose—holds onto her bunny tightly as she eats her spaghetti, sauce smeared across her face. But for now, at least she's fed and smiling.

When the line dwindles and the cleanup is done, I step back out into the city streets. The air is cool and brisk against my heated skin. It isn't much—just a few meals served and some donated hours of my time—but I feel good about having spent my afternoon doing something that makes a difference in someone else's life. Still, as I walk home, I can't shake the feeling that Dani lingers at my side. Sometimes, I can swear I feel her, though I know that's impossible. I'll just have to settle for the ghost of her.

CHAPTER TWENTY-THREE

DANI

I've been in the Boston area, waiting for a job to open in the hospice department. I was told that they'll have something soon, as the woman currently holding my dream position is finally expected to retire. From what I hear, I have some very big shoes to fill. For now, I'm settling into a per diem nurse role in the emergency department, which is just as busy as the one I left in Houston. There are a few differences in the lingo, but the job itself is the same. The first time one of the nurses asked me to pass her a "Johnny," I stared at her like she had sprouted two heads. Only when she pointed at the blue-striped hospital gown did it click.

"You mean the gown?" I asked, brow furrowed.

She laughed. "Yeah, that. It's a Johnny. What do you guys call it down South?"

I tilt my head sideways, giving her my best *Are you serious* look. "Um, a hospital gown," I deadpan, because isn't it obvious?

She chuckles, "Well, you're not in Kansas anymore, Dorothy," she teases, walking off and down the hall. Hell, don't I know it. When I first moved here, people kept asking me if I was "all set," and I had no idea what they meant. A water fountain is called a bubbler, and soda? They call it tonic. Back home in Texas, everything is just Coke. Want a Coke? Which kind? A Sprite? You got it. Coming right up. So I guess she's right. I'll get used to it...eventually. Though if someone offers me some Dunkin' Donuts caffeine through an IV line, I might get on board with that. Speaking of, where is my coffee order?

I'm searching for Shioban, who should be coming with my beverage any minute, when I see him. All the air is punched right out of my lungs, leaving only a hollow pit. He prowls down the corridor, a dark presence radiating a "devil is a gentleman" vibe. His polished black shoes and flashing red soles strike the floor with sharp, commanding strides, abruptly coming to a stop at the central nursing station. He lifts a clipboard, flipping through it with focused precision, until he stops, almost mechanically, and extracts a 12-lead EKG tracing. His cold, calculating obsidian eyes scan it from top to bottom, assessing the rhythm. With his elongated fingers, he flips the paper aside, places another sheet on top, and saunters off with one hand clasping the chart as his white coat trails behind him. His athletic legs take him into one of the trauma bays, where he pauses briefly. His head tilts slightly before shaking it off and disappearing into the room.

For a minute, I thought he was going to turn, and his eyes would find mine. Did he feel it, too? The possibility makes my pulse quicken, and a restless energy sparks and electricity hums beneath my skin. An ache so profound consumes me, demanding that my body follow him. The sensation makes my skin prickle as I fight off my intense attraction to claim him here in front of everyone. My Vic. Mine.

Even after he disappears into the trauma bay, I remain frozen, rooted to the spot, my breathing left shallow from the encounter. I stare at the space he left behind, mesmerized, as my body finally awakens after feeling nothing for so long. This electric current of need and longing surges through me, reviving every nerve, every synapse just from the sight of this man who's tormented my dreams for years. Though he's gone, my body still burns, branded from the mark he left on my heart years ago.

Just then, Shioban appears with my coffee. Her cool, green

eyes study me with amusement. "I see you've had the privilege of witnessing Dr. Flores in action," she teases. I turn my gaze to her, my face blank as I try to school my expression, but it's no use. Shioban sees right through it.

"Um," she says, lifting a finger and swirling it in the air toward my mouth. "You have a little drool—" but she doesn't finish as I break into laughter, shaking my head. Popping the plastic tab of my medium regular coffee cup, the steam wafts upward, curling in the air. I take a long sip, letting the warmth seep down my throat, settling my stomach.

Shioban smirks with her arms crossed over her chest. "Don't bother trying to hide it. Most nurses go weak in the knees when he walks by." Shioban leans in closer, poised to tell me a secret. "Just watch out for Bethany," she says coolly. My brows lift, silently asking her to elaborate. She lifts her chin toward a knockout of a woman walking toward Vic. She's slightly older, but her face screams Botox. Her smooth skin is taut against her strong cheekbones, and her plump, collagen lips are shiny with a coat of pink lip gloss. I see Vic stop outside the trauma bay as Bethany places her hand on his arm. I watch and fight the urge to rip her hand away. He hands her the chart and strolls away as we all watch his tall, muscular form walk down a back corridor that leads to the darkened stairwell and up to the operating rooms, no doubt ensuring the staff is setting up his case in preparation for his patient.

"Are they dating?" I ask Shioban before I can stop myself.

She shrugs. "Don't know. I guess it depends on who you ask," she replies, noncommittally.

My grip tightens around the coffee cup. "What's that supposed to mean?"

She begins to say something, but then stops herself. "Just be careful with that one. He's not what he seems." Shioban smiles like she's said too much.

I nod, understanding, settling in, knowing this conversation is over. "Okay, let's get back to work. Shortest fifteen-minute break ever," I deflect, my voice laced with humor.

Agreeing, she starts to walk away, but then turns back. "Oh, hey. We are going out after work." She lifts her coffee in salute.

"The Holy Grail after our shift ends. You should come." Her smile is warm and inviting. I realize I'd like that.

"Sure," is all I say, and she disappears into the same trauma bay Vic was just in as I leave in the opposite direction.

My shift wraps up quickly, and before I know it, it's seven. I find my replacement to report on my patients. I honestly didn't plan on going, but sometimes the loneliness is too much. The voices in my head are too loud, and I need something distracting to quiet them. I don't plan on staying out late tonight, but since I have the day off tomorrow, anything could happen. My soft, velveteen black leggings hug my thick thighs as I throw on my sweater that hangs off one shoulder. I slip into my favorite pair of black combat boots, and a scarf is thrown haphazardly around my neck.

Grabbing my work bag, I decide to leave it in my locker, walking out with only my small crossbody around my shoulder. As I step out in the crisp September air, I walk a couple of blocks to the tavern to meet up with everyone. My combat boots strike the cobblestone walkways with straightforward strides as I quickly pace through the night. The cold air bites at my cheek, causing my eyes to water. I wish I had brought some gloves, but it's only September, and we aren't even into the cold weather yet. The temperature is vastly different from Texas, and I've updated my wardrobe to accommodate the lower temperatures. I hear laughter coming from the green illuminated sign. A couple of women are outside smoking, and I deride their commitment to a vice that forces them to inhale toxins in the cold air.

The bell jingles above the door as I step inside. The hostess stands at a podium that looks more suited for a Sunday sermon than seating patrons, but I wave her off, already spotting my coworkers sequestered at a high-top table along the side wall of the tavern. The tavern itself is a blasphemous contradiction, having once been a church converted into a pub. The stained glass windows cast colors across the room, clashing with the foul language and clinking pint glasses. The bar is centered, like an altar, in the middle of the tavern, set in high-polished wood trimmed with ornate gold scrollwork. Even the floor seems to mock the sanctity it once held, copper pennies set in epoxy speckled into its surface like an unholy offering.

Searching for a certain familiar face, the details of the bar fade into the background once I spot Shioban. She lifts her pint in greeting, calling me over with that mischievous grin of hers. I bump her shoulder with mine as I slide past, and she carries on her animated conversation with one of the nurses from our shift like I hadn't interrupted. Turning to the woman beside her, I lift a hand. "Hey, Jill," I say, and she flashes me a warm smile.

"Hey, hon. Glad you made it out." Her smile is friendly, but the corners of her mouth pull down as she turns her attention away toward the door. Bethany walks in. Shioban groans audibly, lifting her beer for a long pull, knowing she'll likely need it to endure the night. The waitperson approaches, pen ready to take our drink orders. I order a bloodytini. Bethany sits across the table, crinkling her nose upward with a subtle hint of disapproval, as if I just ordered tap water instead of a bottled sparkling one. She surveys the table, her eyes lingering on each drink, finally settling on the one she deems the safest choice.

Shioban looks at me over the rim of her glass, her green eyes alight with mischief. "So Beth," Shioban begins, then pauses just enough to tip back the last of her beer. She sets the glass aside with a heavy *thunk* and leans forward onto the table with a calculating grin. "You just getting out of work?" She patiently awaits whatever story Bethany is going to spin. I've been around her enough in my short time here that Bethany loves to inflate her ego any way she can. Bethany straightens in her seat. She glances over at Shioban, then at Jill, gathering her audience, and I catch the way her tongue presses against her front teeth. She drags it slowly across them, giving her a moment to contemplate the story she'll weave to gain admiration.

The waiter reappears with our drinks, and Shioban wiggles her empty beer bottle at him. "I'll take another when you get a chance," she says easily as he sets my bloodytini in front of me. The glass is chilled, the rim is salted. The cocktail itself resembles a bloodier, stronger relative of the traditional Bloody Mary. A skewer of olives, pickle, and onion is set neatly across the top. Bethany's sparkling white wine arrives next. She lifts it delicately, taking a prim and proper sip, leaving a red lipstick stain on the rim. I noticed this about her. Her lipstick is nearly the same shade as mine, but where mine is a matte stain that doesn't smear as easily, hers is a glossy lacquer. I've worn this shade since high school, and it's so much a part of me that I rarely wear anything else.

Bethany smirks, glancing around the table and looking over at the women, with a smirk playing at her lips. "Well," she begins, flickering her long, blonde hair over her shoulders, "I wanted to make sure Dr. Flores had everything he needed for surgery."

Shioban places her hand dramatically to her chest. "Oh, Bethany, how thoughtful of you," she coos. "I'm sure he was positively lost and oh-so-grateful to have your help and expertise."

Bethany straightens at her words, her posture lifting from Shioban's praise. Under the table, Shioban's hand jabs me in the leg. I glance at her and see the effort it takes for her to keep a straight face. I bite back my own laughter, hiding it behind the rim of my glass as I pull my drink off the coaster, letting the bloodytini burn warmly down my throat.

"Come to think of it," Bethany says, her lip twitching as if savoring the memory, "he kept staring at my red lips. Entranced is the word I'd use. He just couldn't look away. And then," she pauses for effect, "he said something about stained kisses."

The words hit me like a slap, dragging me awake to that moment. Vic and I are in the kitchen. How he kissed me, blood and secrets coating our lips. The thought makes my stomach knot, and the spicy bloodytini goes down the wrong way. I cough, attempting to set the drink back on the thick coaster. But I miss it. It tips in slow motion, and Shioban lunges to catch it but knocks it harder, sending a crimson wave splattering across Bethany's cream-colored cashmere sweater. There's an audible gasp around the table.

Bethany freezes, her mouth agape. Red streaks drip down her torso, staining the perfect knit sweater like something from a horror scene. Sending Stephen King's *Carrie* vibes, as the horror show flashes through my mind, and I have to bite my lip from laughing. Shioban fumbles with some napkins, only managing to smear the stain deeper into the expensive fabric. Bethany's eyes snap to mine, burning with contemplative murder. And honestly? Seeing her dripping in fake blood is a sweet form of poetic justice. Her coated in my bloodytini is the most fun I've had all night. "Excuse me," she hisses, stomping off and away from the crowd and our table of coworkers.

I fish out thirty dollars from my bag and drop it on the table like it's hot. "And that's my cue," I announce, giving the group a little wave as I stand. A couple of my coworkers wave back, and one bites her lip to stop from laughing. Behind me, Shioban cups her hands around her mouth and yells, "Coward!" I pause mid-step to glance over my shoulder and flip her the bird. Her cackle follows me all the way to the door as I push it open and step out into the night.

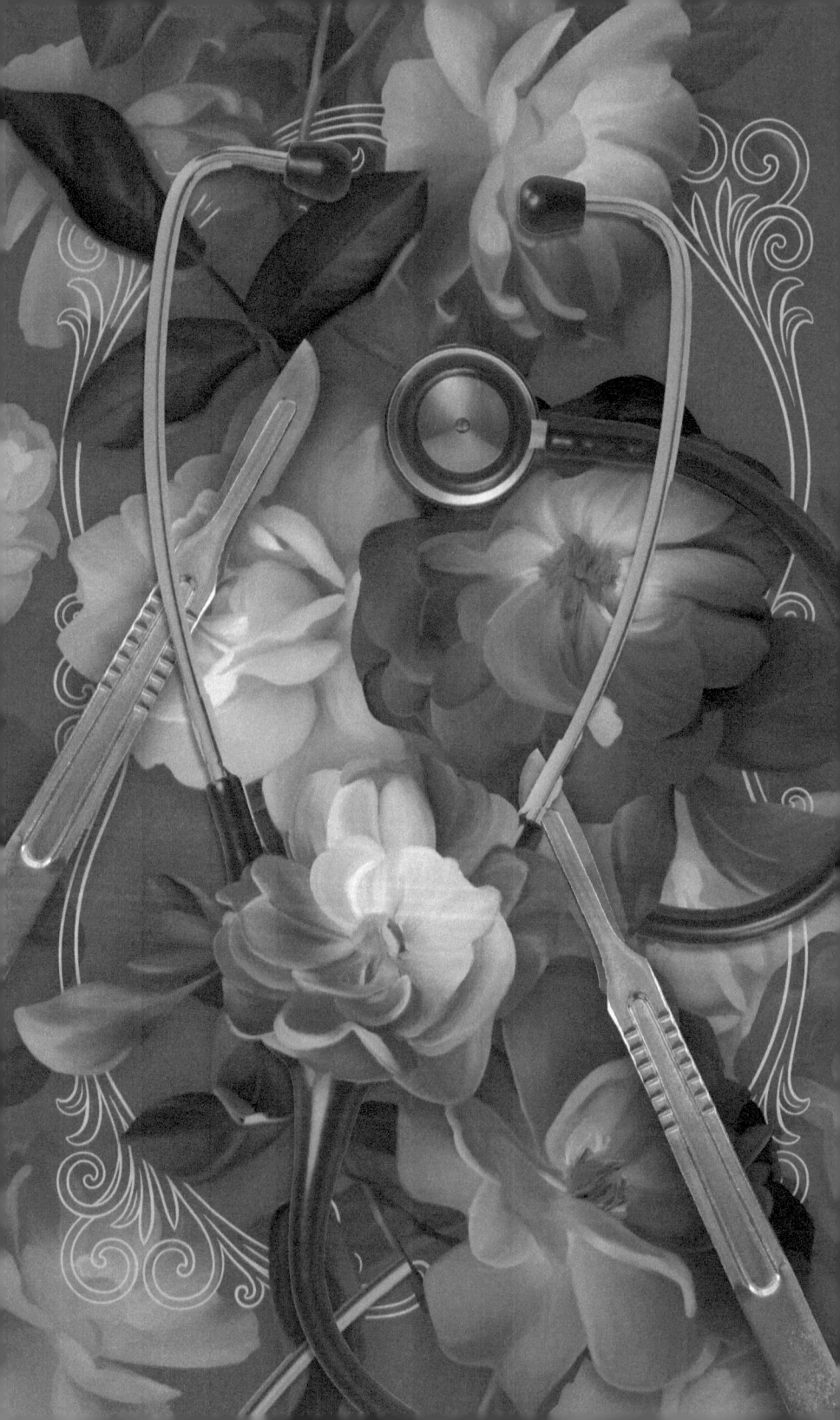

CHAPTER TWENTY-FOUR

VIC

It's Friday, and my day off is a single reprieve from the relentless week's burden of operating with minimal rest. With no obligations holding me down, I intend to lose myself in small indulgences. The kind of solitary activities that pieced me back together after calling it quits on dating and parties, things other people were doing at my age. The streets, still damp from the morning mist, brought a chill to the air, but my sanctuary awaits. My favorite, dimly-lit corner of the café, where I can people-watch out the window, and remain hidden from the world, here in the shadows of this recessed nook. Determined to finish my new novel, I set my things down. A scarf that I didn't forget this time and my freshly brewed café Americano, along with my psychological thriller that promises blood at the hand of a complex serial killer, litter the table as I sit enjoying the peace this morning brings.

Just as I turn the page on the chapter that is sure to unmask the identity of the killer, a flicker at the edge of my vision causes me to look up. A child's stuffed rabbit swings off the arm of a little girl. Its long, brown ears droop downward, skittering the surface of the cobbled stone walkway. Lifting my hand in greeting, she stills until recognition hits, and she tugs at her mother's sleeve to get her attention.

The woman's eyes follow her daughter's pleading ones. Yet, it wasn't I who caught her longing gaze, but the food that was just brought over to my table. The untouched scone and the steaming cup of coffee sit before me as she clutches her daughter tighter. I rise from my seat, beckoning them to come in, but the mom looks apprehensive, mistrust emanating from her stiffened, protective stance.

The little girl couldn't be more than five years old. Her smile is bright despite her situation, but she is nervous, her body swaying with restless energy. At her side, her mother stays silent, her eyes track my movements, watching for any sign of danger. She's skittish, and I'm afraid to scare them off, so I approach her with caution, hoping to gain her trust.

I offer a faint smile, steadying my voice as I formally introduce myself. "Hi. I'm Victor." I give a little wave. "We met at the kitchen where I volunteer." Her gaze flicks up to me, her eyes rimmed with exhaustion and deep purple shadows beneath them. I wonder if it's from not sleeping at the shelter or from something far worse. Sometimes it's the haunting memories you can't escape instead of the live monsters nearby. I'd know.

She looks ready to flee, clutching her daughter as though I am one more obstacle the world has placed in her path. I don't extend my hand in greeting, so I decide to extend them a little offering of food and a warm place to rest instead.

Before she can turn away, I temper my words into something gentler, almost pleading, because I don't want them to go. "Will you sit with me? Just for a little while?" I lift my hand toward the table I just left, attempting to coax them toward the warmth of the café. "That way, I can get you guys a little something to eat. Maybe a warm beverage until the shelter opens up."

I know too well what awaits her otherwise. Cast out into the streets at an ungodly hour with a child, she's left to wander until the shelter reopens. The staff is forced to kick everyone out at dawn, and they can return around lunch service. The door remains closed, allowing the staff time to strip the cots, sanitize all surfaces, and redress the beds with fresh linen. It is a preventive measure to keep the environment free of germs, especially as flu season approaches—a necessary act, but one that is nonetheless cruel.

The little girl tugs on her mom's frayed sweater. "Can we? Mama, please?" she asks, with more plea in her words than a question. A tremor passes through her already thin frame, and that little shiver was enough to shatter her mother's resolve. Enough to have the mom agreeing to it, she gives a low, reluctant nod. Her head bowed and broken with shame.

I step ahead to the door and pull it open, and at once a rush of warm air escapes from the vents above, rolling over us. The little girl releases a soft sigh as they walk through, and I know I've made the right choice. I gently guide them to the counter. The mom's voice is soft and unsure as she orders a hot tea and the little girl a hot chocolate with whipped cream. I know she's trying to be grateful and not order anything else, so I step up to the counter beside them, adding to their order. I get two bagel breakfast sandwiches and muffins for them, along with a new drink for myself, and gather it all into a single tray.

Carrying it back to my corner table, I set it down beside my neglected items, where the coffee had grown cold, and the scone remained untouched. The little girl's gaze lingers longingly on the tray until I slide the items toward her. She blinks as if in a trance. She looks up to me in silent permission as I nod once. Her little hand extends outward to reach for the hot chocolate. She wraps her hand around the cup, holding it as if it were something magical. She bites into the sandwich urgently, then quickly abandons it for the muffin.

The sight breaks my heart, and my chest aches with the urge to tell her to slow down. To promise her that the food won't vanish, but maybe it's something she's used to, and I don't want to lie to her. I just want her to know that this time it's okay. This time, she is safe. I don't do any of that, because it's best not to make promises you can't keep. These are the ones that break you. Instead, I bring my own cup to my lips, swallowing the bitter liquid going down hard along with the bitter fury boiling inside in a world full of indifference.

Her mom finally picks up her sandwich, her movement hesitant, expecting someone to rip it away at the last minute. Through every careful, controlled bite, I can see her restraint in trying to maintain her composure. To not seem too eager and appear too hungry. Wanting to ease some of the heaviness I feel and the emotions that threaten to rise to the surface when I recall similar memories I've tried to suppress, I attempt to offer them a glimpse of my life, perhaps allowing them to feel a sense of safety in my presence.

"I started at the shelter about a year ago," I tell them quietly as if I am remembering a story instead of chatting up conversation. "I wish I could do more, but my hours are spent at the hospital where I work. I work as a surgeon at Boston Hospital, and my schedule is time-consuming." I let the words hang in the air between us, hoping they can reassure them that I am somewhat trustworthy. People often mistake my composure and distance for indifference, and perhaps they are not wrong. More often than not, I appear tough, as if nothing touches me. But this? This matters to me. I want them to know, for the first time in a long time, that beneath the mask of the emotionally detached surgeon, there is still a man who cares, although it's been a while since it has been about anyone in particular.

Her eyes shift, softening. She clears her throat, the sound rough, like a voice without practice. Being silent or unseen can wear a soul down.

"Thank you for this." She lifts her bagel, then tilts her chin toward the one clutched in her daughter's hands.

"It's nothing," I answer quickly. I don't want her gratitude. Not for something so simple as an act of kindness. Food and warmth should never require a thank you. Nor should compassion toward another fellow human, but here we are.

She hesitates, then offers, "I'm Sonya, and this is my daughter, Rose." I incline my head in acknowledgement, committing the names to memory. Not Dani, Rose. Got it.

"Call me Vic. That's what my friends call me." I offer a small smile. The little girl meets mine, whipped cream resting on the tip of her nose. I tap my own, gesturing to my nose, making her look down. Her eyes crossing most endearingly, she notices it, and before she can remove it, her mother reaches over and wipes it clean.

I didn't dare reach over myself to clean it off. The bruises on her arm give me pause, and the last thing I want to do is make her uncomfortable or remind her of it. She is just about to take another bite of her muffin when her mom motions for her to follow her to the bathroom.

"Can't I stay here with Vic, Mom? I just want to eat my muffin," she whispers hesitantly. Her mom's eyes flick to mine, silently asking for permission before she gets up.

"I'm not going anywhere," I tell her, meeting Rose's gaze. "I'll be right here and watch over her. Go to the bathroom. Take your time."

She nods once, placing a protective hand over her daughter's shoulder before walking toward the sign with the arrow pointing to the bathrooms.

Rose kicks her feet back and forth beneath the table, a small carefree motion that makes her look happy. Like a little girl her age on an ordinary day, without the worry of hunger or fear. Trying to engage her in conversation, I ask, "Will I see you tomorrow? I'll be serving lunch on Saturday."

She shrugs her shoulders, glancing toward the bathroom where her mom had just gone. Her hesitation bothers me. I lean a little closer. "Is everything alright?"

For a moment, I think she might look away, retreat behind her furry stuffed rabbit, but then she meets my stare. Worry flicks across her features. "What is it?" I press further.

Sparing one last glance at the bathroom, she turns to me, "My mom is thinking about taking us back to that house."

I stiffen, a knot forming in my stomach. Carefully, I ask, my voice trying to be calm. "With your dad?"

She nods once. The shadow of a frown graces her lips. "And that makes you scared...because you're afraid he might hurt you? Or your mom?" I ask, letting the words hang between us. Another nod, followed by silence that speaks more than words, fills the room. The tension is thick and suffocating. Her fear is palpable, and the fact that she trusts me with this secret makes me act before I can second-guess it.

I grab a business card with my information on it, scrawling my cell phone number on the back, and hand it to her discreetly. "I'm going to give this to you. I want you to hide it, okay?" She nods, the only sign she is listening as she continues to nibble on her muffin. "My number is on the back," I continue softly, "so you can reach me if you need to." She takes the card, folds it in half, and tucks it inside her little stuffed toy, where there must be a tiny hole in the stuffing. Once she rights it, she presses the toy under her arm again and sips her hot chocolate.

"You'll help me?" she whispers, barely audible. But I hear her. Loud and fucking clear. Her gaze lifts to mine, and in those eyes, I see something I hadn't seen there before–hope.

I bring my hand to my heart. "I promise," I tell her. She smiles briefly before her expression turns to a thin line as her mom slides into her seat across from us.

CHAPTER Twenty-Five

DANI

I could hardly believe it when the email finally came. "I got the job!" I do a little dance. I had been waiting, knowing it would arrive, as the director had smiled and told me I would be hearing from them soon. But the confirmation last night felt like a salvation after the heaviness of my emotions. Hearing Bethany go on about Vic had my blood boiling, so this huge victory was a much-needed win to help elevate my mood. And if I'm being honest, the memory of Bethany dripping with my bloodytini was its own kind of sadistic satisfaction that will long live rent-free in my head. Smiling, I ready myself for the first day of my dream job.

In a grey knit dress and my favorite black trench coat, a bargain I scored for a ridiculous price at Marshall's, I walk down the street toward the hospital. The morning air is crisp, heavy with a hint of autumn's chill, and a sign for Café Nero catches my eye. I slow my pace, wondering if I have time to stop before my orientation begins.

As I walk to the door, I see him, and I stop in my tracks. I freeze watching him through the window as he sits at a table with a woman and a little girl. There's an unease in their postures. The woman's shoulders are held tight and guarded, and the little child is restless.

My mind spins. Who are they to him? A lover?

I spot the small, thin wedding band around her ring finger that tells a different tale. Vic doesn't have one. I know he isn't married, so there is more to the story here.

They rise to leave. That's when I notice some obvious things. Their clothes are clean, but worn. It's the kind of careful presentation that attempts to mask hardship. The little girl echoes her mother's words as she holds a stuffed animal firmly with one hand and her mother's hand in the other. Once they get to the door, she breaks free, rushing back to Vic. She presses her arms around his waist in a quick embrace. For an instant, he looks rigid, unprepared for her touch.

The mother's expression shifts from sorrow to a glimmer of hope, as she sees her daughter latch onto Vic, someone whose kindness offers a brief comfort in a life that has shown little compassion. Before Vic can react, she returns to her mother, grabbing hold of her hand once again. She gives him a small smile and wordless wave, nothing else to be said, before leading her daughter back onto the unforgiving streets.

I shrink back, not wanting him to see me, at least not like this. But then, as if drawn to one another, he turns toward me, eyes wide—my heart free-falls. I turn sharply, raising a hand in greeting to no one, and hurry off as though late. And I might if I don't leave here soon. The glass reflects his movements, and I walk off hurriedly around the corner and disappear, as my breath catches in my throat from nearly being found out this way. "Stupid," I curse under my breath, the word rising bitterly into the crisp morning air. Being more reckless because at this point, I've lost all common sense, I risk a glance back. Vic rushes outside, eyes searching the street with a frantic urgency, haunted as if he'd seen a ghost. Perhaps in some way he has.

I slip away quickly, vanishing down the alley and into the morning fog, just as suddenly as I had appeared. Stopping at a Starbucks instead, I steady myself and regain my composure with an espresso topped with thick non-dairy foam before continuing my walk toward the hospital, carrying more than this unit orientation on my mind.

My thoughts weigh heavily, burdened with questions about the man Vic has become. I always knew this softer side of him, the one he only revealed to me. So different from the figure I witnessed in the ER. His expression was cold, his steps precise, honed with clinical detachment. He walked those halls untouchable, yet I am the one who has tasted his tears. Who knows what he feels like when he places his long fingers around your neck, squeezing as you climax, all while whispering how much he loves you. This man is such a contradiction, but to me, he's perfect. The memory stirs a deep ache and almost unbearable longing to turn back and find him. To let him know that I am here. That I have returned to him, and the future that I still believe to be ours. There has and will never be another man for me than Victor Flores.

The elevator carries me to the hospice unit, with its slow ascent, taking in and spitting out people on each floor. I step out and follow the signs leading to the unit, where Mrs. Meyer is waiting for me in her office. Her door stands half open, and I rasp my knuckles softly against it. She stands from her desk with graceful movement, and a radiant smile greets me as she opens the door wide. I love this woman at first glance. Although she is about to retire, nothing about her says retirement. She wears a bright, patterned dress beneath a white coat, name stitched in blue embroidery along the front lapel. The color suits her dark complexion and warmly contrasts the unit's grey, dreary color.

I extend my hand. "Hi, Mrs. Meyer, I'm Daniella. It's so nice to meet you."

Her grip is firm, and her smile tilts at one corner. She takes my hand in hers, a firm shake and a tilt of her lip. "Please," she says, gesturing toward the chair, "call me Samantha. Have a seat so we can get the boring stuff out of the way first."

I nod and settle in as she returns to her desk. Along the wall, I notice a stack of boxes that catches my eye. Her career is in boxes that wait to be carried out, and mine is to be carried in on Monday. Today must be her last day. She opens a drawer, retrieves my new badge, and hands it over to me. I reach for it, seeing my picture dangling from the lanyard, pride evident in my eyes as I achieve my goal.

"This will get you into most departments in the hospital. As a hospice case manager, you will navigate various areas of the hospital, depending on your patient's caseload. You'll report directly to Mrs. Nolan, the director. She oversees the unit but is less involved in direct patient care, instead focusing on the business side. Insurance, reimbursements..." She trails off. She waves a hand, dismissing the thought with a soft chuckle. "That part is complicated. I don't want to think about it."

I offer her a tentative smile. "Mrs. Nolan must have really been impressed to bring you on with so little experience, although you do have the certification. That definitely helps," Samantha says warmly, rising from her chair. "But she assures me you'll be a perfect fit. And that's good enough for me." She crosses to the door as she gestures for me to follow her. "Come on, let's get you around so you can introduce yourself to everyone before you start on Monday."

I trail behind her, the sight of her stacked boxes still lingering in my mind. My thoughts drift involuntarily to Vic, his secrets, his shadows, the complexities of a man only I've seen. All of our memories reside in similar stacked boxes, brought with me, quietly waiting until the right moment to be uncovered. Full of truths I ache to touch, and almost within reach.

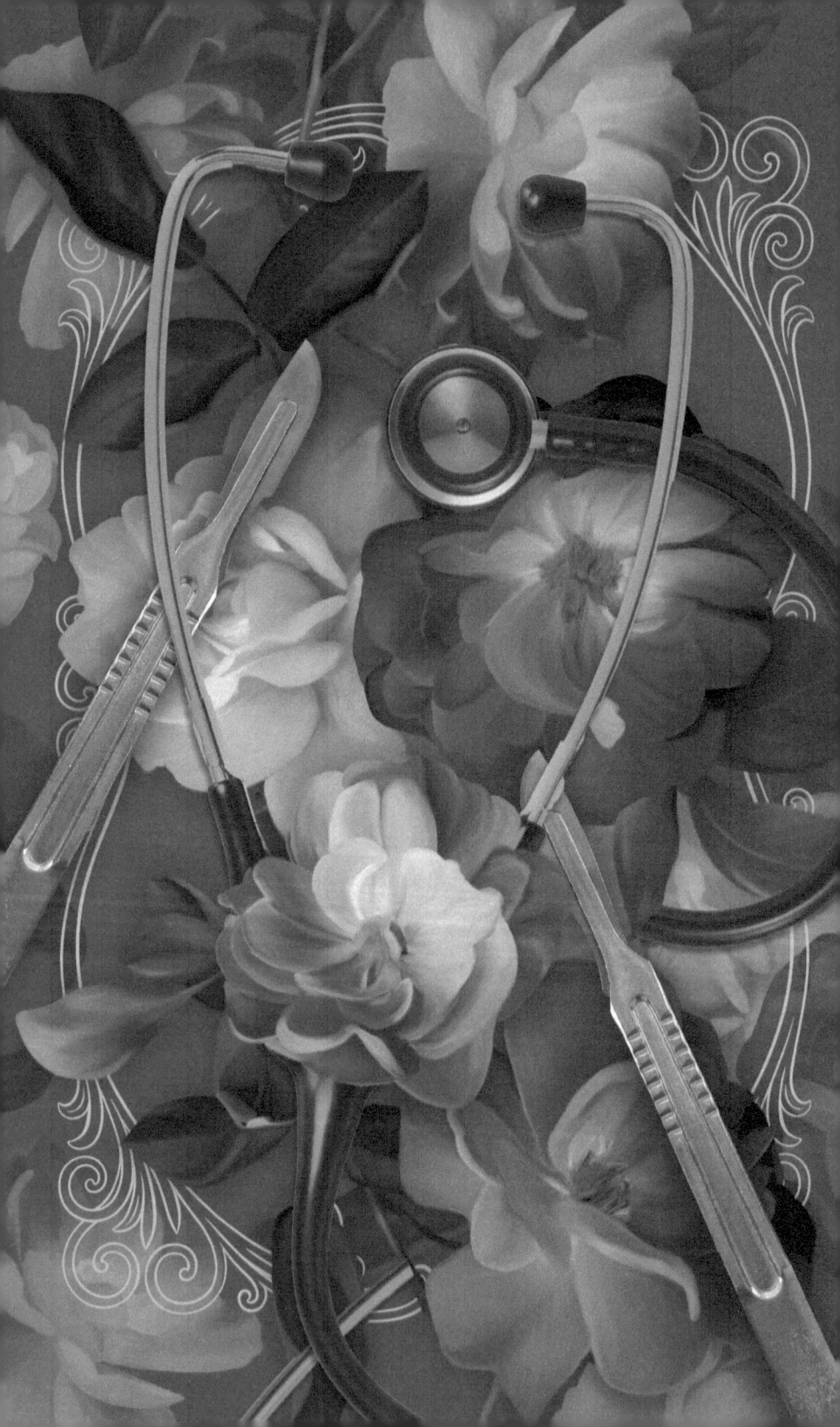

CHAPTER
TWENTY-SIX

VIC

I've been at the hospital all night. Being on call offers no promise of rest. Of course, my pager went off at seven p.m. yesterday evening, as soon as my call shift started, and I have lost count of the hours since then. I'd hoped to see Sonya and her daughter, Rose, at the soup kitchen, but I missed my volunteer lunch service there. The staff knows I am sometimes on call, and while they need all hands on deck during those times, the volunteer pool is small. When I do show up, they are appreciative, but they understand that if I'm not there, it's because I am working or have been called in for surgery.

Instead, lost in a sea of blue sterile drapes and arctic temperatures that make up the sterile rooms of the OR and its inner core. The hum of the machines and beeps of the heart monitors have been on a constant loop through my fourth case as I stand here suspended in time until each suture is tied and our end sign-out is completed. The music is cut off abruptly as the circulating nurse performs the final count of all instruments, and I provide my estimated blood loss for the record.

After she confirms that it's correct, I strip the blue gown from my shoulders. The impermeable material feels stuffy, and my scrubs remain sweaty beneath it. I discard the two sets of bloodied gloves, snapping them off like a second skin and throwing them into the trash. My hands are white and wrinkled-looking from the long hours my skin has lain beneath. The patient is now stable, left in the physician assistant's capable care as the last layer of skin is sewn and glued before a dressing is applied to the incision. I step out of the cold tank and into the corridor beyond, where the skeleton crew is sparse. Only the call teams are present today to handle cases requiring immediate attention before the regularly scheduled cases come in on Monday. Carrying the weight of the night's events and faceless patients hidden underneath the drapes with only the prepped skin visible for the scalpel I've been trained to use with precision, I walk out of the operating room to speak with the patients' family members, who look just as weary as I feel.

It's time to go. I need sleep after being awake all night. My car is parked in the on-call spot in the ER, so I have to cross the department to reach it. I'm so tired that the corridor seems to sway with each step. The fluorescent light emits a greenish hue, bringing the shadows to life. I blink, and the images fade. Fuck, I'm seeing things. Then...Dani? Or the shape of her standing at the nurses' station talking with Bethany, that woman who always gets under my skin. I halt mid-stride as Daniella walks away, and Bethany catches my double-take. She lights up, sure that I was looking at her. Nope. You're still you, Bethany. She breaks away, moving toward me in long, steady strides. I move, but only in the opposite direction, hurrying away before she reaches me, disappearing across the hospital lawn.

"Dr. Flores," she calls out, but I don't stop. I'm too tired and too unhinged to be confronted by her. I practically sprint across the lot as I can see her searching for me in the ambulance bay. Fingers fumbling with my key fob until the car unlocks, I drop into the driver's seat and pull out of the spot without letting the car warm up.

I must be more sleep deprived than I thought, because Dani's face is everywhere tonight. I know it isn't her, but still a small, stubborn part of me wants to believe that fate finally nudged her back into my path after all those years apart.

I pull into one of the most coveted spots at my building and take the elevator up to my high-rise. The door opens onto a silence that rings louder than any club or crowd. I drop my keys into the little ceramic dish by the entryway, strip off my clothes, and stand under the hot spray of the water until the exhaustion of the day leaves my body. Toweled off and half awake, I pull on joggers and a T-shirt. I can't take it anymore. I have to know.

I pull up my socials and type in her name, *Daniella Andrande.* There's nothing new. It's just her old account with no updates. The same photograph stares back at me, the one she took with her mother. Memories flood me with the sad look in her eyes, her brilliant light fading to low-burning embers. It's similar to the photo of the last time I saw her, when I left her standing in her driveway, tears streaming down her face. I can't unsee that, and every time I wake from a nightmare of my father, this feeling is a close second to remembering her that last time. The feed is covered with unanswered birthday wishes, each one a reminder of her continued silence. I take a sharp inhale when I see a memory she commented on.

"No. No." I stand when I see the picture of her and her mom, with the caption: "Until we meet again." With a date set—wait, what? Her mom fucking died? I pace the room back and forth, my hand atop my head, as I try not to hyperventilate. "How did I not know this? Fuck!" I throw my fist into the desk, and it groans as if a sentient being, feeling the rage from my fist. Then it clicks. I stop pacing, envisioning the conversation I had with Brandon, the one he told me I had to hear about from her. That was the reason she sold the house. The dots began to connect. She knew her mom was sick. Did she not get into Dartmouth, or was that a lie as well? I drop to the floor and sink to my knees, cupping my face in my hands. My selfless, selfless angel. She stayed behind to take care of her mom. I look up to the room's ceiling, trying to stop the tears that threaten to spill from my eyes.

I stand, desperate to find out more, and eager to learn why she did this and anything else I can discover about her and her whereabouts. I continue to scroll. Then I see the tag. My pause hovers over the button. My pulse stutters as I finally click on the image. The enlarged picture takes my breath away. It's a recent one of my Dani on the screen before me, seated on a velvet couch in a dimly-lit club in Houston.

"Wow!" I touch the photo reverently. She was stunning then and has grown into a more stunning woman. Her legs are crossed, with tight black, fitted jeans down her legs and hugging her thick thighs. Her black combat boot plopped heavily against the upholstered chair. A velvet rope glints in the picture's corner, announcing that it must be a VIP section, roped off from the other customers. What catches my eye is that she isn't posing. She isn't smiling, but her interest is held by something on the floor below, and I can't help but wonder what that interest is.

I pinch the screen, zooming in closer, greedy for every little detail I can find. She is so beautiful, and still mine. The friend who posted it, Liv Johnston or something like that, hardly matters. Only the information that might bring me closer to learning more about my girl.

I click on her profile, and the screen floods with photographs. Most of her friends are laughing, posing, crowded together under strobe lights. Dani is there, too, only in fragments. A shoulder at the edge of a frame. The curve of her face half turned into a smirk with her "fuck me" red lipstick. I groan at the memory of my dick streaked in red, and my full-mast erection becomes painfully hard. She is always present, but never meant to be seen. It's as if she wants to stay hidden in the shadows. It's probably why her posts are not up to date. I scroll faster through the picture until I spot her.

There! I stop as my pulse quickens. Focusing on the picture before me, the image strikes me like I've been hit. Dani stands there, this time at the center of the photo, surrounded by friends. My body bolts upright, my chair scraping against the floor, and my box of belongings toppling off the bed. I lean closer until the screen illuminates my reflection in the window pane before me. My reflection stares back at me from a dark sky. How long have I been at this?

They are celebrating her, but what? I can see the way their

eyes were fixed on her, a mixture of adoration and love. These are clearly her people, and I have no idea who they are. My gaze scours the picture until I click on the caption. It says, *Good luck, Dani!* Then I see it buried in the hashtags. #Boston. The word stabs me through the heart—the feeling of shock and then excitement.

I drop my phone and snatch it back up. I knew it. I fucking knew she was here. My little angel has been following me. She's been here. At least now I have proof that I'm not losing my mind. I hadn't seen her that day, but I felt her presence. This small electric jolt always crackled between us, the pull of two opposite ends of a magnet aching for each other until they finally snap, bringing each other into its polar field of attraction. That's always been us.

Dani and I were always in sync. I used to lean out my window across the way, and find her staring out hers, searching for me the same way that I ached for her. Years pass, but the thing we have doesn't fade. It hardens into insistent longing, a hunger that will not be soothed. A craving for what is gone and the memory of what could still be. It isn't nostalgia, it's fate, and I can't pretend it is anything else.

With that thought, I make up my mind. I need to keep a closer eye on things. I go to the closet and pull down the box. The one I swore I would never open again—my box of Dani. One by one, I draw out the photographs, setting them around the apartment until her face surrounds me. The picture on the nightstand has been the only one I allowed myself, the only reminder I could bear to keep in plain sight. The rest I buried, the loss too great. At the very bottom rests a small velvet box. I lift it carefully, almost reverently. The small hinges creak in protest when I open it, stiff from years of sitting idle, waiting for her. Inside, the diamond ring still waits, a half-carat stone in total, small by any standard measure, yet once bought with all my love for her. For us.

I purchased it for her when I left for college. A promise ring, not an engagement one, although in my heart it meant more than either. I never found the courage to give it to her before I left. By the time I returned, on the night everything in my life shifted, I thought I would finally place it on her finger. Instead, I left that night with a shattered heart and broken promises.

Now I laugh under my breath, bitter, yet strangely amused. What I could afford today makes this little stone almost laughable, and yet at one time it felt priceless. The cut is flawed, the quality imperfect, but it was bought with everything I had and with every intention of giving it to the only woman I have ever loved.

I slip the little box back into the drawer, closing it softly this time, and return to the glow of the phone screen. I fall further down the rabbit hole of her friend's socials, then friends of friends, chasing every tagged photo, every possible glimpse of her. Hours blur together, my eyes burn, and the apartment is dark with night. Still, I scroll, caught in the chase, my pulse thrumming with the thrill of the pursuit, as I follow her through the endless maze of posts that might somehow close the distance between us.

By the time my phone flashes a red 1%, the sky outside is dark, and the moon is high. I put the phone on the charger and drag myself to the kitchen. The silence in the apartment seems louder than before. I pour a glass of whiskey. The amber liquid catches the dim light of the crystal glass, shooting a thin prism across the wall. I take a long, slow swallow, anything to calm my racing mind and the heartbeat in my chest, to quiet the surge of excitement from seeing her on my phone screen. I tell myself this drink is to decompress, but I know better. My mind won't rest until I have her with me once again.

CHAPTER TWENTY-SEVEN

DANI

I've been at my job for about a week now. Too many close calls with Vic in the emergency room have left me grateful to be away from that chaos. The whole reason I moved to the Boston area was to reconnect with him, yet I still haven't managed to do so. I keep finding excuses, telling myself it's not the right time. But deep down, I know the truth. I've been a coward.

I didn't confess before he left, thinking I was doing the right thing. But all I did was make us both suffer. It doesn't seem like he has moved on either. From the few glimpses I've had, watching from afar, he has almost become detached from all emotion, and in a way that makes him nearly untouchable. I was the only one to experience his softer side, and he hasn't shared it with anyone else. No girlfriends. No partners. There are no traces of a life someone his age would lead. No public social media. No distractions either. Just work, a grueling schedule, as though he's drowning himself in it to keep everyone away.

Today, my coworkers from the ED are here for department continuing education. They must maintain their trauma credentials because we are a Level One hospital, designated to receive patients with the most severe injuries, supported by the necessary facilities and skilled staff to meet those demands. As a per diem nurse, I'm not required to attend. I'm due to meet them for lunch in about thirty minutes, and I'm excited to catch up. My full-time job is going well, and I've settled comfortably into my new office space, although I can't bring myself to let go of my per diem work.

I have a plant in the small window, a motivational sign, and three pictures that hold deep significance on my desk. The first is of my mom. She represents my past. The photo was taken on the day we moved out of my childhood home, which we shared with my dad. After her divorce, she told me that we should never look back on what we've lost. I have since learned that it isn't true. If I could change the past, I would in a heartbeat. I would have her with me, recognizing how she hid her sickness because she was all I had, forced to keep working instead of taking care of herself. Most of all, I would change how I handled everything with Vic.

The middle picture represents my present. It's of my found family, the guys and gals who have become everything to me. They know my past, yet they still love me, darkness and all. They saw the parts of me that no one else did, applauded my efforts, and never thought I was crazy.

Lastly, there's the picture of Vic and me lying in bed. I snapped it one morning, the sun just beginning to spill across the room. I stare at the phone while he snuggles into my neck. His dark trestles hang over his eyes, but it's his smile that gets me. His lips pull up in a smirk as he pretends to be asleep. Even though this photo belongs to my past, I cling to the hope that it will still be my future. I raise a hand to my lips, then lightly touch the frame that rests front and center on my desk, reminding me every day of the memory and longing that remain.

I glance at the time. Only fifteen minutes left until I meet the girls in the deli downstairs. It's a small place tucked into the main floor, serving sandwiches, soups, salads, and Starbucks products. We agreed on noon, their lunch window, and I've been looking forward to it. I gather my tote, ready to leave when a soft rap of knuckles draws my attention to the door. It isn't fully closed, just as Samantha used to keep it, slightly ajar. That way, it was always open for anyone who might need her. Only now, it's Samantha standing there.

"Hey!" I stand, walking over there with a grin. "Aren't you supposed to be retired?" I narrow my eyes at her playfully.

Her hand lifts in mock surrender. "Yes, I am. Believe me. I have no intention of ever asking for my job back," she laughs brightly. "I just had to meet with human resources, and I thought I would stop by to see how you're settling in." Her smile is radiant, and her face is soft and well-rested.

I glance around the room. "I'm settled. I love this job."

"I'm glad," she smiles warmly. "It's good to know that someone truly passionate about end-of-life care has taken over."

I grab my bag off the chair, about to suggest she take a seat, when she cuts me off with a slight shake of her head. "No, I just wanted to drop this off." From her bag, she pulls out a metallic envelope, the weight of the paper evident before it even touches my hand. I look up at her, curious, and she flicks her finger toward it. "Go on. Open it."

I tilt my head, studying her expression before sliding a finger beneath the seal and looking at her. "Okay," I murmur, unfolding the ornate cardstock inside. The embossed lettering catches the light as I begin to read the invitation aloud.

"Admittance for one: *Masks Under The Stars Masquerade Ball…*" My voice trails off as I look at her quizzically.

"What's this?"

Samantha's eyes sparkle with mischief. "I thought it was self-explanatory," she chuckles.

I tilt my head, weighing the card in my hand. "Well…yes and no. What am I supposed to do with it?"

She steps closer. Her hands come to rest lightly on mine, still holding the invitation. "You go and have fun." She gives my hand a firm squeeze before letting go.

I nod, watching as she retreats toward the door, only to turn back suddenly. Her eyes glint with playfulness. "Who knows," she teases. "Maybe you'll find a charming doctor to chat up." She waggles her brows, and then she's gone, leaving the room quiet as my thoughts are roaring. I look down at the invitation, the metallic shimmer, making it appear magical, and my thoughts slip to Vic, wondering if he'll be there. A smile curves at my lips as I begin to imagine how the night will unfold. Just then, the alarm from my bag chirps, where my phone is nestled in the pocket, reminding me that I need to leave if I am going to make it to lunch with the girls.

Walking into the hospital deli, I immediately spot the girls in line. Not wanting to cut, I give them a little wave, letting them know I'm here before heading straight to the to-go counter for my online order. I find a table big enough to fit all of us, Bethany's ego included, before settling in. Unwrapping my chicken teriyaki special, I pair it with the Green Monster smoothie that Shioban swears tastes like grass. A wry smile tugs at my lips. Moments later, the girls flitter over, each collecting their own carefully labeled order. I shift in my seat, sliding over to make space for her to sit beside me.

"Hey, love. How's the new job going?" Popping the top on my bowl, I reach into my bag for my little wooden utensil set. I catch her amused glance because my eco-friendly quirks always invite comment. However, I'll let this one pass, even though protecting the environment is no trivial matter.

"It's great, actually," I say, spearing a bite of chicken with my little skewer. "I really like it. Nothing too much yet, I'm still learning the ropes. However, I have my own caseload, and it's going well. So far, anyway."

She nods approvingly. "Anything fun going on with you? Been out lately?"

I hesitate, then reach into my bag again. "I'm good on the wooden sporks, babe." Her hand is placed upward.

Rolling my eyes, I continue to retrieve the metallic envelope and slide it across the table. "Here, I got this today. Thought it might constitute fun." I say blandly.

She takes the invitation, her eyes widening as she opens it. A low whistle escapes past her lips as she hands it back. And that's when Bethany flicks her head sharply in my direction, her full attention on me and the invitation in my hand.

"Are you going to the ball?" Her tone is almost too casual.

I shrug, trying to act nonchalant. "Maybe?" Now the card

feels almost too heavy with the weight of her stare. "I just got the invitation today."

She nods as if trying to piece it all together. "Well, I'll be there," she gloats. "I was just talking about it with Dr. Flores the other day." She flicks her hair over her shoulder, taking a small sip of her soup from her plastic spoon.

That catches my attention. "Really?" I deadpan.

"Yes," she says, sensing my sarcasm. "I was helping him out at that soup kitchen for the homeless where he volunteers—"

I cut her off sharply. "You mean people experiencing homelessness." My anger flares at her casual, insensitive phrasing toward the unhoused population.

"Um…yeah, that's what I said." She stares at me like I'm missing a few brain cells when it's clearly she who's lacking any shred of compassion. My eye twitches, and for a split second, I wonder how hot that soup really is. "Dr. Flores is going, but he didn't have another ticket for me to go with him, so I bought one. They're kind of expensive." She eyes me up and down, and I feel the similar weight of her scrutiny. Here we go.

Really, all I can think about is Vic. I've already tuned her out, her words are nothing more than background noise. I pretend to look at my watch. "Oh, look at the time." Standing, my appetite now gone, I pack up my food to eat later.

Shioban stares at me, like I'm a puzzle she is intent on solving. "You going to that meeting you mentioned?" she asks, one eyebrow arched, giving me an out.

I smirk, pointing a finger at her. "Yes. That would be the one." The group waves casually as I walk away, not giving it too much thought, waving behind me while I plot the next move forward. And I know exactly who to ask for help.

> Me: What do you know about
> masquerade balls?

The reply comes instantly.

Emma: Random. Why?

I can just see her now, multitasking and texting, a smile on her lips, making me give out too much information. She has a way of dragging it out of you.

> Me: I need to go to one. Most importantly, what should I wear?

I bit my lip, excited for the first time in a long time because I know that this will be a pivotal moment, and I need to look my best.

> Emma: Oh. When is it?

When is it? I pull out the invitation, and my brow furrows at the close approaching date.

> Me: Next week. It's called Masked Under the Stars.

I look up at the ceiling, praying that she has an idea of what I could wear.

> Emma: Got you! You can borrow something of mine. I'll send it today. Oh, and the other thing you wanted, too. *wink emoji*

And just like that, my found family has come through, and I like that for once, I don't feel alone.

When the package arrives, just as promised, excitement rolls through me in waves. I'm shaking at the prospect of what tonight could mean. As I sit at the vanity, carefully applying my makeup, I try to steady my hand. My eyes are smoky with a winged black liquid eyeliner. I've spent years perfecting my lines so that I never have to use a stencil. My hand is steadfast in my determination to ensure perfection, as I finish the last upward stroke. And my lips are my signature color, sinfully red—black strapless gown with feathers that trail the floor. I smile as I walk out the door, hope blooming in my chest like a newfound spring as I leave to take back what's mine.

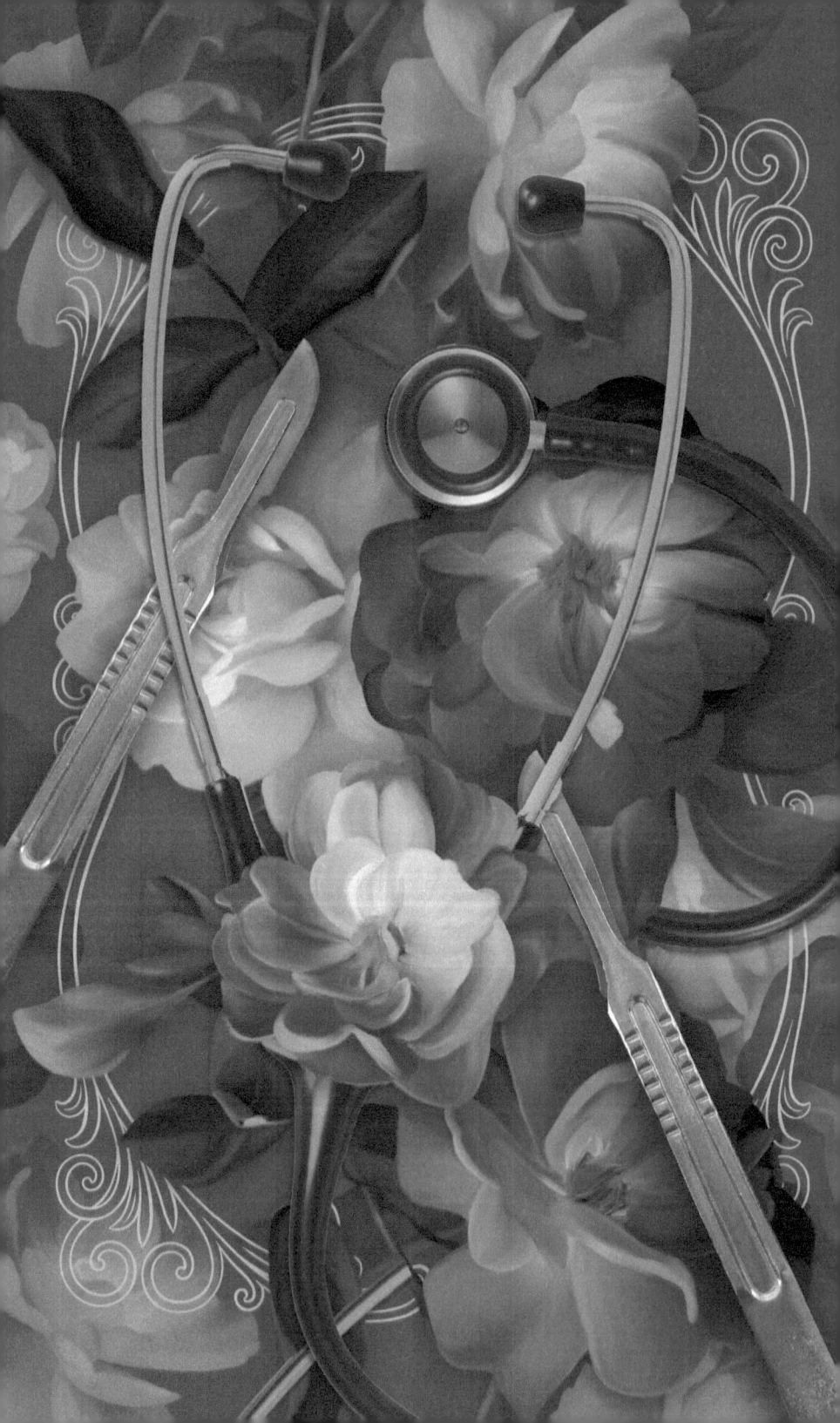

CHAPTER TWENTY-EIGHT

VIC

I'm beginning to worry with each passing day that I haven't seen Sonya or Rose since that morning at the café, when I pulled them in from the cold and offered them food. I had promised I'd see them that weekend, but my call schedule betrayed me, turning me into a liar as it unraveled into a blur of emergencies. Night bled into the next day, and by the time I stumbled out of the hospital feeling hollowed and exhausted, the shift at the soup kitchen had already come and gone. Unfortunately, I never made it, and I regret breaking that promise. I should have known better than to make promises I can't keep. After all, I'm not good at it.

Perhaps it wouldn't have changed anything, but the unease gnaws at me all the same, much like it did all those years ago. And after that last conversation with Rose, that apprehension only intensifies, leaving a sinking feeling in the pit of my stomach. An emotion I can't quite place burrows inside me. It wraps around memories I've tried hard to suppress, dragging them forward no matter how hard I try to forget them. That emotion is fear, but not for myself. It's for the innocent, for those the world has once again failed to protect.

When I spoke with Arthur at the front desk, he informed me that he hadn't seen them in over a week. Betsy, from food service, confirmed it, and she always works the food line. There had been no sighting of Sonya or Rose since the day that I first met them here. The unease coils tighter in my chest. Rose mentioned that her mom was considering going back to her husband. I close my eyes, and the unwelcome images rush back to the blooms of varying shades of purple on her arm, and I can't unsee them.

I blink, looking back at the clock on the nightstand. How long have I been standing here like this? Shaking my head in disbelief when I see the time, I stand in front of the mirror, my thoughts continue to wrestle in my mind as I wrestle with this fuckin' bow tie. How the hell did I let myself get roped into going to this event? I hate these things—the forced smiles, the small talk, and Bethany. But I know it's for charity, and that's the only reason why I endure it.

I smooth down the lapels of my Tom Ford tuxedo, the luxury twill sharply hugs my toned frame, and I give myself a once-over. I look stylish enough to pass with the crowd tonight, but I feel like an imposter. I lift the mask out of the box that arrived just yesterday. It's ebony, molded into the face of a devil, ribbed horn curving upward with a wicked kind of elegance. I smile at the detail. The moment I slide it on, I can't help but feel a firm satisfaction, no imposter here. It's fitting, considering the season so close to Halloween, and well, there's me. The reflection staring back at me is almost unrecognizable. I feel like I'm putting on armor as well as a suit.

My hair is slicked back, though one stubborn curl keeps falling across my forehead. At least the mask pins it into place. I adjust the pentagram cuff links on my French-tailored cuffs, silver against the black poplin shirt. Finally, I snatch the keys from the desk and step out into the night.

I decide on an Uber. The venue might be within walking distance, but it feels odd to stride through the streets of Boston in a tuxedo and a mask, being put on display before I even get to the event where I'll be watched and silently judged. Driving also seemed pointless. With a sigh, I pull up the app, and my ride is set to arrive in three minutes. Right on time, a sleek, black car eases to the curb with a license plate match. Without hesitation, I open the door and slide into the cool leather interior, setting tonight's wheels in motion.

The event is held in the historic Grand Ballroom of my own Back Bay neighborhood. The architecture rises with old-world prestige, a blend of elegance and power, bustling with busy commercial business that offers a lively atmosphere. But tonight, the hotel hosts physicians, staff, and benefactors whose money and influence fund the hospital's mission. The evening aims to raise support for equitable healthcare, extending that care to the city's most vulnerable and underserved populations. A noble cause, one I am proud to support. And yet, beneath the polished veneer of charity, I can't help but sneer at the obscene amount of money poured into an evening like this, all under the guise of generosity. Crystal chandeliers, champagne flutes, and elegant trays of canapés are luxurious overindulgence paraded as philanthropy. My lip curls. Sickening.

Unfortunately, Bethany Sinclair's father is on the hospital's board of trustees, and she has somehow attempted to insert herself into my life. She hinted countless times about tagging along, being my plus-one, but I made her buy her own ticket, claiming I wasn't sure I'd attend. Truthfully, I knew I would all along. It's none of her business, though. I suspect her father slipped her a ticket anyway, but with any luck, I'll avoid her tonight entirely and make it home unscathed.

Donning my mask before stepping out of the car, I'm let out at the front and make my way up the steps, escorted to the ballroom. From here, I can hear the delicate strains of Beethoven's "Moonlight Sonata," echoing throughout the vaulted ceilings. I step inside, and the sight stills my breath. The crowd is a sea of tuxedos and gowns, each face concealed by elaborate masks. Midnight blue lighting washes over the room, casting shadows that dance across silvery drapery suspended in peaks from the ceiling—specks embedded in the fabric glimmer like stars, mimicking a night sky. Ornate chandeliers hang in cascading layers, emitting soft, ethereal appearing light. Moons and stars are suspended between the panels of cloth, adding another layer of enchantment. The tables are adorned with glowing centerpieces resembling constellations, casting a warm, otherworldly glow across the tables of seated guests. Sateen tablecloths and velveteen chairs complete the effect, giving the entire space an almost celestial elegance.

I wander through the ballroom, admiring the artistic planning and flawless execution that have brought this event to life, stopping occasionally to discuss work or the strides we've made in the trauma program. I'm just about to speak on our significant improvement in preventable deaths this year when the words catch in my throat—a woman in a black strapless bustier gown strides into view. The fabric is flowing with a dramatic slit up the middle, adorned with ruffles and feathers. A black feather shawl drapes elegantly over her shoulders as she slides it off to the waiting attendant. Her face is hidden behind a simple black mask, tied with a silk ribbon, which catches the light just so that her brown eyes catch mine through the slits. Every movement, every shimmer, holds me captive. Her eyes twinkle in recognition, and her red lips curl into a mischievous smirk.

For a moment, I straighten instinctively because there's something about her. When her eyes find mine once more, in the sea of masked faces, I know that it's her. Time slows, and the administrator tapping my shoulder fades away just as his words are lost beneath the rush of blood echoing the pounding swoosh of the beating organ growing louder in my chest. The crowd becomes a blur. All of it is background noise, behind the singular pull drawing me toward her.

I take a step forward, and she takes a step back. Faster now, I move, and she retreats again. Except this time, I won't let her disappear—the haunting melody, building in a crescendo. I quicken my pace, weaving through the crowd, with each stride a silent vow to find her. To claim her once and for all.

I run toward the front entrance, the door slamming with a resounding *thunk* as the music is but a soft hum. My eyes seek hers. But she's gone. Until I see just a flash of black that darts down the hall before vanishing. I glance left and then right as I reach the end, but still I see nothing. Moving cautiously to the left, I notice a black feather lying on the floor. I pick it up, twirling it between my fingers. *My little angel.*

I take off down a corridor until a door, left partially open with a low light bleeding beneath, catches my eye. I push it open, expecting the room to be empty. Instead, she's there, standing still with her back to me, and gazing beneath the balcony. Men are gathered outside, smoking cigars, and women hide in the shadows of the night, their actions concealed from prying eyes.

I walk toward her slowly with carefully measured strides. A predator sizing up its prey. I assess her, having once misjudged her, but this time my eyes are wide open, and I see her. All of her. I see her for everything she's done, and for the crimes committed in the name of love and passionate desire. I've had years to imagine this moment, and now it's here, and I can hardly believe it. I stop just behind her, and for the first time in my life, I'm hesitant when it comes to her. If only for this fragile and impossible thing between us. It's been years, and the thought of it slipping away again makes my hand shake with a vulnerability I vowed never to show to anyone again.

I whisper her name. "Dani?" and it falls from my lips like a prayer. My voice cracks with longing. "Angel?"

This time, she turns. Mist gathers in her eyes, and I freeze, drinking her in. I stare into the brown eyes that hold me prisoner. In that instant, all the years of loss, of pain, and worst of all, the deadening silence, fall away. I'm finally home where I belong, and it's with her. She's my eternal resting place in this worldly prison.

CHAPTER
TWENTY-NINE

DANI

He speaks my name, and I almost crumple to the floor. How many nights have I woken with it echoing in my mind—the sound I've imagined a thousand times, only to find my bed cold, and the silence that accompanied it deafening. To hear it now, alive and spoken from his lips just feet away, strips my defenses. Seeing him from a distance was agony, a sweet penance, an atonement for my sins committed in the name of love. One I accepted freely. But seeing him up close…it's my undoing. He sees the tears threatening to fall, and his eyes soften for me. I know it's only for me.

I lift my hand to him, desperate, and his fingers find mine. Then my body, pulling me into him. I sink into his arms, the comfort is a memory made flesh, and I have no intention of ever letting go.

"Vic," I whisper, but my voice dissolves as sobs spill freely. I can't stop them, nor would I want to. After all these years, this man who holds me now deserves every one of them.

"Shh, baby," he coos, voice low and reverent, and I melt into him a little further. "You've been so brave, my little angel, and I know what you did for me." His words fall like absolution, yet they burn through me like a confession with sobs that wrench from me with desperate pleas. I cling to him, trying to get closer, clawing at him with a need to be inside him, not physically, though I expect that, too, but spiritually. To be stitched into his heart, fused where nothing could ever rip us apart again.

Somehow, I'm lifted, set upon the desk. His body stands between my parted legs, like my protection and tether all at once. The air is cool against my skin, ghosting up the slit of my gown, turning the ache in me to a molten desire.

Through the black slits of his horned mask, his eyes are black, hollowed pits devouring me with one look. His mouth curls, not quite a smile, but a premonition of what's to come. I swear I can hear his unspoken vows, spilling from the darkest recesses of his mind.

His hand glides upward, deliberate, along the ruffled edge of my gown. A single, featherlight touch brushes my thigh, and a shiver overtakes me. He hums approvingly because he knows it not just from the contact. As I shift my legs slightly, hoping he will move them in the direction I want, a breeze travels up my thigh and hits my panties, starting to soak from just the closeness of Vic, causing me to rock when I feel his cock harden. And when I look up at his devil-horned mask, his hand gently drifts up the slit of my dress.

I inhale sharply, anticipating him to touch me where I need him to. Still, then he pulls back, his hand changing course and traveling up the side of my waist and up my ribs, barely touching the outside of my heaving breast that arcs involuntarily, presenting it to him in offering, as I fight the urge to lean further into his gentle touch. His fingers continue trailing to my neck, then cheek, and then he holds himself there. Touching the side of my mouth, he rubs at the red on my lips, but it doesn't smear. He stares at me for a moment before he wipes away some tears and then rubs my lips with the moisture, smearing it slightly at the corner. His cock twitches in his pants at the memory of what I assume is me taking him in my mouth and the sight of the red around his base as I swallowed him down, his hot cum shooting down my throat as his head tilted back, roaring with his release. I'm reliving the same memory, and when he looks at me, it's like he wants to devour me whole. And all I can think is,

Damn, please do.

His fingers slide into my hair, searching until they find the silken ties of my mask. With a slow tug, the ribbons loosen, and the mask slips away. My face is bare to him now, revealing my mascara-streaked eyes that flow like dark rivers of secrets between us. Every fractured piece of me is laid bare under his scrutinizing gaze. I look up, caught in his gravitational pull, and I want to live in his orbit forever. He crushes a thumb underneath my lower lids, smearing the remnant of my tears. I don't know if he's trying to stitch me back together, much like he does with his practiced surgical precision, wipe away the evidence of how I unraveled in front of him mere moments ago, or maybe he just has the innate need to touch me. Just to remind himself that I'm here in the flesh, not another dream, or conjured up memory.

For a moment, I can't fathom the years that have passed between us. Time feels irrelevant, just a cruel trick of distance and silence in the time apart. Because here he is, looking down at me with the same obsessive devotion and the same raw hunger, as if not a single second has passed since he last held me. Every fiber of my being still belongs to him.

This time it's my turn to reach for him, and he doesn't hesitate. He surges closer, closing the gap, until his body pins me against the desk. His cock grinds against my core. He's so hard, unrelenting, and I bite back a cry at the sheer pressure of it. My panties are already drenched, clinging to me, not doing much to soften the reality of how badly I want him inside me.

Instead, I lift my hand to his cheek. He leans into the touch like a starved man, like a child deprived of love, and sometimes I forget that he was. His vulnerability was exposed and reserved only for me to witness. His hand grips my thighs, spreading me wider and dragging me closer to accommodate him. My fingers find the clasps of his mask, and even though I am desperate to claw it off, I undo them one by one, and he helps me—tearing it off and tossing it aside.

Suddenly, there are no barriers between us. No masks and no obstructions. No more walls and no more lies. Only his eyes burning into mine, with a wild hunger that makes the breath seize in my chest. He clings to me like I'm still his entire world, but the rigid length straining against me tells me another truth, a darker, more primal one. His hands tremble with reverence, yet grip me with desperation. It's the duality of him, the man who wants to protect me, and the beast within him that wants to devour me. When he leans closer, I can tell that we are beyond remembering now, and beyond tenderness. His mouth crashes onto mine, and I moan into him, clawing at his jacket, at his shirt, and anything in my way, frantic for bare skin. Frantic for him. He presses into me harder, cock grinding against the thin, soaked fabric that does nothing to protect me from him. I rock helplessly against the pressure, chasing the friction, chasing the years we've lost with every thrust of his hips. It's his demand. It's my plea. But it's our surrender.

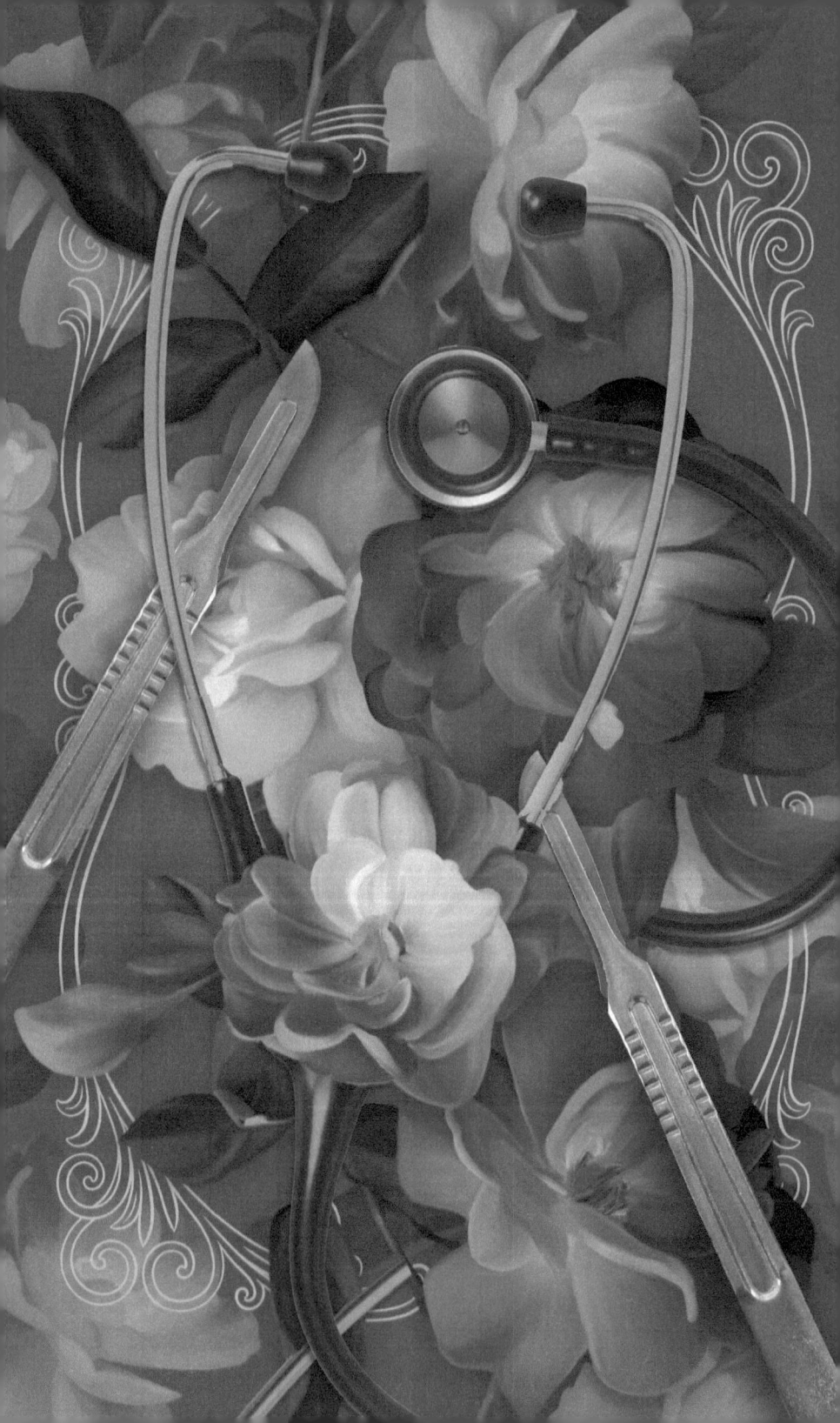

CHAPTER THIRTY

VIC

I close my eyes and let the world dwindle to the two of us. To the heat of her body pressed against mine, and to the ache in my chest that has lived there for years. This is it. This is the moment I've dreamt about and hoped for. She presses against me, and I can feel her wetness through her soaked panties. It's the last straw, and I can't hold back.

"Baby," I breathe, the word more prayer than a demand. My lips trail hot kisses along the hollow of her throat. She throws her head back, and I taste the saltiness of her skin, her tears, and everything else I've missed. "I need to be inside you," I confess with raw emotion. "I need to feel you wrapped around me."

Her lashes flutter. When she turns to face me, her eyes burn with a wickedness I've missed. The dangerous, familiar spark I've hungered for is there, and I'm so ready for her. A smile quirks at her mouth, edged with the residue of her tears and my handiwork. "God," she smiles, "I've missed your filthy mouth."

"Say it." I clamp my hand around her neck, holding her gaze prisoner. "Say you're mine," I implore.

She answers first not with words, but with movement, bringing me toward her, as if the closeness will erase all those years apart. Then, barely a whisper, she announces, "Vic, I'm yours."

The last of my restraint snaps. My mouth devours hers. My hands find the band of her silk panties, and I tear it free with one easy snap, the thin fabric crumpling to the ground at our feet. She hisses sharply, a sound I've always loved to hear between our kisses. I ease back, just enough to kiss her, my lips bruising hers as my fingers fumble at my belt, the ache in my cock nearly unbearable. She presses closer, desperate for me like she's been starved all these years. When I'm finally free, the air sizzles between us as I line my length against her heat.

I press myself into her, feel the shudder of her through nothing but the meeting of our joined skin, and enter the space between us with a movement that rocks the table, with the need to force away the loss of all our nights apart. The first push steals my breath. I want to watch. To see her body open around me. To witness the way she stretches, the way that she takes me like she was made for it. Her whimper slices through me, nearly unraveling me on the spot. Her legs snake around my waist, heels digging into me with commanding urgency. I obey without thought, driving forward in one thrust that buries me to the hilt. The sensation wrecks me. It's hot. It's tight. And it's so perfect.

A groan rips from my throat. There is no gentleness now, only the furious, hungry rhythm we once knew and have been starving for. She meets me in every thrust of our bodies, answers each claim of my heart with hers, as our bodies meld together with their own familiarity. I watch her, savoring how her face twists with pleasure, the way she bites her lip to hold back those tiny, maddening sounds. My hands lock around her hips, holding her in place as her back bows in abandon. I drag her against me, my grip bruising and unrelenting, grinding deeper with each thrust. My cock finds the perfect spot inside her, and I fight the pull of my own release, desperate to wring her climax before surrendering to mine.

"God, you're so tight, baby." The word tears out of me as each thrust tests my control. Then I still my movements, remaining buried deep inside her, my breath sharp against her ear. "Tell me, angel...have you been only mine?" My pace slows, deliberate, punishing, as I drag out the truth I already feel in her trembling body and how she squeezes my cock. Her tears spill, hot down her cheeks, and in that instant, I know my answer. She hasn't let another man touch her. In all these years, she's been mine and only mine. Just as I've been only hers, too scared to forget her in someone else, or worse, let the darkness that has always been a part of me take over. Only she could calm the beast within me. My chest tightens, my cock pulsing with the force of it, begging for release. But I grit my teeth. No, not yet. She deserves more than that. She deserves to be worshipped.

I bend forward over the desk, hovering above her, and caging her in. She gasps beneath me as my lips claim hers in a searing kiss. It's not tender, it is consuming. I let her feel every ounce of regret, rage, and devotion poured into the way my mouth meets hers.

"It's only been you, baby. My angel. Only ever you." The confession tears for me as I drive into her. The words are as urgent as the pounding of my cock inside her. My mouth trails her throat, licking up and down her neck, before tugging at the top of her bustier. The fabric gives way, and her breasts spill free into my hands. I knead one, and tug at the other greedily and frantically like a teenage boy with his first crush. That's how it's always been for us. Her legs lock tight around me, dragging me deeper, and I clutch the edge of the desk with white-knuckled hands to steady myself against the flood of sensations in me. I haven't felt this much in years, and now I'm overwhelmed by a merciless sensory overload. Our kisses turn frenzied, frantic. I feel too much of her—her lips, her breath, and yet, I still can't get enough. My teeth graze her neck, biting down until she gasps, then I soothe the mark with my tongue, circling, claiming, and branding her all at once.

I roll my hips, grinding into her with deliberate precision, hitting her clit in the way I remembered she always loved. Her body answers me as she shivers, tightens, and fights its surrender. She shakes her head as if she can stave off the inevitable, but I grip her jaw, holding her steady, forcing her to look at me when she comes. And then I feel it, her walls pulsing around me. The unmistakable grip of her body giving in. "Baby," I groan, as I stare her down as she rides hers out. "I'm going to come."

"Come inside me, Vic, please." Her plea is the last thread holding me back. I lose myself with a roar, driving into her until I spill, filling her up with my cum and hoping selfishly that she gets pregnant. I know there is no one else that I'll ever love. No one will ever truly understand me, except for this woman.

When we come back together, it's something brutal, yet beautiful to witness, all the same—a collision of our mixed grief and lust that feels like a punishment and a reclamation. The room blurs until only the two of us remain, moving and clinging to each other, as we both ride out the high of our orgasms, until the world comes back into focus, and we're exactly where we belong.

When I pull free, I watch the slick sheen of us clinging between her legs, my seed dripping out of her in a slow trail. Possessiveness burns through me, searing every nerve, as I look at her utterly wrecked beneath me and thoroughly claimed. Her make-up is smeared, her dress pushed down, her panties in tatters on the floor, with her leaking my cum down her leg. She's never been so beautiful as in this ruined state. The sight makes me hard all over again.

"Fuck, baby." The words rasp out of me as I drop to my knees, picking up her ruined panties and stuffing them in my pocket. Pressing a kiss to her swollen pussy before, slowly licking lazily through her folds, she props herself on her elbows, watching me with a look that is both tender and wicked. The smile she gives nearly undoes me. When I suck gently at her clit, teasing with light flicks of my tongue, she lets out a breathless laugh.

"Vic, you tease," she whispers, her voice thick with affection and need. I rise, my mouth still wet from her juices, and crush my lips to hers. She pulls me in deeper, sucking on my tongue, until my knees threaten to give way. She sits up, and I tuck myself back in, my eyes catching on the dark wetness seeping into my trousers.

"Oopsie," she sings, biting her finger as her eyes sparkle with mischief.

"Hm." My brows raise in question. "Try again, angel." I coax, lifting her

chin upward to look at me.

"Sorry?" she offers, but it sounds more like a question than an apology.

And for the first time in years, I laugh. A real laugh, one I thought incapable after the day I thought she left.

"Are you though?" I ask, and she shakes her head.

"Nope." She moves to stand, but I'm already there, steadying her, and righting her dress with the utmost care. It's almost surreal that no one has come in. Perhaps they heard us and retreated, or maybe the time was but a blip in their radar. But to me…To me, the minutes stretched into something eternal.

I help her fasten her mask ties, and she helps me with mine. When we step back into the muffled ballroom, something between us has shifted. An old bond, now reinforced, made stronger with this unspoken connection that was always there, but now is so much more.

"Do you want to get out of here?" I ask, my voice low, hoping she'll say yes because I plan on having her again tonight. Before she can answer, an aggravating, familiar voice cuts across our precious bubble.

"Dr. Flores." Bethany threads through the crowd towards us just as I tighten my hand around Dani's. Her gaze drops to our joined fingers. Her eyes track the possessive way I clutch onto Dani, and in turn, the way she climbs me instinctively as she steps closer, placing her hand on my chest. The contact sparks something electric between us, and my body answers with a thrum of excitement.

"Oh," Bethany steps closer, feigning surprise. "I didn't know you came with someone." She looks at me, then at Dani, not catching the hint. "Wait," she says, "Daniella, is that you?" Her tone shifts to shock as she takes Dani in. "How do you know—" I cut her off before she can ramble on.

"Bethany, sorry. Let me introduce you to Dani." I keep my hand on Dani's, my grip deliberate.

Bethany straightens, forcing a smile. "Oh, I know who she is." The flatness in her voice betrays irritation that has no business there. I've never given her a reason to think I'm interested in her. I tried to be civil and gave her a chance to redeem herself, but she couldn't even manage that. By volunteering for a good cause, such as when I offered to take her to the charity house I commit my time to, which she also claims to support but perhaps only in name, as seen with tonight's gala. If I never hear from her again, it would be too soon.

Dani steps forward, calm and steady, but I sense the undercurrent of her darkness, which I also feel within myself, yet not from her. This is new, and I'm beginning to feel fearful, but it's not for me. It's for Bethany. Dani's gaze is dark and resolute. "Sorry, Bethany," Dani says evenly, "but Victor and I go way back. I just moved back, so we're actually together again." Bethany freezes at her words, caught between disbelief and humiliation. Dani and I stand hand in hand, finally claiming what's always been ours. She smiles at me, and I press a gentle kiss to the top of her head.

"Come on, angel," I murmur, and we step away, leaving Bethany frozen, her mouth agape. "Let's go home."

CHAPTER THIRTY-ONE

DANI

We leave the gala without further goodbyes or apologies. There is nothing there for us. We stand at the entrance as Vic takes out his phone.

"Where to, baby?" he asks as I look at him, confused. He just chuckles, shaking his head while his fingers stroke the screen, before putting it away in his trousers. I look up at him questioningly. "We are going back to our place," he says casually. And before I can ask anything else, the rideshare pulls up and he opens the door for me. He throws his arm around my shoulder as we sit closely, our bodies melded together. It feels so natural and so right. He sighs, placing his chin atop my head, and I snuggle in a little closer, breathing in his scent. Damn, this feels good. After having no one for so long, this feels like coming home. I have my friends, and my found family is in Houston, but this is different. Vic is my person.

The ride is over just as soon as my eyes are starting to close. "Come on, sleepy head," he jests, "let's get you to bed." There's a glint in his eye, and I'm here for it.

"Yes, please," I counter, and the rideshare guy coughs, clearly picking up on our terrible attempt at hidden innuendos. I guess we really are that obvious. As he extends his hand, I take it in mine to step out of the car. I look at where he's been living all this time, noticing how close it is to my place, and wondering if I even need to call it that anymore. A tall, high-rise building with sleek, modern designs awaits us as the concierge opens the door. He nods at us both in greeting as Vic and I walk hand in hand to his place. The elevator ride up is quick as I wrap my arms around his waist, pressing closer to him. He places his arm around my shoulder once again as if it's always been there.

"This feels nice," he says, and I purr in approval.

Once inside, I place my bag on the table, and he drops his keys down next to it. He takes my hand in his, leading me to his bedroom. There is a large bed in the center of the room, with minimal furnishings in neutral tones of black and grey. I walk toward his desk, which rests off to the side, and plop into the chair by the window that overlooks the city. I slip off my shoes and set them neatly together on the floor. I hear a drawer close, and turn my attention to the sound as Vic prowls toward me with a shirt in one hand. I look up at him, the shirt offered up with a smile. It's one of his favorite bands, and it tugs at my heart to see that he still has it after all those years. I loved sleeping in his old punk rock band shirts. The fiend's skull is vanishing from the black cotton, but I stand stripping off my clothes and discarding them onto the floor, standing naked in front of him as he watches me pull the shirt over my head. It is just long enough to cover me, but if I bend over, all bets are off. He stands there, biting his lip as he removes the cuff link from his shirt and places it on the bedside table. It's then that I see the picture.

The sharp intake of air must have caused Vic to stop undressing to see what's upset me. He looks from me to the picture, his eyes softening. My hand covers my mouth as I hiccup. My emotions are all over the place, and when it comes to this man, I can't help it. He evokes a multitude of feelings in me.

I walk over to him and move past, bending over to pick up the picture of us. It was one day after weeding in the backyard, where I was planting flowers, specifically peonies. Oh, how I loved pink peonies, and so we decided to plant them in abundance. The town had a garden sale that the senior club likes to host once a year. For a relatively low price, mainly from a group of friends growing them from seedlings or dividing them, you can get the plants at a very affordable price. For us, that was the only option since we were on a budget.

He had just cut me a bouquet of peonies, and I held them as we shared Jarritos soda. The hot sun was shining down on us, but as the late afternoon approached, just before sunset, it bathed us in a golden glow. We looked happy, content, and very much in love. I smile at the memory, my hand touching the photo as it holds on to those feelings in a single picture frame. I look up, but I don't find him there. He comes out of his closet, dressed in grey sweatpants and no shirt. My mouth waters at the thought of having him again, and a smirk shows at the corner of his mouth as he walks toward me. He takes the picture from my hand and stares down at it, his eyes tracing over every inch of it before he places it back on his dresser.

"You kept it there?" I ask, and as he reaches into his drawer, he pulls out something I can't quite make out from here. His large hand covers most of it.

"I kept a lot of things." He turns toward me, and I stand there transfixed. "Here." I look down at a velvet box sitting in his outstretched hand. I'm hesitant to open it because it can't be what I think it is. I expected that to go so differently. As if reading my mind, Vic places it in mine and folds his fingers on top of it.

"It's not an engagement ring, Dani." He removes his hand, and I feel the loss of his warmth immediately, or maybe it's the cold realization that I want one from him, even though I might not deserve it.

I hold it between my fingers and open it. Inside lies a white-gold band, its front set with a delicate half-band of diamonds intertwining with an infinity symbol. I pick it up and see that it says something inside. "When night comes," I say aloud. Vic picks up the ring and places it on my left ring finger. I stare up at him, waiting for him to explain, because I don't know what this all means.

He brings my hand to his lips. "This is a promise ring. I bought this for you when I came down to visit. I wanted to surprise you with it." He stops, as if reliving that time. "I wanted to give you something tangible to hold onto, and remember that I want eternity with you." He rubs his fingers along the band. I want to ask for more, but I know he is trying to get this all out and needs a moment after waiting so long to finally say it. "It says, 'when night comes' because it was always then that I was scared. Scared for my mom, scared for me, and scared of the monster I became after they died." He shakes his head. "When the dark comes, you are my light." I move into him.

I wish we'd have had that conversation. That, and he just needs to know that I never had anything with Brandon. "It's always been you, Vic. You know that, right?" He nods, smiling, but it's a sad one.

"I do, but I was in a bad place, and I missed you." He shrugs. "Can you forgive me for thinking the worst of you?" He looks hopeful, as if he thinks I can do anything but love him.

"There's nothing to forgive, Vic. I should be asking you to forgive me. I thought the same thing about you when I heard some woman pick up your phone." Vic's face looks murderous.

"I could have killed her for that. I never touched her." He says with disgust. I wonder if he is joking, but that is the least of what I want to talk about.

"I also lied to you." I swallow a lump forming in my throat." He nods, bringing me into him. He rubs my back as I cry into his chest.

"Shh, baby," he coos. "I understand why you did it, but I wish you had given me the choice. If you had told me, we could have worked it out." He continues to rub my back. "I wish I could have been there for you. Like you were there for me." I nod because I can't speak. The words are stuck. "You got into Dartmouth, didn't you, angel?" And I nod, crying harder. "My smart, beautiful angel," he murmurs, and I melt into him more.

I thought that when I came over to Vic's place, we would continue with him ravaging my body, but instead, he demolished my walls. The emotions came pouring out in a tidal wave as I told him about having to sell the house, about my mom being sick, and how I tried the best I could to take care of her and be a good daughter. I told him about my found family and confessed to the sins I had committed to protect others. I don't know what time I fall asleep, but we wake up wrapped in each other's arms in the warmth of one another. The sound of an intrusive beep wakes us from our cocoon of bliss, much like the warning alarm that precedes a storm.

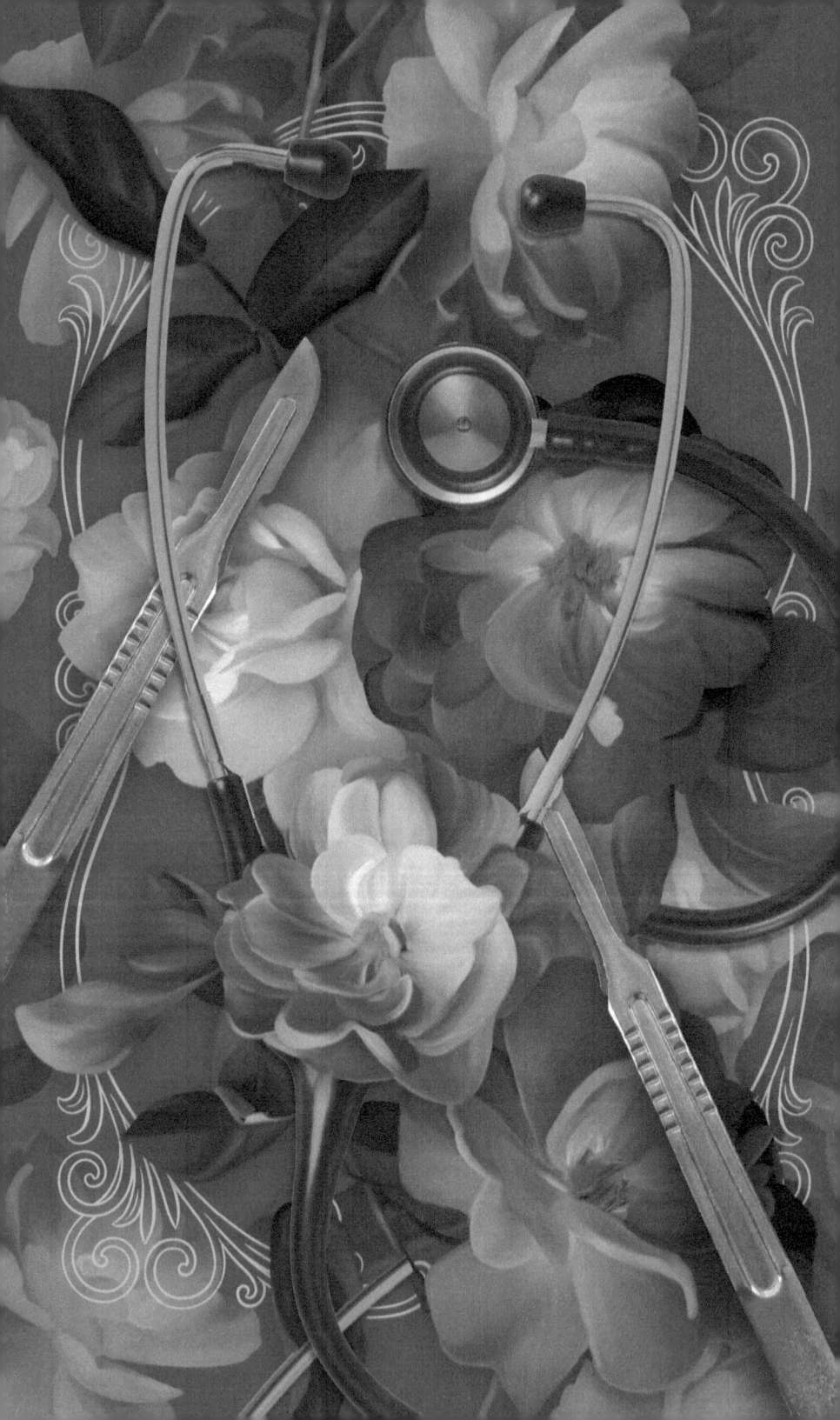

CHAPTER THIRTY-TWO

VIC

"Fuck," I mutter, recognizing the alert flashing across my pager. A trauma. I press a quick kiss to Dani's shoulder, her grip tightening on me as if she can sense the shift in my body—the way my heart rate spikes, and the adrenaline coursing through my veins. She reaches for me as if she could shield me from the devastations I am all but certain to witness when I arrive at work. I break away, dragging myself out of bed, reading the message as I move. The closet door creaks as I yank it open and reach for my clothes. Muscle memory takes over, my body moves on autopilot, and my mind fails to keep up. Dani sits up. She's silent, but her eyes track my movements, waiting for me to speak the words aloud.

"I'm on call," I mutter, dropping into the chair to tie my shoes as quickly as my hands will allow. I make a sweep of my usual items from the dresser. My wallet, phone, and watch as I fasten the strap onto my wrist. The movements are mechanical, drilled into me from years of repetition, except this time is different. I break that familiar cycle when I stop and walk over to her. Leaning down, I hook an arm around her and tilt her head back into a kiss, lingering long enough to feel the worry, trembling behind her lips. When I pull away, her eyes search mine. I try to calm her nerves with a smile that I don't quite feel.

"Stay here as long as you want. Maybe bring some items over if you'd like," I add sheepishly, because it sounds too soon. But I've already wasted too much time without her, and I don't want to waste another second. She nods, settling her head back against the pillows, and for a moment, the chaos outside these walls doesn't exist. At the door, I pause, stealing seconds that I don't have. She's framed in the low light that peeks through the sheer curtains of my bedroom window. Her hair is spread across the pillow, and I want to memorize this moment forever. "I like the way you look in my bed, baby," I tell her softly, fingers brushing the door frame as I force myself to leave.

I make it there in record time, and the ER is chaos. Bethany comes running toward me, but she's in work mode now, or maybe she's taken the hint. Shioban and a cluster of nurses bypass us, disappearing into the trauma bay. I follow in pursuit of them and the crisis that brought me here. I am a surgeon, it's what I'm trained to do. But what buckles my knees isn't the trauma, it's the face hidden behind the blood and bruises. I know her.

"Update and prep the OR if you haven't already," I snap, forcing my voice to stay level. This morning, Bethany, the charge nurse, falls in beside me while others administer fluids, push medications, and work to maintain hemostasis.

"Neuro's already been by. We are trying to stabilize her for transport to the CT scanner." I glance at the chart, noting the arrival time, mechanism of trauma, vitals, and any items already flagged in the pre-hospital alert I received half an hour ago. Cold, lifeless facts on a page. Nothing prepares me for the reality before me as the memories return unbidden, ripping their way up from the darkest pit.

"She's got multiple contusions to the face, chest, and abdomen," Bethany says in a clipped voice with precision and efficiency—years of delivering this information. I usually want only the facts—the evidence of what occurred. But the words fade as I remember my mother, who equally suffered in life. Is this what she looked like when she came here? She had no one with her. I was at home, and my father was taken in for questioning as she was left there all alone, fighting for her life. Now I look at this woman, Sonya, who has a similar fate. My past collides with my present, because through the swelling, the bruises, and the blood, she is barely recognizable. She could be anyone. And that thought makes heat erupt in my chest, scorching the cold numbness that has lived inside me for years. A fury so strong, it outweighs common sense. And what it leaves must be a basic animalistic instinct, because what I want now more than ever is revenge.

Snapping out of my memories, I scan the ER as if Rose will pop up any second. Before thinking, I ask. "Where's her daughter?" Bethany glances at me in confusion.

"Her daughter? You know her?" she asks.

I nod. "She was a patron at the soup kitchen I volunteer at…" I trail off, looking around. "She has a daughter."

Bethany leaves my side, rushing over to Shioban, and together they look back at me. I force myself into the practiced calm of a surgeon, hiding every flicker of emotion. Leaving to consult with the ER doctor quickly, I track down the neurosurgeon, and together we formulate a plan as we await the results. I step back, letting the trauma care team probe her with tubes and needles, securing access for life-saving medications. All the while, I stand on the edge, ready to act and doing everything I can to keep her alive if surgical intervention is needed.

Shioban and Bethany are speaking with the on-site case worker, who returns with an update. For once, I am grateful to see her approach me. "The victim's sister was here visiting—"

"Sonya," I state.

She nods, continuing. "Sonya's sister had the child at the time. She wasn't home when this happened, but they suspect it was her husband who committed the crime. There had been multiple calls for domestic violence at the house in the past years." Bethany hesitates before she continues, "His brother is a police officer, and apparently, her husband likes to throw around his name when they are called to the house. He would never get arrested, and I guess she stopped calling."

Bethany looks at me, then at Sonya, as they wheel her off. A person at the head of the bed squeezes a bag to provide ventilation because she can't breathe on her own. Anger starts to build, and the urge to find him and punish him overwhelms me, but I can't think about that right now. I have to help her live. So that she can be there for her daughter and, most importantly, live the life she deserves.

Blunt trauma was the cause of her head injury. In the CT scanner, she had her first seizure. They were able to control it with medication, but that wasn't the extent of her injuries. She had some broken ribs, which collapsed her lung, making her unable to breathe on her own. She didn't have internal bleeding, but several bones are broken that are splinted and set in traction to fix at a later time, if she makes it through brain surgery.

I stayed at the hospital, waiting for her to come out of the operating room, and I watched from the inner core window as they worked on her. It is surreal to stand outside the OR while someone else operates, looking in and hoping they make a difference in the outcome. Sometimes, in cases such as this, it's a wait-and-see game. I hate feeling helpless in this situation. I wonder how Rose is doing. When the neurosurgeon takes his gloves off and discards them in the trash, removing his headlight and specialized loops, he sees me standing there. A frown forms on his face as he walks out to meet me.

"How did it go?" I ask nervously, and he sighs. One that comes with the long hours of operating, even though you have no concept of time at the moment —just the bone-dead tiredness I am familiar with once it ends, and then the fatigue starts to set in.

"I guess we wait and see, but..." He trails off, biting his lip. "I don't think she will recover from this. The damage was too extensive and the swelling too great." He rubs his eyes. "We will know more in the next couple of days. He places his hand on my shoulder and squeezes reassuringly. "I hear you know the woman and her daughter," he says as his kind but tired eyes meet mine.

I nod. "Acquaintances," I hear myself say, even though it's true. I felt a connection to her daughter, a familiar bond that recognized her pain, and felt the phantom one in mine as if reaching out in mirrored recognition.

"They went to the soup kitchen I volunteer at," I continue. "I met them there, and the daughter told me she was afraid that her mother was going to go back home. She was scared for her." I swallow, because she knew. Rose felt unsafe, and no one would listen. I had hoped to talk to the mom that weekend, but when I heard she wasn't there, even though I'd missed the shift due to work, I knew she had already made up her mind. With nowhere to go and the unkind streets, sometimes it's better the devil you know than the one you don't.

When I step inside my home, an ache erupts in my chest. The keys clatter on the entryway table, louder than I've ever heard them as they echo through the emptiness of the apartment. I've done it a thousand times before, but tonight everything feels different.

"Dani!" I call out, but there is no answer. My pulse spikes as I run to the bedroom, flinging the door open. The bed is neatly made. Her clothes are gone, but her scent lingers, wrapping around me with familiarity. I sink onto the edge of the bed, burying my head in my hands. The room feels too quiet and too still. The silence is louder than ever before. When I finally lift my gaze, the clock draws my eye. And that's when I see the folded note. Breathing out a large exhale, I bend to retrieve it shakily.

> I hope you are okay. I had to
> go to work. You can find me in
> the hospice department today. I
> love you, Vic.
> -Dani

Relief floods me. I let the note slip from my fingers, discarding it with the rest of my clothes as I strip down. In the bathroom, the steam curls around me as I step into the shower, letting the hot water hit me, and willing it to wash the day away and the memories with it.

CHAPTER THIRTY-THREE

DANI

After not hearing from Vic all of Sunday, I knew something was wrong. After his confession, after our promises of commitment, there was no way he would simply vanish without a reason. But just to make sure, I had Emma send me one of Jameson's GPS trackers when she sent me the dress for the gala. I needed something that didn't need Bluetooth so it couldn't be easily detected, and he's the best, according to Evie. I won't risk anything happening to him, us, or our future.

Still, I remind myself that we are not the reckless teenagers we once were. We're adults now, bound by responsibility as much as by love. He was likely caught in the endless demands of his work, a busy surgeon saving lives while time simply slips away from him. With my new role demanding diligence, I rose early and went about my morning with the dedication this job deserves.

I won't let silence unravel us the way it once would have. Not anymore. I refuse to fill the space between us with assumptions or fear. We'll talk. We'll face it, and each time, we'll choose each other again. That is what it means to love him now, not as a girl clinging to reassurances, but as a woman standing firm in her place at his side.

Just as I'm thinking of him, a shadow falls across my desk. And when I look up, he's standing there. Dark half-moons sit under his eyes as exhaustion clings to him, but when he smiles, it is somehow brighter than the weariness. He crosses the room, leans down, and presses a quick kiss to my lips. When he pulls back, his gaze drops to my computer screen, and I see the change as his face shifts and eyes widen in surprise. He reaches for the photograph of us on his desk, lifting it with care, as if it's something precious to hold onto. He touches the frame with tenderness, reverently tracing the edge as if he is in that moment, frozen in time all over again. For a few seconds, he simply holds the picture, and when he looks up at me, his eyes are soft with apology, and I know it's for all the time missed in between and a longing for what could have been. My eyes meet his in understanding, feeling everything unspoken between us.

"I've always loved that picture," he murmurs, setting it gently back on the desk with such care, afraid it might shatter otherwise. His gaze drifts to the one beside it—the one of my mother. I watch the muscle in his throat tighten as he swallows hard.

"I'm so sorry, I wasn't there, Dani," he says, eyes closing, as if the words themselves rip him apart. His voice trembles thick with grief and guilt, but it wasn't ever a burden he was meant to carry. I ache at the sight of it. He blames himself. But how could he? He wasn't supposed to know. I never wanted him to know, yet he still feels guilty over it. I never wanted him to glimpse my own darkness. I was always meant to be his light. He had his own burden to carry. I will not be the one to add more weight to his.

"I know, Vic." I touch his hand, grounding him as I did in the past. He tilts his chin to the last remaining photo on my desk.

"Who are they?" he asks, as he stares at the group of strangers in the photo.

"It was my last day there, and they threw me a party." My finger drifts across the glass as I list them in a single breath. "Emma, her husband Eduardo, Emma's sister Evie, her boyfriend Jameson, their brother Mateo, Liv, and her husband Dax." The names tumble out too fast as I point to each one. Vic picks up the picture, studying their faces, searching for something I don't see.

He tilts his head. "But who are they to you, baby?"

I smile, taking the picture gently from his hands. "My family," I say without hesitation, shrugging my shoulders because it's the only way to describe them.

His lips curve, and he smiles knowingly. Because sometimes blood isn't what binds, it's the bonds we form through friendship, help, and healing. And this group? They've had my back more times than I can count.

"I'd love to meet them someday." The corner of his mouth lifts in sincerity.

"I'd love that. I think you'll like them." But my mind drifts back to that night outside the club. The visual of a body cooling in the dark, and Eduardo's boot striking the corpse before he spat on it, returns quickly and floods my mind. No one called the cops or even flinched. They just helped me. Calm and unbothered by it all, as if the ugliness of death is nothing new to them. It was proof of their loyalty. Proof that when the world turned violent and cruel, they stood by me, and in my choices, unafraid to carry the burden in the shadows of that alley together.

He leans over to kiss me, and I wrap my arm around his neck, pulling him deeper into it. When he finally pulls back, his eyes lock on mine, his voice low and raspy.

"I missed you, baby. I have so much to tell you about last night. Can you come home with me?"

I nod, and the faintest smile tugs at his lips before he gives me one last chaste kiss and straightens.

"Meet you out front?"

"Yes," I answer softly, making sure he hears the certainty in my voice. I don't want more confusion ever again.

"At five?" he confirms, and I nod again, sealing the promise between us. Then he's gone, and I'm left with the lingering warmth of his mouth on mine. The quiet thrill of knowing that we're no longer circling what we want. We are claiming it.

The day passes in a blur of patients and consults. I help where I can, set appointments for family members flying in, and ease the burden of those who must navigate the transition of a loved one into end-of-life care. Easing their burden is what makes me feel better about my job.

When my shift ends, I ride the elevator down to the lobby to find Vic waiting by the front windows, watching the traffic. I slip behind him, wrap my arms around his waist, and lean into the familiar heat of his body. He exhales and turns, folding into me in a return hug that dissolves the stress of my day. "I missed you," I tell him, because it's true. I've missed this man for years. Now even hours feel too long to be apart. Every time I get the chance, I want him to know that.

"And I've missed you, baby." He brings me into him and kisses the top of my head. His hand finds mine as we step out together toward his apartment. But after a few strides, I stop, tugging lightly on his hand. He halts immediately, turning toward me, with concern showing on his brow.

"What's wrong?" he asks, voice careful and body tense as he waits for my reply.

I swallow, searching his eyes. "Vic, do you mind if we go to my house tonight?"

Relief flickers there. He nods, his eyes alight.

"Of course." He nods, lips curving. He extends his hand toward me as though making the choice mine. "Lead the way."

I smile knowingly, a slight flutter in my chest. "It's not far."

He chuckles lowly. "Of course it isn't." I flash him my best, award-winning smile, and he laughs. This time a little bit louder. We may be a little crazy, but only for each other. We walk fifteen minutes past Vic's place until we get to my apartment complex. The building isn't as nice as Vic's, and there is no concierge at the door, but we manage to get in and take the elevator to the second floor. My view is of an alley, but if Vic notices, he doesn't comment. The room is bright and cheery.

"Do you want something to drink?" I ask, as I open the fridge, but when I turn around, he isn't there. "Vic?" I call out. The door to my bedroom is open, and when I walk in, I already know what he is going to see.

He stands there, looking around at all the pictures I have of us that cover every inch of my bedroom. I took every photo and placed them in frames. All the others are displayed on a wall. My favorite ones are on a desk.

"Vic," I say, but this time feeling self-conscious. What if I went overboard and he thinks I'm a stalker? I mean, clearly I am, but I am just as infatuated with him as he was with me, but I never showed it. "Vic," I say again, and this time he turns abruptly, staring at me, but it's not disgust or fear I see in his eyes. It's desire. He grabs his cock and rubs it through his pants.

"Get on the bed, baby, and take your clothes off. I need to fuck you now," he growls, throwing his shirt on the floor and kicking off his shoes. I don't waste another moment, I discard my clothes.

"First, we shower, Vic." He chuckles. "I'm not letting you fuck me with all these hospital germs on me." He prowls toward me, and I shriek playfully, running for the shower. I love it when he chases me. I walk to the shower, quickly turn it on, and let the hot water run for a bit. It takes a while for it to heat, but as he comes through the doorway, he's there looking at me with a lust-filled stare. I lick my lips, my mouth watering at the chance to get him into my mouth. I walk backwards as I hit the lip of the shower and step in.

He follows suit, and before I can turn around, he pins me to the tile. He grabs my hair and pulls me back, licking up the side of my neck and tugging me back further before he plunges his tongue into my mouth. He's merciless, as his grip tightens on my hair. His thick erection nudges my back, and my pussy weeps at the thought of being filled. I feel that hollow ache between my legs that can only be satiated by him. He turns me around and drops down on his knees, throwing one leg over his shoulder as he presses the other against my abdomen, holding me in place as the other spreads me open, as he licks through my folds over and over again. He stops, circling his tongue around the little bud as he sucks on it, and I cry out. He does it a few more times, and my legs start to shake. It's when he scrapes his teeth before flicking it repeatedly, then bringing it into his mouth once again, that I fall over the edge, crying out. When he stands to his full height, he lifts me easily and brings my legs around his waist. He lines himself up and pushes into me. My head falls back. And when he fucks me against that shower wall, there is nothing gentle about it. He holds my hips, pinning them in place as my back moves up and down against the wet tiled wall. As he screams his release, I fall once again to the sound of him calling my name. I look up at him through hooded lashes. I kiss his face, and when he opens his eyes to meet mine. He smiles.

"I couldn't help it, baby. The crazy, stalker-like pictures of me all over the place made me feel feral. I wanted to fuck you so bad and couldn't wait. You have no idea how turned on I was, and am now, just thinking about it." His cock hardens against my entrance. "You ready for round two?"

"Yes, please."

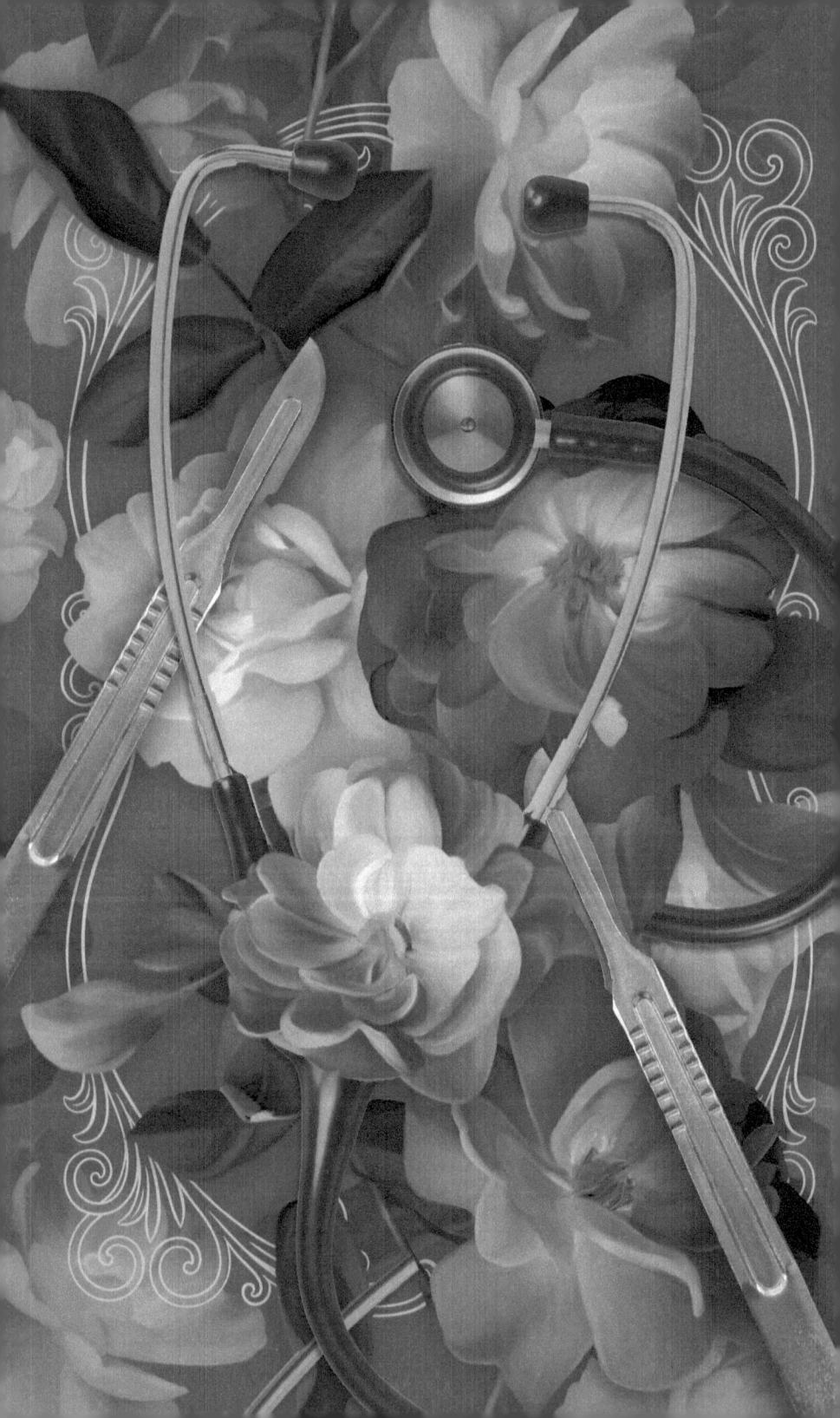

CHAPTER THIRTY-FOUR

VIC

Three days. That's how long we've been holding our breath, waiting to see if Sonya will pull through or slip through this world entirely. Three long days that I've been holding onto this guilt, the ache in my chest that whispers, *Vic, you could have done more.*

The neurosurgeon warned that the days after the operation would decide everything, though it feels like the verdict has already been served. Seizure after seizure rips through her fragile body, and every time I get the call, every time I see her convulse, I'm pulled back to my own mother, who never made it this far. Despite all my years as a surgeon, the helplessness feels the same, as though time has collapsed into one long continuous wound that festers slowly. And I hate myself for it. For feeling this weak, and for the silence that ensues. Some part of me is already grieving, because the outcome is bleak, and miracles aren't wasted on people like us. We are the victims. The forgotten. The ones society fails to help, unless we take the reins and choose our own fate.

I told Dani everything about Sonya and her daughter, Rose— how I met them, and how I tried to help in those little ways that feel like drops of rain on a roaring wildfire. She admitted that she had seen me that day at the café, the day that I bolted out of there thinking I'd imagined her face in the crowd. She confirmed it was real.

I told her about the little girl. How frightened she was. How she clung to her mother with the desperate hope of a new life away from her father, just to have that future ripped away from her. And now Rose's worst fears have come to fruition. There are no comforting words to give, no gentle lies to ease the truth. Her nightmare is here, unfolding in the worst possible way, and she's living it with wide, dry eyes that have seen more than a child of her age should. The stark reality is that she may lose her mom. The only comfort is that she wasn't there when it happened. Because if she had been, it could've been her tiny broken body on that stretcher, or worse. And that makes me murderous.

I walk into the ICU to check on Sonya. The nurse informs me that her blood pressure began to climb yesterday. They're giving her medication to keep it under control. Through the glass, I see Dani, Rose, and another woman. The woman's shoulder shakes as she's racked with sobs, though she keeps nodding at what Dani is telling her. But Rose sits there frozen, staring at the wall as if nothing in this mortal realm can touch her. Not her father's fists, nor the grief spilling out of her.

Her small hand clutches a stuffed toy, worn thin from being squeezed too tightly for too long. Perhaps her only source of solace. In the other, she grips the card I gave her that morning in the café. The one that contains my phone number on it in case of an emergency, or if she should need anything at all. She rubs the edge with her thumb and forefinger, over and over, as if the paper itself could keep her safe. A lifeline she refuses to call, but can't let go of.

As I step closer, Rose's head turns toward me. The moment her eyes find mine, they widen, and she bolts upright out of the chair. Dani and the woman turn, startled, but Rose is already running toward me.

"Vic!" Her voice cracks as she collides with me, throwing her arms around my legs. I freeze for half a second before dropping down to her level. She clings to me with a desperation that makes my chest ache, as her small body trembles against mine. "Please," she sobs, her arms sliding around my neck now. She holds on tight, as if I, too, will vanish, leaving her alone. "Please! Can I see my mom?" Her tears stream freely down her cheeks, soaking into my collar, as I hold her tight, already knowing that there is only one answer. I tighten my arms around her, my voice rough when I finally reply.

I pull Rose back gently, my hands steady on her small shoulders. I force myself to nod, to keep my voice even despite the surge of emotions I'm trying so hard to suppress. "Of course. Let me see what I can do, okay, Rose?" She sniffles, hiccups breaking through her sobs, as she tries to channel a bravery that no child her age should have to. When I rise to my feet, she loosens her hold, watching me with wet lashes that cling to unshed tears. Behind us, Dani leans toward the woman in the room, murmuring. Her voice is a balm, soothing still, even as grief hovers around us. The woman nods, clutching a tissue, and Dani slips out, falling into step beside me. Together, we push through the ICU lockdown doors, where the world shifts into a cacophony of beeping monitors, hushed voices, and the antiseptic smells of the critically ill. Dani stays close, a solid presence by my side. Her silent steps are honed into every pulse of tension in the air as we pass curtained bays and machines that beep with hope and a promise of tomorrow.

"Vic," Dani says softly, though her words strike me with precision. "Things are looking worse. Her sister is requesting comfort measures only. She could die soon, and we need to make sure Rose has a chance to say goodbye. That they both do."

The recycled air suddenly feels heavier, pressing in like a weight on my chest. Her words land with a punch to the gut, and for a second, I can't move. I can't even think. All I hear are Rose's words, looping like a broken record in my head. "Can I see my mom? Can I see my mom?" I look over at Dani, who is already speaking with the ICU nurse to make it happen.

"She can see her?" Rose's aunt asks, her voice shaking, yet hopeful.

I nod once. "The nurse said she needs five minutes. I'll take her in myself." Dani dips her head, her gaze steady on me, and in the depths of her eyes, I catch it. The quiet understanding that this is more than medicine or protocol. It's a mercy, one that I never had the chance to receive. When I step back into the waiting room, Rose looks up at me, clutching her rabbit tightly. Her aunt straightens in her chair, her posture rigid with worry.

She extends her hand, her grip firm despite the tremor in her fingers. "I'm Julia."

"I'm Dr. Flores," I reply before offering her informalities. "But you can call me Vic. I knew Sonya and Rose outside of here. I volunteered at the soup kitchen where they sometimes came." I pause, stopping on the words that don't sound fake. "And I was also part of the trauma team that received the call when she was brought in."

Julia studies me for a long, measured beat before speaking. Her eyes sharpen, determining whether to trust me or not. Finally, she leans in, her voice dropping low, "I need to talk to you for a minute. In private." She nods. Dani reads the room instantly. She calls Rose over, keeping her close by her side, but out of earshot. Her hand rests gently on the girl's shoulder, steadying her as if to remind her that she's safe, while I prepare myself for whatever truth Julia is braced to speak.

When Julia sees that Rose is safely out of earshot, her shoulders sag. She exhales, dragging her hand down her face as though trying to wipe away the years of exhaustion.

"Look," she begins, her voice full of defeat. "I don't know how much you know about her husband—David, Rose's father."

"Just the basics," I answer with a shrug, though the words are a bitter pill to swallow. "He's abusive. Rose told me that she was terrified her mother would go back to him. That he might hurt them both."

Julia's lips press tight. Her lips worry the corner of her mouth before she nods. "Then you understand," she whispers. Her gaze flicks toward Rose, then back to me. Pleading. "You understand why she can never go back to him?"

Her knuckles twist together in her lap, knuckles blanching. Anger burns beneath her skin, barely contained. Her posture is rigid with the strain of holding it all in. When her voice breaks the silence again, her fury is palpable.

"Yeah, that prick's been hurting my sister for years," Julia snaps, her voice shaking as much from rage as it is from grief. "And now he's getting out." She looks up at me with wet eyes. "His brother's a cop. Every time Sonya called, every time she begged for help, nothing happened. She just stopped calling altogether. She stopped hoping someone would help."

My jaw tightens, anger rising in me at the injustice of it all. Julia swallows. Her hesitation is palpable in the space between us. Then the words spill out. "He started going after Rose. He used her to maintain his control over my sister." Her breath hitches. "And when Sonya called his bluff—" Her voice cracks.

The tears come faster now, streaking her face as she wipes them, ashamedly, but unable to stop the flood. "He's going to take her from me, the second he's free. And I—" Her voice shakes. "I won't be able to stop him. There won't be a damn thing I can do." She presses her fist against her mouth, and a strangled sob escapes despite herself. "I'm so afraid."

Before I can answer, an ICU nurse pokes her head out. "We're ready, Dr. Flores," she says gently.

I cross the room, crouching until my eyes are level with Rose's. Her small hand is so tiny in mine, but her grip is firm and resolute in her determination to see this through. "Are you ready to see your mom, Rose?" I ask gently, wanting this for her, but also trying to protect her from what she will see. Is this how she wants to remember her mom? She nods too quickly, too eagerly.

"You're going to see some things in there," I continue, lowering my voice so the conversation is meant for our ears only. "Machines making all kinds of sounds, and tubes that look pretty scary. But none of that matters. Your mom can still hear you, even if she can't answer back. So when you're with her, you tell her everything you need to. Tell her everything you've always wanted to and never have. Okay?" Her fingers curl tighter around mine, a silent promise, as she takes a deep breath in preparation for what she will bear witness to. She follows me with self-assured steps as we move together. The moment is pivotal, and we can both feel its weight pressing down on us with each stride. Behind us, Dani's eyes glisten in quiet solidarity. Her hands are clenched by her side in anger for the little girl who has to witness the monstrosities dealt out unjustly on the weak and neglected. She remains a steady pillar of support for Julia, who is already crumbling. Rose moves out of sight as Dani folds her aunt into her arms.

I turn back around, keeping my focus on the little hand in mine, as we walk the length of the unit, fortunately stopping at room five. The sliding door opens with a slow creak, and the air inside feels colder. Sonya lies still in bed. The sound of the inflatable mattress is a contradiction, meant to protect against pressure wounds while resting beneath the map of violence already inflicted on her body. Bruises in cruel shades of purple, green, and yellow alter her appearance, combined with the swelling throughout, it makes her almost unrecognizable. Her head is shaved and wrapped in thick white bandages. A tube juts out of her mouth, connected to a ventilator that pushes and pulls oxygen into her lungs, giving her a countable number of breaths per minute, rattling against her fractured ribs. IV lines protrude from veins and arteries in her neck and arms, monitoring her blood pressure and carrying the medication that keeps her with us. Rose stiffens beside me because no amount of coaching could have prepared her for this sight. She doesn't make a sound, but I can feel the shaking of her body, and she processes the scene in front of her.

CHAPTER THIRTY-FIVE

DANI

I follow them into the ICU with Julia trailing close behind me. I hang back far enough to give them the space they'll need, though my chest aches at what's coming. I watch Vic crouch down, as he tries his best to prepare Rose for what she'll see. But inside, I can't help but think, *how do you prepare anyone for this? More so, how do you prepare a child?* How can you see your mother in that state with fuck all ability to change the outcome? The realization is that there is nothing you can say that will blunt this kind of impact—no kind words. No steady, yet sympathetic tone can shield her from what waits behind that sliding door.

We hang back, giving Rose the privacy she deserves to say whatever her little heart wants to say to her mom. Julia and I watch in silence, but are ready to move quickly should she need us. But she doesn't. She seems steadier than Vic does in there, as though his presence provides her with the wall she needs to remain upright and strong. And that's when I see their similarities. As they stand there, I know the two of them have suffered so much abuse in their past. Witnessing trauma at such a young age can alter their perception of the world.

This may be the last time that she sees her mother alive. That thought alone squeezes something in my chest, remembering why I went into this profession in the first place. To give people this moment. The last chance to say their goodbyes. Funerals are for the living, but this—this is the real closure. The time when both are given the chance to say their peace. Sometimes it is in a better situation, but nonetheless, this is the real end.

Vic crouches beside her. His hand is resting gently on her small shoulders as he coaxes her forward. When she hesitates, she looks to him for reassurance. Their eyes meet, and something unspoken passes between them. Vic nods once and then stands to his full height, taking her hand in his. Step by step, he leads forward. Then he leans her closer, guiding her shaking fingers, until they meet with Sonya's slack palm. Rose leans in, lowering her head, and mouthing words I can't hear. Whatever she's saying, she's pouring her heart into it. Vic nods, along with Rose's words, which confuses me, but still, I watch on. Then he speaks to Sonya, too. His eyes are sharp as he looks at Rose, making a promise there amongst the three of them.

Finally, he lifts Rose, keeping her steady in his arms, as she presses a kiss to her mother's bruised cheek. My throat tightens painfully, and I blink hard against the sting of tears. Because there is no way to prepare for this. Each time I do it, it doesn't get any easier. In some situations, such as this one, it is even more challenging to bear witness. No child should ever have to say goodbye like this—a life that's cut short by the unjust hand of another.

Vic turns, catching my eyes, and motions us over. We enter the room, and I move with Julia to the bedside, where she takes her sister's hand. Her tears break through the silence of the room, as Rose stands there with her own silent ones flowing down her cheeks. She leans close, whispering apologies, promises, as their shared grief flows in the short distance between them. Beside her, Vic still holds onto Rose's hand, grounding her as she gives her mother's hand one last squeeze before leading Vic out of the room, letting him know she is done.

Seeing that final touch, Julia and I follow them, leaving the ICU together. I linger a second longer, glancing back, just in time to see

Sonya's blood pressure climbing as it flashes in large red numbers on the monitor. The nurse rushes forward, ushering us quickly out of the unit as the alarms begin to sound. We've barely cleared the door when the overhead system crackles. A voice cuts through with its announcement. *Code blue. ICU.*

People run up the stairs and spill out of the elevators, badging into the locked intensive care unit with proficient speed. As the door opens, we see a blur of blue scrubs surrounding Sonya's room. The same room that we had stood in only minutes ago. I glance over at Vic. He's frozen, rooted to the spot. When his eyes catch mine, something flickers as he blinks, bringing him out of his haze. Then he bolts forward, as if he has just remembered who he is, disappearing into the crowd of other medical providers. Minutes feel like eternity, stretching on until we lose track of time, as I stand in the hallway alongside Rose and Julia. None of us speaks. We don't need to. The muffled flurry of activity behind the door is enough to tell us she is fighting. Whether to stay on earth or leave it all behind is yet to be determined. As more people come and go, I hear the loud, clear instructions being called out. The request for epinephrine administration, feedback on compressions, and closed-loop communication of commands are documented in the medical record. I've witnessed this countless times, but never like this, and never in this new role. I feel helpless to ease the burden of the child next to me, who is holding back her sobs, too young to comprehend the events going on, but old enough to understand the gravity of the situation, and terrified enough to know the sadness that will follow the silence soon enough.

The conversation about comfort measures was never finalized, so she remains a full code status. And now it's done. Every measure is being performed to bring her back, just as they were processing the possibility of letting her go peacefully. Sometimes things don't work out the way we planned, yet they have a way of coming to the same conclusion.

One by one, staff file out of the ICU. They return to their station, their rounds, their charts. To them, it's just another part of their lifesaving skills needed for their profession. To them, it's routine, but to the family sitting beside me, their life is forever altered because of this. The noise of the code fades, leaving only hushed voices and the closing of doors as they exit the unit and floor, waiting for the next crisis.

When Vic finally steps back into the hallway, we don't need words to let us know what happened there. His face says it all. She's gone. Rose bolts into his arms. Her cries are raw. Her stuffed toy falls to the floor, forgotten, as she wraps herself around Vic while he tries to comfort her. Julia, who once stood up hopeful when she saw Vic, still holding on, now sinks into the nearest chair, her face buried in her hands. She sobs, her shoulders shake, and all I can do is hand her a fucking box of tissues. Vic gathers Rose close, his arms holding her tightly in reassurance as she releases grief that is much too large for her little body to hold.

I sit beside her and do my best to console Julia. "Maybe she was waiting to say goodbye," she sobs into her tissue, clutching the box tighter. "She heard that Rose would be okay," Julia chokes out. "And whatever her daughter said, whatever Dr. Flores said, maybe that was enough for her to finally let go."

The ICU nurse appears and gently leads Julia away to discuss next steps, as her grief and words remain with me. Silence settles in their absence. I sit alone while Vic and Rose stand together. The girl stares straight ahead with eyes red-rimmed and hollow, seeing far too many things in her young life.

When her father's name drifts by in Julia's and the ICU nurse's nearby conversation, Rose's body begins to shake. Vic's jaw tightens, teeth grinding, as he holds back the fury I am all too familiar with. One that I can say matches my own, except I've always been better at hiding it than Vic, though that in itself says something, given he has had more years to perfect the art. But I know his tells. I've memorized them as surely as I have the lines of his body, the secrets that he hides from the world, as well as the darkest of desires he elicits on my body when we find pleasure in one another.

I stoop and retrieve the rabbit from where it fell by my chair. Its fur is worn, one ear stitched hastily and now forever bent in that crooked tilt, as though it too has weathered some kind of abuse. When I hold it out, Rose finally lifts her eyes to mine. Her small hand reaches for it without a word. Vic meets my eyes and gives me a nod, his hand lying sturdy and firm on her shoulder, offering his support and conveying to me that he won't let her face this alone.

Vic clears his throat gently, trying not to startle her. "Can you tell me where you live, Rose?" I hear him ask, and she nods almost mechanically.

But her reply makes me want to cry. "Yes," she says lowly. "I've had to tell the cops before, and my mom made me memorize it in case I needed help," she says without making eye contact. She repeats the address, and Vic carefully listens to it. The matter-of-fact way she says it guts me because she's not simply repeating an address, she's repeating a kind of lesson no child should have to learn.

"I don't want my dad to take me, Vic." Her small shoulders shake before she looks up at him. Her eyes burn with animosity and her voice with such rage. "I wish he was dead." The words hit me like a slap. She's angry, and I can understand more than I want to, having seen it happen to Vic, I'd still never admit that. "He hurt my mom," her voice tightens, "and he will hurt me, too." She says, as if it's already decided. She pushes her face into the matted fabric of her stuffed rabbit, wiping her tears against it, and trying to put on a brave face.

Vic gently pulls the rabbit away just enough to see her face, which she is using as a protective shield, hiding her emotions. "He's never going to hurt you again, Rose. I promise you." She blinks up at him. He begins whispering words of comfort and reassurance about her future to her. And I stand still, listening to it all. "You stay strong, Rose. This moment doesn't define you, you hear me?" She nods, a little whimper escapes her, as she puts on the face of a soldier, her bravery shining through in the darkest hour. "You can still have the life you want. You can do anything, Rose," he says, and she nods. "Tell me you understand."

"I understand," she relays, her voice faint, but unmistakable in her response to his request.

She stares at him one last time, then nods. Quietly, she walks to her aunt's side. The nurse sees her approach and gives her a sympathetic smile before returning to work and attending to her other patients in the unit. Julia gathers her close, and they proceed to leave all this nightmare behind. Halfway down the hall, they pause. Julia's shoulder shakes as she tries to conceal her grief, but Rose's eyes are dry now. She doesn't cry, nor does she look away. Instead, she locks her gaze on Vic, her small hand white knuckling the stuffed rabbit in her arms. In that silent exchange, a promise lingers between them—the words Vic told her and ones she will carry on into her future.

The walk home is quiet. I called Emma from the office to tell her everything that had happened. Everything I'd feared might come true. She gave me her word that it would be okay and that she'd help. Back at my desk, I'd pinned Vic's location on my phone, watching the little blue dot moving around the hospital, which helped to calm my rising anxiety. Knowing Vic, he's already formulated a plan for revenge. But thanks to Jameson, I can keep an eye on him and make sure he doesn't fall apart on his own. I refuse to lose him again. The device, although small, still has its own SIM card, making it undetectable on Bluetooth and ideal for concealment. Tonight, its presence is a comfort, and I'll take whatever I can get.

That was hours ago, right after it happened, and I'd gone back to my office pretending to work, while the day lagged on. When Vic and I finally left the hospital, he clung to me, whispering how much he loved me, but I could feel his mind wasn't with me. It was with Rose and the silent promise he made to her. We walked hand in hand, as always, but when we reached my apartment, I could sense him pulling away emotionally. He turned off that part that makes him human, the urge to feel too much. Instead, he had only the clinical detachment he reserved for everyone else, except me.

"I've got something to do," he murmured. He didn't have to tell me that. I could already feel it. Whatever type of monster that lived inside him had already stirred awake, and he was slipping away, becoming nothing more than its shadow. I nodded, letting him go, even as every part of me wanted to drag him back.

CHAPTER THIRTY-SIX

VIC

I couldn't stay and play the part of the distracted boyfriend, nor pretend to Dani that I wasn't on a mission to find Sonya's husband and ensure he never hurt another person. Especially not Rose. God, the way that she shook in front of me at the mere mention of her father was heart-wrenching. After asking for her address and finding out where that piece of shit lives, I follow him to a bar. He isn't in the least bit upset about the fact that his wife has died, because they had to call him.

He's a good-looking man, not the type one would envision when thinking of a man who abuses his wife and child. But then, evil sometimes hides behind the pretty illusion of a good career and a well-groomed persona, all the while their insides are black and rotten to the core. A poison that leaks out, infecting anything it touches, hidden behind a white-toothed smile. I can tell. He sits at the bar as a woman comes up to him and sits on the stool. I sit close by, listening to the conversation transpire, itching to get closer and warn her that he is an abusive piece of shit, but I can't. I'm playing the long game, and soon it will be over.

She points at his ring, and he lowers his gaze, summoning a

mask of grief—one that is full of manipulation as he tells her he's a widower. Her hand clutches her chest in sympathy, while her other slides onto his leg, desperate to comfort him. He stares at her hand on his thigh, and she can't see the smirk that plays at his lips, I can from my view in the darkened booth next to them. The game he plays to get women into his bed. His wife died hours ago, he was the reason she was there, and didn't care about her enough to see her go, nor be there for his daughter. We have established this isn't the type of man he is. He chooses to pick on the defenseless, the ones who can't fight back, and I remember all too well how that feels. To not be big enough or strong enough to protect someone when you can't even defend yourself.

The woman leans closer. "It looks like you could use some company for the night." She looks down at his hung head, hope filling her lust-filled gaze. And when he looks up, he meets her eyes as his darken. He leans over to whisper something in her ear. I can't make it out, even from here, the effect is apparent—she likes it. Her cheeks flush crimson with heat as her thighs push together against the bar. She licks her lips, and he watches it all. He turns away, downing the rest of his dark amber liquid in his crystal glass in one quick swallow. As he stands abruptly from the stool with his hand extended out toward her, she doesn't hesitate. She leaps up, grinning like she won herself a prize. Blind to the knowledge of what it will cost her.

I leave my tonic water and lime there untouched at the table, slipping out after them, careful to keep enough distance between us, so he doesn't sense me trailing behind. Outside, the night air feels heavier, cloaked in low-lying fog. My car purrs to life, headlight low, as I ease from the spot a minute later. His taillights illuminate with a red hue, a beacon guiding me along the path I've already memorized back to his house. He leads me back to his street. I don't park near him, instead, I slide onto the next block. Pulling up beside a house that rests empty on a corner lot behind his. A "For Sale" sign is placed in the front yard, yet the house remains dark. Staged amidst the greenery and annuals that appear freshly planted, perhaps to showcase the house with its well-maintained landscape, giving the illusion of what it could be.

I walk in the shadows of the night, my feet make no sound on the concrete walkway, as I round the corner of the back yard and onto the darkened porch around back. There are no cameras here. That would only provide proof, evidence of the atrocities that happened in this place.

I give it thirty minutes before I come in. The back door is unlocked because predators rarely worry about becoming prey. They grow too sure of themselves, too reckless, that they think they are untouchable. Getting away with the abuse because his brother is a police officer has lulled him into a false sense of security, a bubble about to burst before his very eyes. I hear the faint sound of music in the living room as I follow it. I see a glass of wine mostly finished and a glass of whiskey left mostly untouched. I follow the sounds of slapping skin and grunts that come from the bedroom. I wait on the couch for it all to finish, thinking he must be a selfish lover, only searching for his own release. I bet she doesn't even come.

He finally emerges from the bedroom, and still I wait. The sound of his footsteps crosses the hall, unhurried. He opens the refrigerator door, and in the pale light, I see beads of perspiration on his forehead and the sheen of sweat on his skin. From the bedroom, there is nothing, no voice calling out to him. No sound whatsoever. And it's sometimes in that silence that the scream is loudest.

Before I can address that, I need to come here and finish what I set out to do. With that, I take a quick step, stabbing him in the neck with a scalpel. The precision I usually use to fix a patient has the opposite effect as I rip his skin about, slicing through tissue and hitting his major artery in seconds. Before he can figure out what is happening, he slumps to the floor. His blood coats the black and white checkered tiles of the floor as he holds onto his neck, trying to staunch the bleeding. His eyes are wide, scared, and I take deep satisfaction from it. I just regret that he didn't get a chance to feel more of it.

My scalpel drops, and when I bend down to retrieve it, I see it—the same tiled pattern. A sick trick of the mind perhaps, but the similarity all the same. I can't move because I am seeing a different scenario from long ago. One that I tried to erase from my mind, pressed into the darkest corners, hidden forever, but it explodes open as the memories come back in vivid color before me: my mom, her body surrounded by all that blood. I can't move, I'm paralyzed in this spot. My vision blurs and my ears pop. I can't hear, I can't see, all I can sense is the pounding of my heart in my chest as I fight the urge to pass out.

"I can't breathe, I can't breathe," I wheeze out between pursed lips. Then I feel someone by my side, the hand warm against my cool, clammy skin.

CHAPTER THIRTY-SEVEN

DANI

I knew what he was going to do when he left my apartment. It was written all over his face, there at the hospital, and when we got back. I see the blue dot moving, and I already know where he is headed. When he asked Rose for her address, it was already decided that her father would die. Suffer a similar fate, but have the mercy of not suffering as long, so as not to risk the chance of a recovery, because dead men can't talk.

I saw that he was at a bar, so I waited at a restaurant, sipping on a Coke and having a little appetizer. I need to keep up the appearance of being a patron, and honestly, I'm also fucking hungry. I pick the perfect location with a window view of the bar entrance. I already paid my tab and secured the tip, so that when I need to leave, I can. Just as I finish my last dumpling, the bar door swings open. A man leans close to a woman with his arm draped over her shoulder, murmuring something in her ear. She throws her head back laughing, the sound carrying across the street. Her hand rests against his chest as they get into his car, driving off.

A minute later, I see Vic, his face controlled and fury radiating from every pore in his body. He rounds the side of his car, sliding into the seat, and quickly follows suit after the car drives off, carrying the couple inside. I start piecing it together and wipe my mouth, throwing the napkin onto the table. I thank the waitress on my way out and start walking onto the sidewalk toward the blue dot that is moving at a quick rate away from me. I call an Uber, already having an idea of where he's going. The similarities in the man's face and features are close to those of the little girl who was crying for her mother as she died mere hours ago.

The black sedan picks me up, and I give an address for a block away, needing to make sure that I still stay as discreet as possible. I hop out of the Uber, thanking the driver as I pretend to walk up to my house. As he drives away, I round the corner and pull the hood over my sweatshirt, covering my face, as my sneakers make quick work of getting closer to Vic's blue dot on my screen. I see his car parked around the corner, walk around the block to the address on file for Rose and Sonya. The house is dark except for a lamp in one of the rooms and a faint hue coming from the back of the house, which is probably the kitchen. As I walk around the back porch and peer through the window, I see Vic with his back against the wall. He's crouched down, and the man is sprawled out in a pool of blood. I notice the similarities in the title and how he must have retreated into his own mind from the death of his mother.

"What the fuck?" I push the door open all the way which was left slightly ajar with the covered portion of my hoodie. I walk over to Vic, who is crouched over, hyperventilating. He isn't seeing me, and he isn't seeing the dead man on the floor. I know that without a doubt, he is seeing his mother, as she fights for her life and takes some of her last breaths. I drop down to him. "Vic, baby. Look at me," I implore. I take hold of his arm, placing my hand on his, and feel how cold he is. "Vic, please look at me. Breathe, baby, breathe," I beg him as he moves his head in my direction.

His voice comes out hoarse. "Dani?" he questions. And I nod, as tears threaten to fall down my cheeks.

"Let's get you out of here, baby." He nods as he stands to his full height, towering over me. I bend to retrieve the scalpel, walk over to the sink, and use a tissue to turn the knob, rinsing the blood off the blade and flipping the nozzle off as it gleams in the dim kitchen lighting. The refrigerator door remains open, and as I tuck it away in my pocket. The body lies on the floor, with eyes wide and open, but no life remains. As I take Vic's hand in mind to leave, he holds me back, and I stop in my tracks, watching his face take on an expression as if he is just remembering something.

"There was a woman who came with him. I heard them having sex in the bedroom, but I haven't heard anything since he came out, and I am fairly certain she is still here." I notice the concern on his face, and I nod.

"Okay, what do you want to do? She would have heard this commotion, though. Don't you think so?" The music continues to play from the bedroom, and Vic takes a couple of paces out from the kitchen, turning his head to look around. Nothing remains to be seen except his keys, his phone, and a piece of paper that resides atop. I walk over to the table by the sofa, noting the two glasses. One is mostly empty, and the other is almost full of an amber-colored liquid. Upon further inspection, I notice a white film coating the wine glass, and my stomach sinks at the implication. "Vic," I call to him, but he is looking at some papers on the desk under the keys.

"Motherfucker took out a life insurance policy on Sonya," he spits out, and the realization dawns on me that this was likely premeditated. I swallow the lump in my throat, but I walk toward the bedroom, also thinking about what I will find once I get there.

"Vic," I call again, and this time he walks toward me, and I point to the bedroom. "I think she was drugged," I say quietly, and his eyes widen. His face is murderous, and we proceed to the bedroom with caution. The door is left slightly open, but it's enough to see that the situation is not okay. A woman is left naked and handcuffed to the bed frame. I can tell that she is breathing, but she is unconscious. What may have started as consensual is clearly no longer the case.

Vic and I leave the room and walk over to the desk where he left his phone and keys. I pick up the phone and take it over to his lifeless body, unlocking the older phone with his finger and dialing 9-1-1. The operator's voice comes over the line, and I leave it there, wiping it down to remove any trace of my fingerprints. We walk out of the place knowing that help is on its way for the girl who may have been drugged on the bed. But no help will be coming for the man who caused so much suffering and who got away with murder for a possible payout from the insurance company. And no amount of cover-up will help his reputation, or his brother's, when they find that girl passed out and handcuffed to his bed, saved from who knows what kind of abuse he could have caused if given the chance. The undisputable evidence of her body is there on his bed, and it's not one even his brother can deny.

We drive away from the scene with Vic in the passenger seat, and the unspoken promise that this too shall pass. When I arrive at my apartment with Vic in tow, I turn on the light to see Emma sitting there in the dark, twirling her hair. I jump up, and Vic steps in front of me, but I stop him. "Wait." He stops mid-stride on his way to Emma. She doesn't look scared. In fact, she seems amused. "What the fuck, Emma? How do you do that?" She laughs.

"Special skills, babe," she says, pointing to the black dress she lent me a couple of weeks ago, which hangs in tatters on the hanger it came with. "So, I guess you owe me a dress." I laugh, and it makes her green eyes sparkle. Vic looks between us.

"Vic, this is Emma. Emma, this is my Vic." She stands from the chair and walks over to him. He stands still, assessing her. His eyes are calculating, and as she extends her hand, he pulls her into a hug.

"Oof," Emma staggers into his arms, as he releases her just as quickly.

"I recognize you from the photo," he says, as that explains it all. He looks over at me, and I nod, understanding as he shrugs his shoulders. Emma looks at me, her lip curled up, and her eyes alight with humor. "You're her family," Vic says, unbothered by it all.

Emma throws her hair over her shoulder. "Damn straight," she says. She starts walking toward the door, and we follow her. "Oh," I say quickly, just remembering what is in my pocket. "Can you get rid of this?" I hand her the scalpel, and her eyebrow quirks up.

She looks at the skinny scalpel in my hand before taking it with a roll of her eyes. "Please tell me we don't have to get rid of another body, Dani?" She sighs, and I let out a laugh, while Vic just stares at us like we've all gone mad, and maybe he's right.

"No, this one doesn't need disposing of." I snort as she pockets the scalpel.

"Yes, well, that's good. I was here with you all night, right?" she confirms, with a slight smile.

I nod. "Yep, and Vic, too."

"Of course," she agrees. "Now, will you two get dressed and meet us at the Four Seasons? We can't wait to finally see you guys."

I clap my hands excitedly. "Is everyone here?" I ask hopefully, and she smiles widely. "Of course. Even Mateo came this time," she says as there's a knock at the door. I walk to answer it, and then Eduardo comes through. He looks straight at Emma, checking her from head to toe as she rolls her eyes.

"Sorry, Em. You took too long, and I got worried," he shrugs, but I know he isn't sorry. He looks over at me and smiles before coming over to give me a quick hug and extending his hand over to Vic. "Welcome to our family. I'm Eduardo." Vic quirks his lip, trying to hide his smile, and I can tell he likes them already.

"Vic, and thanks. I hear we are meeting you guys at the Four Seasons?" Eduardo looks over to Emma, and she beams at him.

He looks back toward us. "Of course. I heard you also need an alibi." He winks, and Vic lets out a loud laugh.

"Thanks," he huffs. "I guess we do."

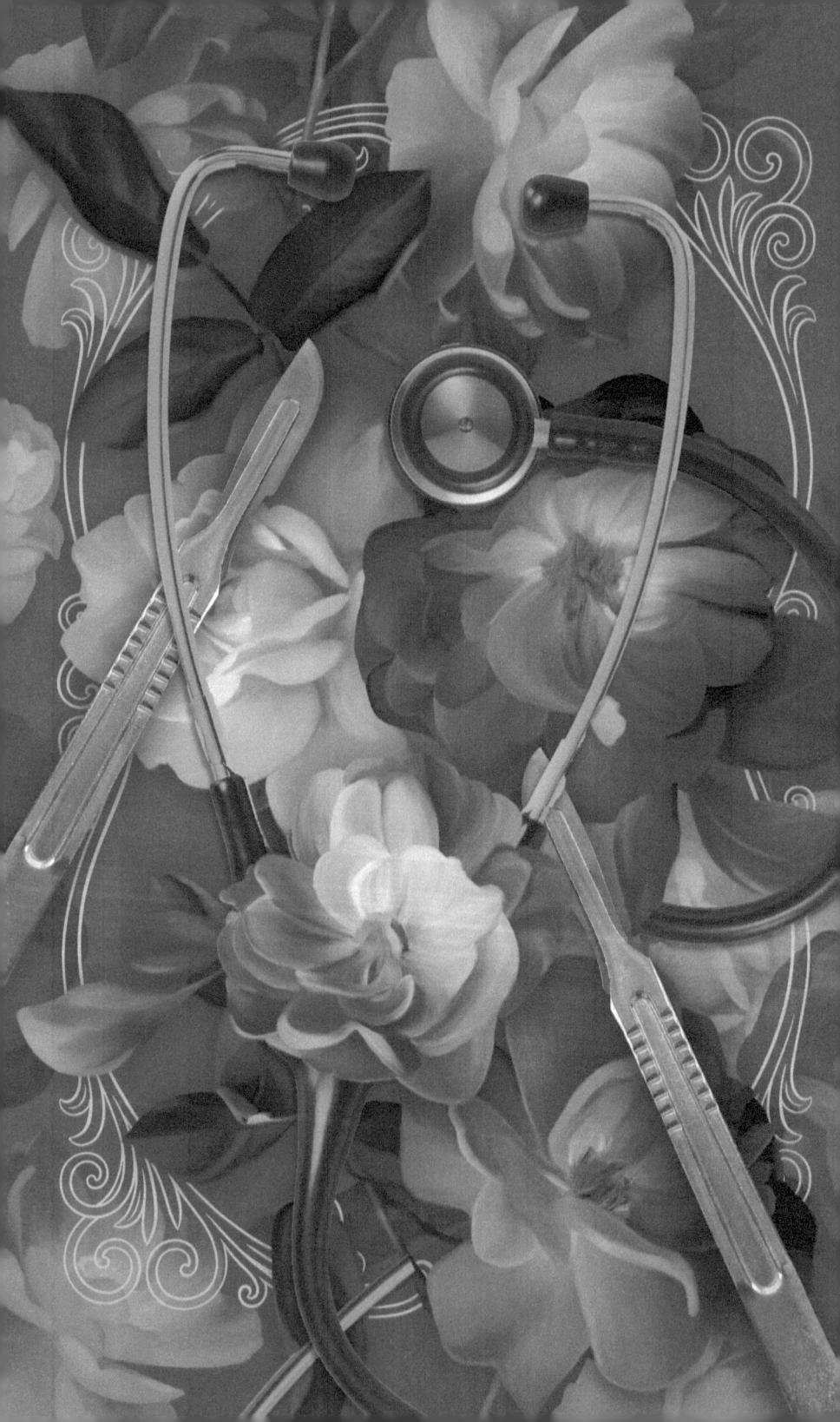

CHAPTER THIRTY-EIGHT

VIC

After having a shit ton of fun with Dani's friends, we make it back to her place and finally let the night settle around us. Within the safety of her apartment walls, the noise of tonight fades into something that is just us. "I miss them all so much," Dani whispers, pulling the blanket higher to her chest. She shifts the pillow beneath her arms, curling into it as the events of tonight take their toll on her body.

I lie on my side, facing her. She has never looked more beautiful than she has right now. In the dim light, her promise ring glints faintly on her left hand. I reach over and tap off the lamp, plunging the room into darkness except for the outline of her face. We stare at each other across the inches of space, but it feels like an eternity between us.

"What are you thinking about, Vic?" she asks softly, already sensing the question burning at the back of my throat. She tilts her head, studying me in only the way she can. It makes me smile as she prepares herself for whatever answer I can offer.

I sigh, brushing my thumb over the blanket where her hand rests beneath it. "Baby, how would you feel about going back home?" Her body stiffens almost instantly, and she flinches, not understanding that I want her with me, of course.

"What do you mean?" Her voice is cautious, but I can hear the ache behind it, the longing for a place that I equally miss. "You work here, and I just got the job that I always wanted."

I nod, forcing her to hold my gaze, to let her know that I am not dismissing her dreams, but knowing that she only came here for me. "Yes, that's true. I know that we have started to build something here together, and I don't take that lightly. But what if we went home, like really home? Surrounded by our friends, with a support system that we can lean on, not just down the road, but now."

She sighs, sinking deeper into the pillow, her eyes searching mine in the dark. "I don't know," she says on a long exhale, "the only place that I wanted to live was sold, and all those memories of us belong there. If it can't be there, then we might as well start over and build new ones." Her lips purse, like she is forced to surrender to the loss of it all over again.

My chest tightens, but this time it is not from grief. I can hardly contain the smile at the secret I've been carrying, waiting for just the right moment to share it because she doesn't know. She isn't aware that I've already reached out to Brandon, our former realtor, to ask if I can buy back Dani's home. It has been at the back of my mind after he suggested it, should I ever have that as an option. When he asked when I wanted to sign the papers, I said, "Now's as good a time as any." He laughed, and as I gave him the down payment, we signed the papers, then took the keys and handed them to me. I reach back behind me and fumble through the dresser.

"What are you doing?" she asks curiously, but I can sense the excitement in her voice. "Is it another ring?" she asks jokingly, but I can tell she wouldn't mind if it was.

I chuckle. "That will be our future soon, baby," I say reassuringly. "The first box I gave you was our past, and you are wearing that." I point lazily at her promise ring. "This box here," I hand her the little black box with a red bow, "is our present, if you'll accept it." She plops herself on one elbow as she stares down at the box in her hand. She looks up at me expectantly.

I chuckle, hands up in surrender. "You're just going to have to open it and find out what it is then."

She pops open the top and picks up the key. She twirls it in her hand. "A key? You want me to move in with you?" she asks, confused. "I thought we were already moving into my place because you are going to sell yours?"

My smile widens. "What if I told you that we can?" Confusion flickers across her face, but beneath it, a little hope shimmers behind those eyes.

"What do you mean?" She pushes herself upright, eyes locked on mine, and waits for me to elaborate.

I lean forward, unable to hide my grin. "What if we could move back to your home? The one that was next to mine in Texas?"

Her lips part, disbelief painting her features as she stares down at the box in her hands. Her fingers wrap around the cool metal resting inside. "Vic," her voice cracks, hopeful. "Did…Did you repurchase my house?"

My smile widens, matching hers as her tears spill over. "Yep. I sure did."

The keys slip from her grasp as she launches herself into my arms.

"Yes. Yes!" she cries, her voice muffled against my shoulder. "Let's move back." Her joy soaks into me as I hold her tight and laugh. And I've never felt more at peace.

She hugs me tightly, and I laugh. "Okay, let's move back."

I'm sitting in Dani's office on Monday afternoon, after we have both submitted our notices at work. The weight of our shared decisions is still fresh, but I know that it was the best plan for us moving forward. Both of us had submitted our notices this morning. I have a two-month notice bound by contract, and Dani has nearly the same, more so out of obligation. Hers was less rigid, but when she told them she was moving back home, they agreed she could stay until her replacement was found, or sooner, if needed.

Now with the hardest part done, I wanted to make today lighter. I'd brought her favorite lunch for the little café downstairs. It's a crisp apple salad with a scoop of curry chicken salad on top, with almond slices scattered across. A small vinaigrette packet rests next to the bag, exactly how she likes it. Her face lights up when she sees it. A huge grateful smile on her face—that is like a punch to the gut, knocking the wind out of me every time. I'm just glad that we got here again.

I decided to give it a shot and grabbed an extra side scoop of chicken salad curry to go with mine. Her iced matcha latte rests next to my drink on her desk —a healthy green smoothie that I pretend tastes much better than it does.

Just then, a slight knock sounds at her door, and Julia, Sonya's sister, comes into view. I rise from my seat, pushing the lunch container aside. Dani is already on her feet, crossing the small space to gather Julia in her arms for a hug.

"Sorry to disturb your lunch," Julia says as she steps inside the cramped office, offering a small smile. Her expression isn't the vacant one she wore when her sister died. "I just wanted to let you know some news." Dani glances at me, and our eyes meet. And in the silent exchange, we both remember the scene of Sonya's husband bleeding out on the kitchen floor not too long ago.

"Oh?" Dani says carefully, voice neutral. "What is it, Julia?"

She exhales as she reveals this truth to us, as if it sheds years of weight off her shoulders. "Well...Sonya's husband was found dead in his home."

Dani draws in a sharp breath, feigning shock.

"What?" I say, my hand flying to my chest in a rehearsed gesture of sympathy, trying to follow her lead. Dani gives me a look that says too much.

She clears her throat, drawing the attention away from me. "What happened?"

"He was stabbed, I guess," Julia says, her voice flat, as though she is still trying to make sense of it. "The weird thing was that someone called emergency services from his phone. When they arrived, they found an unconscious woman who'd been drugged. I asked if she was okay, and they told me she was okay physically, but," she shakes her head, "I don't know how that poor girl is doing mentally."

The silence hangs heavy in the air until I change the subject. "How's Rose handling all this?"

Julia's eyes soften, her shoulders relaxing at the mention of her niece. "I told her her dad had died, and she looked...relieved," she breathes out, with a slight tremor to her voice. "I will be taking care of her. Permanently." Her gaze flicks back to me. "And do you know the weirdest part?"

I shrug, because honestly, it's all pretty freaking weird if you ask me.

"He had taken a life insurance policy out on Sonya a year ago for one point five million dollars." Julia shakes her head as if she can't believe it at all, but I know it's true because I saw the papers there. "It all goes to Rose now. I'm going to set it aside in a trust, make sure she has the kind of life my sister always wanted for her. One with love, and safety...and choices." She sighs. "Friends. Even college, if she wants that, too."

Dani's eyes are glistening with tears as they slip freely down her cheeks. She doesn't bother hiding them. Her hand drags across her face, fingers splayed, catching more tears as they continue to fall.

"I'm so glad for Rose," she whispers hoarsely. "She'll never have to fear that man again. Maybe now...she can move forward." Dani's throat bobs as she swallows down the emotions. "No one can ever take the place of her mom, but I am so damn grateful that she has someone like you, Julia."

"Oh, I almost forgot," Julia reaches into her bag and pulls a folded piece of paper. "She drew this picture and told me to give it to you." I take it carefully, unfolding the crayon lines to reveal a picture of me, Rose, and the coffee shop where I treated her and her mom to breakfast. A stick version of her, rabbit in hand, standing beside a taller stick figure, which is undoubtedly me. A tiny heart floats above us, and my name is written in uneven block letters across my figure. She's drawn herself smiling up at me, while my stick figure eyes look down at her. My throat tightens as tears blur the images on the paper before me. Dani takes it gently from my hands and pins it to the corkboard in her office, smoothing it flat with reverence.

"I'll keep this here, for him, in my office," she says softly, but she smiles through her tears, and there isn't a dry eye in this place.

Julia hugs us both. "Thank you both for everything." With that, she leaves, and Vic and I stare down at our uneaten food, appetites now lost.

"What do you think happens now?" Dani asks.

I shrug, but there is no hesitation in my voice. "Anything she wants." My mind flashes to Rose walking out of the ICU with her rabbit clutched tight, braver than most grown men I've met. "Anything at all."

PART THREE

"WHATEVER OUR SOULS ARE
MADE OF, HIS AND MINE
ARE THE SAME."

EMILY BRONTË,
WUTHERING HEIGHTS

EL CORAZÓN

The Future

CHAPTER THIRTY-NINE

DANI
ONE YEAR LATER

It's good to be back where it all started—those forgotten promises made under the web of darkness in the witching hours between two love-struck soulmates. I was the beacon of light in his stormy sea, leading him to safe harbor. He sees the darkness in me, bringing it to light, causing our souls to intertwine in a macabre of primal urges. Urges we explored together.

I run as fast as my feet will carry me into the pitch-black. A single light shines from a window on the upper level of the house. I can hear his boots crunching through the brush as I swing around a tree, stopping to catch my breath. My heart is beating at an erratic pace, the blood rushing to my ears at the thought of being caught. No, I can't. I need to get away.

I run further into the thicket until I hit a hard wall of muscle. Deep corded arms reach around me, picking me up off my feet as they dangle in midair. "No!" I scream, but there isn't anyone here to hear me out in the country under the night sky. The hoot of an owl echoes through the air somewhere in the mixture of sounds. A low chuckle rings out under my ear as his hot breath wraps itself around me.

"Caught you, my little dark angel." His voice echoes from the closeness of his mouth against my ear as he presses it there.

"Oof." The air rushes out of me as I'm thrown up against a large tree trunk out in the landscape of brush and open field. His erection presses into my core as he wraps my legs around him and grinds against me.

"No. Please stop," I beg, but it's no use. I'm stuck against him. His muscular frame leans into me, making it hard to breathe as I catch a large intake of air, and his body shudders as I struggle against him. He holds my arms at an awkward angle, with a knife in the other hand. The blade gleams in the moonlight, the full moon reflected in the tip, angled against my jugular. I whimper as the blade presses into my skin. He laughs lowly at my meek attempt at a fight.

"Ouch." The knick to my neck is sharp as the heat coils lower in my belly, and the warm liquid drips down my neck. He drops the blade, ripping my little sleep shorts right off me. The snap of the fabric against my skin causes me to cry out once again, foolishly thinking anyone will come to my aid. I feel him shift as he frees his cock. He trails his tongue on my neck, lapping up the blood as he hums in approval. I can feel him there at my entrance, and I brace myself for the intrusion. His thick cock plunges into me on one forward thrust as my back arches against the tree trunk. I'm sure I'll have marks from it as he buries himself to the hilt. He moans, and my head falls back against the tree. Just as he withdraws to drive back in, we hear a piercing wail. He stops, placing his head against my forehead, and he begins to heave in laughter.

The baby monitor is there in the grass as Vic pulls out of me and gently places my feet on the grass. "We can try again tomorrow, if you'd like?" He offers me a small boyish smile that makes me remember him from all those years ago.

"How about a little ride back to the house since you ripped my sleep shorts right off?" I lift my eyebrow. I look down at my exposed pussy, still throbbing from being filled, just to be denied as quickly.

Vic smirks, sensing my sexual frustration. "Sure, baby, hop on," he says, bending and letting me jump onto his back as he hands me the baby monitor. I grab it with my left hand, where my large diamond wedding ring sparkles in the moonlight. I tuck it under my arm as he returns the knife to its holder. He wraps his arms around my legs, and we walk the small distance back to the house where our one-year-old was fast asleep not long ago. Unfortunately, he has developed a love for our arms, and we couldn't be happier to indulge him. Vic, in particular, loves his son something fierce. He is the epitome of the protective dad. I love their relationship, and I couldn't be happier.

As we walk into our home, the pictures that adorn the walls are of our family. From the beginning, with Vic and me as teenagers, until we met again all those years later, both of us were always trying to find each other—pictures of our wedding and the newest ones of our newborn. After we returned to Texas, we reconnected with Brandon, our former realtor and now a friend, who kept his promise to sell us the house back. When Vic's home went back on the market, we bought it just to tear it down. The house and all its terrible memories were stripped down to rubble. We decided to build one house on two lots, rebuilding our dream home where we first met, where we will create new memories together until we leave this earth.

I open the door to find Alexander standing in his crib. He looks pissed, but when he sees us, his tears stop, and he extends his hands outward for Vic to pick him up. He sits in the chair with our son, rocking him and staring out the window. The sky is blanketed in a sea of stars. I stand in the doorway watching my favorite people on this earth, holding onto each other, and I've never felt more at peace than I do at this moment. We may have taken the long way, but in the end, the journey, the heartache, and the reunion were all worth the time it took to get here. Vic got to fulfill his dream, and I—well, I got what I wanted in the end. My perfect family.

EPILOGUE

The doorbell rings, and I halt halfway through packing this box up. "Alexander, can you get that, please?" I yell as a loud thud hits the floor above. I have no idea what he's doing up there, nor do I want to. Rolling my eyes, I hear the door shut loudly before I see him flying down the stairs. His size twelve combat boots echo, hitting each step with a solid thunk as he rounds the banister before flashing me a guilty smile.

"I don't want to know," I tell him as he chuckles loudly to the door. All chuckling stops as he opens it. His posture is stock-still, and his mouth is slightly open. A surge of worry grips me. I stand abruptly, dropping the items onto the floor with a sudden clatter, and I move quickly toward the door. Standing behind him, I see a girl in her mid-twenties, staring back at him. When she sees me, she smiles. She waves timidly. Dark brown hair cascades over her heart-shaped face. Her eyes are the same, but this time, they sparkle, light, and happy.

"You may not remember me," she says guardedly, "I'm R—"

"Rose," I finish for her. "My God, Rose. Look at you, honey." I walk to the door, past my son, and open the screen door, pulling her into a hug. "Come in, please. Vic is here, let me get him."

I run up the stairs where my husband is just getting out of the shower. He drops his towel, and I can't help but be drawn to the sight of him. Snapping myself out of my lust-filled haze, "Babe, I need you." He walks over to me, his cock standing at attention.

"We don't have much time, baby, but you can choke—" I laugh, making him stop mid-sentence, his brows furrow in confusion.

"I'll take care of that," I wave my hand around his genital region, "later, but I need you to get dressed quickly and come downstairs," I say before walking toward the door. I turn to address him before exiting our bedroom. "And hurry. There's someone here you need to see."

With sparked curiosity, he turns abruptly, already pulling his shirt over his head as I walk out, bumping straight into a mousy little girl with pink hair and a nose ring, leaving my son's bedroom. She gives me a sheepish wave as she runs down the stairs, past Alexander, and straight out the door. Alexander doesn't spare her a glance, his focus solely on Rose. Rose looks from him to the girl who ran past, disapproval in her eyes as she turns her head away from him, not sparing him another moment's glance. This makes him smile more, and I feel sorry for poor Rose, who obviously has my son's full attention now.

Vic comes bouncing down the stairs much like his son, but when he sees who is waiting there, he stops. "Rose," he says, almost in shock as he makes his way toward her. Tears run down my cheeks watching them reunite. She runs over to him and hugs him as tears also run down her face. Alexander stiffens, not understanding what this means to us. We lost touch with her, but it's clear that she found us after all these years. He pulls back to take in her appearance. She is dressed nicely. Her frame is still small, but healthy, and she looks good. Most of all, she seems happy.

"Come sit down and let us get you something to drink." She follows us and looks at the pictures displayed on the wall in the hallway leading to the back kitchen area. But she stops at the picture she recognizes. It's one she drew long ago that Vic had framed, and placed proudly along with all our best accomplishments and memories. Her hand goes up to her mouth in shock.

"You kept it after all these years?" she asks, bewildered as if she just remembered the drawing.

Vic comes to stand next to her. She looks up at him, smiling, and he looks down at her. It's almost the same picture, but today, here in this house, after all those years. Alexander stares at them, understanding in his eyes, and something else I haven't seen in him before, besides with his family. Love.

I beckon them to come into the kitchen, as we take our seats at the eight-person island in the center of the room. She is just about to pull out a chair when Alexander comes out behind her and pulls it out for her. She thanks him, her posture stiff, and when he sits next to her, she stares at him. I look over at my husband to see if he is catching this, and he must notice the same thing because he smiles and winks at me. I walk to the refrigerator and pull out four bottles of Jarritos soda. I open each one using the new opener by the fridge, which has a little wooden box that catches all our tops, so there is no need to dispose of them immediately. We bought this at an antique show popular in the area, and it's one of my favorite items that I used to have in my house before we sold it. I hand out each one, and we catch up on all the years that have passed since we were away from Boston and out of the loop in Rose's life.

"So do you still live in Boston, Rose?" Vic asks, and we all turn to her. A smile graces her lips as they tip up slightly, as if recalling something.

"Well," she says carefully, "I actually live in New Hampshire at the moment." She hesitates briefly before continuing. Alexander immediately sits straight up, and I look over to Vic, seeing if he notices, and yep, he does. Nothing gets past that man. "I go to school there," she comments and then looks to Vic. "Remember that last conversation we had, the day before I left with my aunt to go and live with her?" She looks over at me because I was there, too. My hands go to my mouth to hide the gasp that comes, because I think I know what she is going to say. Vic leans in closer as if he could hear her better. He nods, waiting for her to continue. "You told me that this moment doesn't define me. That I make my own path and choose how I want to live my life." Tears start to flow down my cheeks, and my son looks over to me and then at his father. When he turns to look at Rose, her eyes have a sheen to them, but she isn't sad, she's happy. I went to college. I graduated from Dartmouth and am in medical school now." She says proudly, and Vic comes around the corner to hug her. He tells her how proud he is of her and how special she is to him.

Before she tells us she needs to get going, she shares how she came here with some friends and needs to get back soon. We hug and make plans to keep in touch. "I'll walk her out," Alexander says, and I already know this is a bad idea, but we stay close by, listening as best we can, hopeful we don't have to intervene. Our son has some of his father's obsessive qualities, but it hasn't ever been a problem before. She gets to the door, and we lean our bodies into the hallway out of sight, but still in hearing range. He opens the door for her, and he stops her from exiting, her body half in and out of the house as he holds the door. "You know," he says, leaning forward just as she turns halfway to him, waiting for him to finish what he has to say so that she can leave, "I'm going to Dartmouth, too—my dad's alma mater. Guess I'll be seeing you there. Maybe we can hang out?" She stiffens.

"I don't know if your girlfriend would appreciate that."

He laughs cruelly. "Oh, my little Rose, she isn't my girlfriend. Don't worry."

He lifts his hand to her face, staring at her. She doesn't move. They are mere inches away as he tucks a piece of her hair behind her ear so softly. Her eyes soften for a minute before she pulls away just as he starts to lean in.

"Maybe I'll see you around, little Alex," she taunts. He rises from the doorframe, and Vic and I can't help but chuckle.

"Nothing little about me, baby," he says, standing tall at his six-foot-four frame.

"Promises, promises," she sings as she rounds the corner, meeting his stare and waving as she drives off. We walk out of the kitchen as he stands there in the doorway, his head hung down. He hears us approach and stands upright, closing the door, and not meeting our stare.

"You are so fucked," Vic says as he laughs, taking my hand in his, leading me back up to our bedroom.

"Alex, finish packing up these boxes, please. I need to help your father with something," I say as Vic tries to stifle a laugh.

"Gross! I don't want to know," we hear him yell up the stairs as the door to our bedroom shuts. Vic comes prowling towards me and pushes me down onto my knees. His eyes sparkle with humor.

"I hope he knows what he's getting into," I say, before pulling his cock free from his joggers. His eyes darken with lust as his hand comes to cup my cheek, tilting my head up and looking down at me adoringly.

"I hope he does," he murmurs affectionately, "because maybe she is the only one that can calm the beast within."

I take his thick cock in my hand, giving it a firm stroke, as he hisses through his teeth. I look up at him, as he stares down at me through hooded lashes, "And what if," I press a kiss to the tip of his cock, licking the precum that's collected there, "the monster is the only man you need?"

Acknowledgments

To my readers/bloggers/influencers—Thank you for taking a chance on my book. With so many stories out there, the fact that you choose to spend your time with mine means the world to me. I am deeply grateful for your time, trust, and interest. A special thank you to my content team for the amazing posts and all the hype that kept me motivated.

To my family—Thank you for giving me the time and space to write, even when it meant cheering at your games while wearing a headset and looking completely ridiculous. Your pride in me never wavers—even if my books never make it into a brick-and-mortar store. Because of you, I feel like a best-selling author every single day. You believe in me when I lose faith in myself, and for that, I am so grateful for your love and support.

To my PA—Morgan Evans, you are without a doubt the best, and I'd be completely lost without you. Your feedback, thoughtful comments, and help with all things author-related are invaluable. I am so grateful that I found you—your steady support, reassuring words, and problem-solving skills make all the difference. I appreciate you more than words can say.

To my alpha/beta reader—Jena Morrill and Ash, thank you for your thoughtful feedback, insightful recommendations, and sharp eye for detail. I'm incredibly grateful for all the hours you've spent reading my rough drafts, which is no simple task. I am so lucky to have you by my side during this process.

To my besties—You know who you are. My circle is small, but close. Thank you for being there when I need you. Your constant love and support never go unnoticed, and I'm beyond grateful to have you in my life.

Also By L. Renée Richard

STAND-ALONE
Waves of You
The Cruelest Truth

SERIES
Black Wave (Book 1)
Twisted Tides (Book 2)
The Complete Forged Heart Series

ANTHOLOGY
The Lovesick Anthology

NOVELLA
Heart-Shaped Box

About the Author

L. Renée Richard is a Hispanic author who lives in rural New England with her family. She's a born and raised South Texan girl who implements BIPOC characters into her books, imbued with her cherished Mexican-American culture. She is an avid reader, complete with her never-ending TBR, and a romantic at heart who appreciates strong female main characters and good book boyfriends in the books she reads or writes. She loves summers in New England, sitting on the beach with a book, driving with the windows down through rural roads on cool autumn nights, and iced matcha lattes. Her books promise angsty romance where the journey to a happily ever after isn't always easy, but it's worth the trip.

KEEP IN TOUCH

AUTHOR PAGE:
www.authorlreneerichard.com

AMAZON:
http://www.amazon.com/author/lreneerichard

FACEBOOK PAGE:
https://www.facebook.com/Author-L-Renee-Richard-105887815914160

INSTAGRAM:
https://instagram.com/l.renee.richard?igshid=OGQ5ZDc2ODk2ZA==

TIKTOK:
TikTok @l.renee.richard

JOIN MY HYPE TEAM:
https://forms.gle/9cnsA4gSfbezY7a17

SIGN UP FOR MY NEWSLETTER:
https://mailchi.mp/authorlreneerichard/signup